THE
GHOST
APPLE

THE
GHOST
APPLE

A NOVEL

AARON THIER

BLOOMSBURY
NEW YORK · LONDON · NEW DELHI · SYDNEY

Published by Bloomsbury USA, New York

All papers used by Bloomsbury USA are natural, recyclable
products made from wood grown in well-managed
forests. The manufacturing processes conform to the
environmental regulations of the country of origin.

LIBRARY OF CONGRESS CATALOGING-IN-PUBLICATION DATA

Thier, Aaron.
The ghost apple : a novel / Aaron Thier.—First U.S. Edition.
pages cm
ISBN 978-1-62040-527-7 (hardback)
1. College students—Fiction. 2. Snack food industry—
Fiction. 3. New England—Fiction. I. Title.
PS3620.H546G46 2014
813'.6—dc23
2013036240

First U.S. edition 2014

1 3 5 7 9 10 8 6 4 2

Designed by Simon Sullivan
Typeset by Hewer Text UK Ltd, Edinburgh
Printed and bound in the U.S.A. by Thomson-
Shore Inc., Dexter, Michigan

For my family—
Mom and Dad,
Ruthie and Dave,
my grandparents,
and my wife, Sarah

THE
GHOST
APPLE

Letter from
ISRAEL FRAMINGHAM TRIPOLI
to
ZEPHANIAH FITCH

July 24, 1788

Dear Sir,

Not knowing how God in his Providence may dispose of my life, but praying that it may not be protracted beyond the usual span, for I suffer with the Gout, & the Strangury, & a most painful suppurating Boil in the centre of my forehead, & also a periodical ague, I venture to rely on the many proofs of friendship I have received from you, in all the years of our long acquaintance, in order to ask one favor more. I would have you destroy my last Will and Testament, and to please write another, as I will describe.

I assure you this is no rash jerk of my pen. I am lately returned from the island of Saint Reynard, where as you know, Sir, my Grandfather, the Esteemed John Morehead Tripoli, chanced to spend a year of his life. Having been (God keep him) somewhat imprudent in his own speculations, my Grandfather was never able to realize a design of which he spoke often and with the most agitated absorption, namely that something be done to improve the circumstances of the Carrawak Indians, at whose hands he had received such gracious treatment during his year upon the island. The Carrawak are now much reduc'd, even to the precipice of

Extinction, in consideration of which, & as I believe my Grandfather would have wished, I have instead decided to lavish my charity upon their brethren the much abus'd Wapahanock, whom I have known during my long residence here in North Town. Therefor it is my Will to promise the Complete sum of my whole fortune toward the establishment of a Free School, to be intended Solely and Exclusively, in Perpetuity, for the education of the said Wapahanock Indians, believing as I do in the myriad and subtle advantages of a liberal education, & hoping thereby to throw a small stone into the balance that has weighed so heavily against the Indian these three centuries past. I am Greatly concerned to have this accomplished, & I commend the matter to your care knowing that you will do your utmost to see it executed. As I have said, I do not know when God may call me to his bosom, and yet I pray it shall be soon, having been all my life, as you know, more anxious than is perfectly convenient to leave the place I am, and to arrive at the place where I am going. I shall conclude by recommending my self to your prayers, and you & your Dear family to the Divine protection. I am, with great Esteem,

Your honor's most Humble & most obliged servant,
                                        Israel Framingham Tripoli

P.S. I could wish also that some money be provided for the benefit of North Town, in consideration of which it is my hope the Governour and General Court will give to said town the name of Tripoli.

P.S. I would make allowance also for bribes, with which the Indians may be induced to attend the school. The benefits of this education will serve afterward to keep them in attendance.

TRIPOLI COLLEGE OFFICE OF ADMISSIONS
Information for Prospective Students

Why Tripoli?

We know that picking a university or college is one of the most difficult, not to say challenging, decisions of your life. So why should you pick us?

Founded in 1794 as a free school for Native Americans, Tripoli College opened its doors to tuition-paying students of all backgrounds in 1795. Today Tripoli is a fully accredited private institution of humanistic and scientific learning. We graduate outstanding young men and women with a high degree of civic responsibility, diversity, character, and commitment to leadership, in a student-centered learning environment that strives to foster the "teacher within." We offer challenging courses in a large number of reputable degree programs, almost all of which are taught by full-time faculty. We have a strong Division III football program, guaranteed on-campus housing, and self-serve pudding bars in every dining hall. In addition, Tripoli students participate in a large number of extracurricular activities. Whether you want to play the carillon, compete in varsity crew, or just "make the wound" with a few of your fellow students, you'll find plenty of ways to fill the winter nights.

Should any of that matter to you? Doesn't every college or

> *"Every college I looked at, the students were like, 'Whoa, this place is awesome!' Then I came to Tripoli and everyone was like, 'I don't know. You get used to it. It's not so bad.' So I thought I might as well come here."*
>
> —Adam Pressman, Class of 2011

BY THE NUMBERS

Number of students: **1,987**

Number of faculty members: **180**

Faculty to student ratio: **180: 1,987**

Percentage of students born outside the U.S.: **9**

Percentage of students who speak a language other than English at home: **18**

Of those students, percentage who speak no English: **13**

Percentage of students who speak no language at all, not even ASL: **.2**

Unemployment rate among Tripoli graduates (2009): **8.5%**

Zimbabwean unemployment rate (2009): **95%**

Number of deaths from yellow fever at Tripoli, since 1905: **0**

From malaria: **0**

Annual number of deaths from yellow fever worldwide: **30,000**

From malaria: **1–3 million**

university say the same thing? What makes Tripoli special?

In addition to a traditional liberal arts education, we offer unique opportunities for "experiential" learning, including our innovative Vocational Writing Program, which teaches workplace-specific writing strategies. Our branch campus in the Caribbean, Tripoli's Proxy College of the West Indies at St. Renard (formerly University College of the West Indies at St. Renard), provides students with unique opportunities for ecological and anthropological fieldwork. A large percentage of Tripoli students also choose to study abroad in places as diverse as Australia and the Falkland Islands. We strongly believe that in an increasingly globalized world, an appreciation and understanding of other cultures is essential.

Finally, a Tripoli education is great preparation for the "real world." Our graduates go on to distinguished careers in almost every field. According to the latest estimates, only a small fraction (less than 3 percent) are homeless within five years of graduation.

So does any of it matter? You tell us.

FALL
SEMESTER

HISTORY DEPARTMENT COURSE LISTINGS
Fall 2009

HIST 215 / *How to Make a Grapefruit: An Introduction to Atlantic History*

KABAKA

Grapefruits are a hybrid citrus fruit produced by crossing the sweet orange with the pomelo. They were first cultivated on the island of Barbados in the eighteenth century, and in some parts of the Caribbean their association with the British colonial regime, and more importantly with slavery itself, persists to this day. The grapefruit—like the sugar plantation and the big banana farm, like the United States, like chocolate, like cowboys and Indians and Italian food—is a creation of colonial history. This semester, working exclusively with primary sources like slave narratives and early travelogues, we'll discover the pain and horror that underpin the most banal features of daily life. We will try to put the thing in perspective. Ten million murdered slaves howl in their unmarked graves as we drink our grapefruit juice. How could it be worse? Education is about learning outrage. Turn over a rock and nightmares come out. But turn it over.

UNDERCOVER DEAN: BLOG POST #1

This is my very first "blog" post, but I figured it was about time I joined the Internet. After all, I'm a college student now!

Last Thursday night, I met my suitemates for dinner at Longman Hall, where we enjoyed some of Tripoli's distinctive menu offerings and talked about everything under the sun: boating, contraception, Hegel, a sophomore named Maria, the recession, and the excitement of our first week as Tripoli College freshmen. One of my suitemates, whom I will call "Akash," told us all about his childhood in Southeast Asia, and I kept the discussion going by sharing some of my experiences in the Vietnam War. After the meal, we sipped delicious fair-trade coffee and agreed to go on a road trip to Los Angeles at the end of the academic year.

But I didn't have time to sit around "shooting the breeze." I had an evening class. I bussed my tray, grabbed a delicious 80 percent vegan cupcake, and headed off to "Crime and Justice," an eye-opening sociology seminar taught by Professor Malinka West. I was a few minutes late because I stopped to admire the silhouette of Sheridan Tower against the darkening sky, but sometimes it's a good idea to pause and enjoy the little moments. I know that from experience!

Tripoli students benefit from small class sizes (an 11:1 student-to-instructor ratio), which provide opportunities for lots of intimate discussions with distinguished faculty like Professor West, author of the controversial memoir *Fucking the Police, and Other Diversions.* Thursday night's class was part lecture, part debate, part movie screening, and I had to struggle to keep up. The life of a college freshman is so exhausting and fast-paced that I actually fell asleep for a little while at the seminar table!

THE MASKED MAN

If you were to pay a visit to Tripoli and see me hanging out with my new friends in front of Pinkman Hall, you might say to yourselves, "That fellow looks a little older than most incoming freshmen." And one or two of you might actually see through my disguise (I hope not!) and ask yourselves what on earth a seventy-year-old dean is doing attending classes and hanging out with undergraduates. To explain that, I'll have to wind the clock back a few weeks.

As the dean of students, I'm always looking for ways to improve the Tripoli experience. We face more challenges than ever this year, with an unprecedented budget deficit and numerous personnel issues. But the last thing I want, as funding dries up and half the endowment vanishes overnight, is for our commitment to our students to get forgotten in the general panic. Student life remains my top priority, and I'm dedicated to maximizing the scant resources we have at hand. Every day, I ask myself the same questions: What do our students want? What do they need? What are we doing to make life at Tripoli as comfortable and safe as possible?

Obviously, we can't begin to address those questions if we don't have a clear understanding of what's happening on campus. But getting the lay of the land isn't as simple as it may sound. I attend College Council meetings, I'm a member of various faculty-student committees, and I deal frequently with sports teams and other campus organizations. The trouble is that young men and women are not always very forthcoming when speaking with an "adult," especially an authority figure like the dean of students. And truth be told, no matter how much contact I have with young people, I can't help but think that as I've gotten older, I've gotten more and more out of touch.

Last summer marked the third anniversary of my wife's death, and as I thought about her and reflected on how I'd spent those last three years, I began to feel that it was time for a change. My office just wasn't doing its job as well as I thought it could. Plus, I worried that if I went through the same lonely routines for another year, I'd go absolutely batty! That's when I decided to try something new. Call it a "thought experiment," but with real things. I set my bifocals aside and got some contact lenses. I bought denim trousers, a Boston Celtics mesh uniform jersey, "boxer" shorts, and a baseball cap that I turned backwards on my head. I even dyed my hair a rich chestnut brown, the color it had been in my youth. As a final touch, I obtained a gold-plated Tripoli College logo chain. Then I pulled some strings and got myself assigned to a suite in Hogbender Hall, Entryway C, with Akash and two other first-year students, whom I will call "Burke" and "Lehman."

What's the only way to find out what a typical student's life is like? To become a student myself. By move-in, I was ready to begin. I told my friends and neighbors that I was leaving the country for a few weeks, put an out-of-office reply on my e-mail, and went undercover as an entering (or, since I'm a Tripoli grad myself, reentering!) freshman.

MOVE-IN

I share a bedroom with Akash, while Lehman and Burke share the bedroom next door. At first, this was a bit awkward because Akash is such a smash hit with the ladies, but luckily he's also a polite and considerate young man. And anyway, when he's entertaining a young woman in our room, I can always hang out in the common room. We have a futon, a comfy chair, and a nice window seat. Plus, there's always someone to talk to, whether it's Lehman, Burke, or just someone stopping by to say hello.

No disguise is perfect, and it's only natural that I've had to do some explaining. As I was laying out my pill organizers and other toiletries on move-in day, I looked up to see Akash staring at me from the doorway.

"Are you a parent?" he said.

Indeed I am, Akash! I'm the proud father of two girls, both of them Tripoli College graduates! In fact, one of my daughters lives just half an hour away in Manchester, which has been a great comfort to me since my wife passed away. She was the one who showed me how to set up this blog.

But I had to stick to my cover story, so I said, "I'm a freshman like you. I'm a little older because I took some time off after high school. My name is William, or Bill."

Then I asked him if he wanted to do any drugs or drink some wine, in the hope that I might be able to learn something about drug and alcohol abuse among incoming freshmen, but he said he was going out to meet some people he knew from TOOT (Tripoli Outdoor Orientation Trips). The TOOT program has been a big hit since it was established eight years ago.

Akash wasn't the only one who had questions for me. Later that day, I was sitting in the common room with Burke and Lehman. The two of them were looking through the course catalog and I was enjoying a light doze on the couch. Suddenly I was startled by the sound of a book slamming shut, and I opened my eyes to see Lehman squatting in front of me.

"Hey, man, listen," he said. "Don't you want to tell us what this is about?"

I thought I'd play dumb, so I told him I wasn't sure what he meant.

"What are you, someone's grandfather?"

I saw Burke cringe, but I reassured him. It was a fair question, after all. I told them that I'd taken a few years off after high school.

(And no, I don't have grandchildren yet, but I've got my fingers crossed!)

It was naïve of me to expect a disguise to fool these young men, but now that the subject was out in the open, they seemed to take it all in stride. Soon, it almost seemed as if they had lost interest. I've been amazed to discover that most of the other freshmen I've met have reacted the same way. Today's students are remarkably open-minded about deviant lifestyle decisions. Of course, I've been spending all my time with freshmen and I have yet to run across students I've known in my capacity as dean. I'll have to improve my disguise!

Now Lehman was explaining how relieved he was that his parents had finally gone.

"College is a time to be independent," I agreed, "and pursue a journey of self-discovery that could lead you to an activity or course of study that might become your consuming passion."

"Yeah," said Burke. "I mean, it's like, maybe you know some guy in high school, and he's just this weedy little guy, and then he goes away to college and next Thanksgiving he comes back with a bow in his hair and he's like, 'Oh, okay, I self-identify as a female water buffalo.' "

Lehman nodded. "What I've never understood is what's a beefalo?"

I didn't react to these turns and surprises in the conversation. One thing I've noticed as I've gotten older is that it's become more and more difficult to adjust when the topic of conversation changes.

"This can be a stressful time for parents and new students alike," I said. "I wonder if the move-in process could be improved or streamlined in any way?"

"A beefalo is just what it is," Burke said. "It's its own thing, like a squid or a periscope."

I pressed on. "What are the three things you would change about move-in or about Tripoli College orientation activities?"

This got Lehman's attention. "I've had some trouble with the RA," he said.

As far as I could tell from his confused account, the residential adviser had made a disparaging comment about the New York Knicks. There was no indication that this remark had been disrespectful or mean-spirited. The problem was only that Lehman, to use the old phrase, couldn't take a joke. I tried to explain that the RA must have simply misjudged the degree of Lehman's devotion to the New York Knicks franchise, but Lehman only rolled his eyes.

"What about you, Burke? What are three things you'd change?"

I had already seen that Burke was less self-possessed than Lehman, who hails from New York City, and I could tell that he wasn't having such an easy time with the transition to college life.

"It seems like all they serve in the dining hall is pudding," he said. "Also I don't know where to get my schedule signed. The third thing is that coming here was a mistake."

I reassured him, as I had reassured so many students over the years. "You'll discuss your schedule with your adviser, and I'm sure he or she will contact you soon. You're going to do great here, Burke. We all are. Tripoli's self-serve pudding bars are famous."

I told him that everything would get easier as he grew more familiar with the rhythm of life here at Tripoli College. I also encouraged him to get involved in one or more of the 200+ student organizations on campus, one of which might turn out to be his consuming passion. Then I reminded him that the counseling center was a great resource that many students took advantage of at least once in their four years at Tripoli.

Lehman was drinking from a bottle of white rum. He said, "You want a nip, Grandpa?"

I wanted more than a nip: I wanted the inside story on the drinking habits of our students. But I'd have to leave it for another time. I needed to catch up on some sleep!

REFLECTIONS

Over the last few days, I've settled into my new life. On a personal level, I feel better already. It's great just to get out of my empty house! Of course, as a seventy-year-old man trying to keep up with young men and women in their teens and early twenties, I do face some challenges. My days are so full that I hardly have time to think, and I feel as if I'm always rushing, whether I'm eating an early breakfast at Pinkman Hall, walking to class in the chill of the morning, hitting the books, attending dramatic performances, surfing the net, or just talking about sports and metaphysics with my suitemates in the common room.

My fellow students have been very welcoming. I've started to feel like I'm the only one who cares about my age, so I've given up my disguise and started dressing more casually. Most days I just wear my old loafers, a pair of chinos, and a very old tweed sport coat over a T-shirt. That way, if students I know see me out on campus, they'll just think I'm taking a stroll in my capacity as dean. Burke thinks I look great, incidentally, and he tells me I'm fitting in better than he is.

As I relive all the trials and tribulations of selecting classes (exclusively freshman seminars, so I won't risk being recognized by an upperclassman), getting to know my suitemates, and familiarizing myself with the routines of student life, I've been thinking about my first experience as a student at Tripoli College, fifty years ago. A lot has changed—Tripoli is now coed, we offer a greater variety of courses in a greater variety of subjects, our student body is diverse and technologically savvy in a way that my generation would have found hard to believe—but a lot has also remained the same. The anxieties, fears, and frustrations are different in substance but the same in essence. Who am I? we ask ourselves. What do I want? What am I interested in?

And whatever the answers are, they're bound to be exciting.

From: "Maggie Bell" <mbell1990@tripoli.edu>
To: "Chris Bell" <cfb456@mercurylink.net>
Date: September 6, 2009, at 2:06 AM
Subject: (no subject)

Chris!

Somebody asked me yesterday what it's like to have a twin brother, and I told her, "Well, you know, I don't know what it's like *not* to have a twin brother."

How are things at NYU? It's hot as hell here. I'm glad to hear everything's good with Max. I know reunions can be weird. What's it been for you guys, like a year and a half? I wish you could tell just Mom, too, but you know she would tell Dad right away. Whenever you feel like you're ready, that's the right time. They'll be able to handle it.

I finally got moved into my new dorm. It's all right (I've got a single and AC and a beautiful view of the loading dock and dumpsters behind the post office) but now I'm with these three girls I don't know at all. You know how there's that fourth person sometimes in a room with three friends? Now it's me. I probably should've just roomed with Becca again, but we were fighting so much, which I realize I didn't tell you anything about, but it's only that it wasn't real fighting, it was just mutual irritation, like who got toothpaste on the toilet seat and you left this hard-boiled egg to rot in the fridge and are you peeing a ton in the shower because it's turning yellow. Now Becca's in a suite with Liz and Francoise and I'm in my bedroom with the door closed while these three turnips are out there hanging pink feather boas on the walls. I mean, it's OK, really. They aren't bad people, and we're on different schedules, and I'm excited about my classes, but you know how it is—one of them is in the choir and I mentioned I sang choir in high school and then they asked if I liked Rihanna, if I could "like, sing, like, just a little bit" for them, and I felt pretty suspicious of that. They all seem to have the same name. Chloe? They're all named Chloe.

Anyway. Ugh. I don't know what's the matter with me. I feel more and more closed off and depressed. And I'm worried I'm getting fat. I just want to be slim and well dressed so that everyone knows I'm just like all the other privileged upper-middle-class morons. One time last year, I never told you this, but one time I had to do my laundry across the quad and I was going to change it and I forgot my key. So then there I was in my laundry-day clothes, dirty and wrinkled, and nobody would let me in! They thought I was, like, some crazy person off the street trying to steal their clothes! So now I just want to activate as few prejudices as possible. I don't want anyone imagining that I overcame terrible odds and struggled and worked hard and got myself out of the ghetto and into Tripoli, either. If I'd worked hard and struggled, I'd be at fucking Wesleyan or something.

But classes are great, yeah. Whatever other problems I'm having, I do feel more committed to school. I'm taking this class on Atlantic history where we read slave narratives. It's brutal but I've decided I have to face it. This week we're reading the *Narrative of the Life of Henry Box Brown*. This man, a slave in Virginia, mailed himself to freedom in a wooden crate! The professor is this super-impressive guy from St. Renard, Professor John Kabaka, who looks sort of like Peter Tosh. Extremely handsome and commanding. He's got one of those cheerful Anglo-Caribbean accents, which seems very much at odds with his burn-the-cane-fields-and-hang-the-overseer way of talking, but I guess that's the paradox of reggae. Island rhythm and island anger! Maybe that's why people like it? Anyway, there's something mesmerizing about Professor Kabaka. He could talk the husk off a coconut. I feel like I'd do anything he told me to do.

That's *got* to be it. Say hi to Max for me.

XOXO,
M

From
THE TRIPOLI COLLEGE TELEGRAPH
September 8, 2009

Poor Tripoli!

This Wednesday, President Richmond announced that the value of Tripoli's endowment has fallen by as much as 35 percent this year, a result of the global economic crisis.

"These are trying times for all of us," she explained. "We're all going to have to tighten our belts."

Asked when we could expect the endowment to return to pre-crash levels, Provost Alexander Kosta said, "Certainly not in the foreseeable future. This is the reality now."

After the crash last year, the president instituted a hiring freeze, a decrease in the operating budget, and a suspension of merit raises. These measures remain in effect, with layoffs and additional cuts to come.

But after almost a year, many students, and even some professors, are scratching their heads.

"Wasn't all the money imaginary to begin with?" said Jerry Black '12, articulating a misconception shared by many. "Why would it be so bad to lose it?"

"It's going to be difficult for a lot of people to understand," said the provost. "The world of high finance is complex, nuanced, and abstract. Many of our investments were derivatives three and four times removed from the assets to which their value was linked."

Many, but not all. Tripoli lost nearly $500,000 on its investment in Consolidated Paper Products, one of the companies that prints the toy money used in the board game Monopoly.

"Just before the economy collapsed," said Professor David Monahan of the Economics Department, "Tripoli was literally printing Monopoly money."

The provost acknowledged the mistake: "We just did not fully understand how many young people are playing Monopoly on mobile wireless devices, computers, etc. The board game itself turns out to be much less popular than we thought."

Some members of the community have dismissed the current crisis as just one of the many periodic adjustments inherent in the "boom and bust" cycle of capitalism. But there is reason to believe that it may have more lasting effects.

In order to overcome a potentially disastrous budget shortfall, the college has had to seek support from for-profit corporations. Administrators and trustees are now in the final stage of negotiations with the multinational food and food services corporation Big Anna® Brands. Tripoli already has a number of formal and informal relationships with the snack food giant, notably a shared interest in the island of St. Renard and a technology transfer agreement with Big Anna® subsidiary Genutrex®. It is expected that the new partnership will solemnize and extend these existing relationships, although the terms and conditions of the agreement have not yet been made public.

From
ENGLISH DEPARTMENT COURSE LISTINGS
Fall 2009

ENGL 110a / *Freshman Seminar: An Introduction to Disputation*
(MULTIPLE SECTIONS)

Argument, whether constructive or acrimonious, is an essential part of any collective enterprise, and learning how to express a considered opinion in writing is critical to your success at Tripoli. We are not going to entertain the notion that real consensus is ever possible, but we may discover that some of our convictions overlap in ways that strike us as mutually acceptable. Readings will vary across sections but will likely include Professor Beckford's memoir, *Inactivity Is Death*, and passages from *Jeremiads*, a volume of his occasional writings. Some sections will discuss the Tripoli Summer Reading Program selection, *Tan as Fuck: A Surfer's Tragedy*, the authorship of which is unknown.

ENGL 215 / *Introspection and Atonement*
ANONYMOUS

Each student will perform a searching and pained examination of his or her own conscience. The results of this examination will be private and may not be recorded, especially not in the form of weekly response papers. Readings will include selections from Professor Carlyle's poetry, with special emphasis on his postmodern epic, *Frangible Me: A Problem in Hexameters.*

ENGL 300 / *Imaginative Writing: Poetry*
CARLYLE

The essential elements of our poetry will be courage, audacity, and revolt. Literature has up to now magnified pensive immobility, ecstasy, and slumber. We want to exalt movements of aggression, feverish sleeplessness, the double march, the perilous leap, the slap, and the blow with the fist. The poet must spend himself with warmth, glamour, and prodigality to increase the enthusiastic fervor of the primordial elements. We are on the extreme promontory of the centuries! What is the use of looking behind at the moment when we must open the mysterious shutters of the impossible? Time and Space died yesterday. We are already living in the absolute. We want to glorify war—the only cure for the world—militarism, patriotism, the destructive gesture of the anarchists, the beautiful ideas which kill.

ENGL 367 / *The Phenomenology of Feeling: Taking Stock, Taking Action*
(MULTIPLE SECTIONS)

Are you feeling down? Do you have persistent neck pain? Doesn't Russian roulette seem like a reasonable pastime? If everyone else were jumping off a bridge, wouldn't you just shoot yourself instead? If you answered yes to any of these questions, you may be eligible to participate in a clinical trial that could help to relieve you of some of your most aggravating symptoms. We're looking for nonsmokers between the ages of eighteen and twenty-two, with no history of yaws or high cholesterol, to help us test a nutritional supplement and mood additive derived from the Carawak Apple tree of St. Renard, a tree long prized for its effects by the indigenous people of that island. For inclusion/exclusion and reimbursement information, contact GENUTREX® nutrition at ghostappletrial@genutrex.com and include your name, student ID number, and undergraduate major (if known).

Letter from
ISRAEL FRAMINGHAM TRIPOLI
to
ZEPHANIAH FITCH

September 24, 1788

Dear Sir,

I have received your letter of the 18th. I am very grateful to you, not least for your cheerful acquiescence as for your understanding. As to your question, I would have our Professors give to these Indian Scholiasts instruction in every branch of learning, excepting only Moral Philosophy, which I do not hold a true science, preferring rather to imagine that a sense of right and wrong, though present in every man, be he Indian or White, to a greater or lesser extent, is present nevertheless from birth, & tends only to become vitiated by artificial ideas.

You ask me to give an account of the island of Saint Reynard, which I will do without disguise, tho fearful of offending against Your Honor's good nature. I was the guest of a Mr. Sturge, whose cousin I knew at Boston, and stayed with him in the town of San Christobal for the whole period of my residence there, excepting only a brief journey to his plantation in the county of Binghamshire. The aspect of this town is very bad. Every second edifice, as it seems to me, is a house of negotiable affection. The streets, which are of white sand, are bestrewn with Ordure, and abound with Brigands and Carbuncled Scoundrels of the worst description. I saw a man

Killed in the squalid piazza, not ten paces from where I strolled, for no crime other than that of standing where another wished to pass. The planters are no better than the transported criminals, and some are worse, for if they are not indolent, chicaning, and voluptuary, then they are Bedlamites. Their government is a burlesque, their rhetoric and conduct at perpetual handicuffs, and the only law they cherish is that of Profit, tho all in all I think it is not the very great wealth to be obtained from the Sugar cane that renders the island insusceptible of civilization, but the Mortality of the place, by which a man waking in the full strength of his youth may find himself wasted and hollow-eyed at the sun's meridian, and dead at its final decline.

Every man will speak of the fair as his own market has gone in it, & perhaps I judge the island too harshly, for I was much incommoded by the heat, which frustrates the operation of the animal economy and makes walking impossible in the noon-day, with the result that between the heat of the daylight hours, & at night the Unbearable Torment of those teasing trumpeters the moskitos, a man verily becomes a Prisoner in his smoky oven of a chamber. Do not think that the prisoner's couch may be his asylum, for sleep is a comfort to be sought fruitlessly, night after night, as one seeks a fabular creature, or the knowledge of God's inscrutable will. If the moskitos are not molestation enough, one is startled at the first sweet presage of repose by the most discordant piercing yells & shoutings from the street below. An old man is thus thrown upon his recollections of better times, and I thought, my Friend, long and longingly of those palmy days at New Haven, when we were young.

Of the natural world I can speak more kindly, for there is an incredible variety of luxuriant vegetation, including a great many extraordinary fruits, tho I did not sample the ill-famed Carrawak- or Ghost-Apple, which my Grandfather remembered with such a peculiar compound of fear and fascination. Most remarkable to me was the *Ficus* tree, which overspreads an acre or more, and lowers columnar roots to secure itself the more firmly in the island's impoverished soil. But this mention of the soil prompts me to relate an astonishing occurrence, viz. that last year, when the canes were ripe and the Negroes preparing for the harvest, there was a tempest, causing heavy rain, in consequence of which a full three acres of Sugar cane, which stood upon the plantation of a Mr. Howth, became somehow detached from the earth, or perhaps came to float upon it as butter floats upon milk, and the whole field then slid a distance of one mile down Trowbridge Hill and came to rest in a fallow field belonging to a Mr. Price. Seeing that the cane was not one cherry stone the worse for its journey, Mr. Price thereafter maintained that it was his to harvest and process, being now upon his own acreage. Mr. Howth pled his own case just as fervently, & because the dispute could not be adjudicated in a timely fashion, there being no precedent, the cane was left to rot.

Of the plantation which I visited myself, I am of divided mind. Surely it was very beautiful, the new cane being green and vigorous in the rains, and the plantation house splendid, & surely it was a pleasure to see the Negroes working in the fields, for they are a marvel of cheer and natural gentility, but one pities them terribly, knowing that their labor is forced, and seeing how Brutally they are punished for the smallest infraction. I could have wept to see their miserable huts, which are almost as bad as Irish cabins, and indeed sometimes just as bad.

I beg your forgiveness for my unseasonable meditativeness, Sir, and the rhapsodical nature of this letter, but to these descriptions I must subjoin a reflection of my own. I have, as you know, greatly enriched myself in the manufacture of pot-ash and sundry other commercial goods, & I am now grown apprehensive on this account, for as it seems to me it is the commerce of Europeans which has transformed Saint Reynard from the bless'd isle of my grandfather's recollection to the Malarious Rock it is become, & I fear that because there is some cotton raised here, tho not a great deal, and mayhaps it is my own pot-ash that is used to whiten the cloth produced therefrom, in whatever far-flung manufactory this whitening is done, then it may be said quite truthfully that I myself am a participant in the very commerce that has brought the island low. Is it not strange and terrible to think so, Sir, and to reflect that I must therefore participate in a system which I have come to abhor, having seen by what depraved measures the Negro is made to labor? Since you ask, my Friend, it is this difficulty of knowing what we do in the world, and what resonances and reverberations our actions may have, even including those we deplore, that have altered my mind as to the disposition of my fortune. It would be unction indeed to my bruis'd conscience if I could be sure that such money as I have, whatever the uses to which those articles of my manufacture have been put, should itself serve the cause of right. You may wonder why I do not then set aside some portion for the cause of the Abolitionists. I am afraid that in doing so I might give my brothers pretext to have me pronounced a Madman, and to break my Will on that account.

I am filled, Sir, after seeing for myself the yellowed coco-nuts, and the peculiar beauty of the tropic sea, and all that passes upon the island, with misgivings of another kind, for I can appreciate as never before that the world is wide, and my acquaintance with it almost entirely limited to this small corner of earth, New England, and I cannot dissemble my apprehension that there might have been a more diverting way of spending my time than in the manufacture of pot-ash.

I am not certain I understand the comparison you draw between Atheism and Demonism. Please do enlighten me. Fortune, that ungracious duchess, harrows my habitual sufferings with new torments, for I suffer with a Tissick, & Glossitis, & to-day I have done some violence to my foot with a hoe, and I have nothing to do but lie abed and think of these things. I am, with great esteem and friendship,

Your honor's most Humble & most obliged servant,

Israel Framingham Tripoli

MINUTES / SEPTEMBER 2009
FACULTY MEETING

———————

President Lillian Richmond called to order the first faculty meeting of the 2009–2010 academic year. As she did so, the faculty secretary, author of these minutes and himself a professor of geology, felt a titter of excitement and uncapped his pen.

The president began by welcoming the faculty and expressing her enthusiasm about the upcoming semester, adding that Dean Brees, who could not attend the meeting because he was undercover on campus, felt the same way. The upshot was this: Times were tough, and we were facing significant financial challenges, but this was also an exciting moment at Tripoli College.

If it had not been a restful summer, the president continued, at least it had been a very long summer. Some thanks were due to William Beckford, professor of English and acting chancellor of the English Department, who had directed the Summer at Tripoli program for the thirty-first consecutive year and who, as always, had kept that program running smoothly. Professor Beckford had also been playing a larger administrative role at Tripoli's Proxy College of the West Indies at St. Renard, to which he would be traveling several times this semester.

Francis Amundsen, professor of English, rose and began to applaud Professor Beckford for his service to the college. A large percentage of the faculty, probably something like 90 percent, quickly followed suit. All of those abstaining from this show of approval were English professors, reminding us of the deep divisions within that department. Professor Beckford himself smiled like a jack-o'-lantern and thanked the president for her kind words. His voice was powerful and authoritative. He seemed, as always, unnaturally vigorous for a person so manifestly advanced in years, and the secretary wondered if perhaps there was some truth to the rumor that he had served on the Italian general staff during World War I.

When the applause had subsided, the president updated us on the financial situation. While exact figures were not available, recent estimates were that the endowment would be down at least 40 percent this year. This was a very substantial loss—indeed, almost an incomprehensible loss—and the secretary would have found it hard to believe had he not also seen his personal investments melt away to nothing.

There was one bright spot. Tripoli was in the final stage of negotiations with Big Anna® Brands, which, although it was an independent for-profit corporation, was very supportive of higher education. If we could arrive at a satisfactory agreement with Big Anna®—an agreement that would not only reinforce and extend the arrangements and accommodations we had already made with that company, but would probably also lead to significant cooperative ventures on St. Renard, where the company had a substantial interest—it would represent a big step toward financial security.

Speaking of St. Renard, the president was pleased to welcome Professor John Kabaka, who was a Renardenne himself. Since earning his doctorate from Cambridge, he had been teaching Atlantic and colonial history at the University of the West Indies, Jamaica, and we were lucky to have him with us as a visiting professor this year.

As the faculty clapped and called out "Welcome!" or "Hi!" Professor Kabaka rose to his feet and asked for silence. Speaking quite loudly in his mellifluous Caribbean accent, he professed himself "extremely angry" about the proposed agreement with Big Anna®. He said that he had not heard anything about this—if he had, he would not have accepted our offer. He could only conclude that he had been lured to Tripoli under false pretenses. He would not disparage the intelligence of the faculty by detailing the many abuses and depredations of that vile corporation, but he did feel impelled to mention, since apparently no one had bothered to acquaint themselves with his work, that he had spent his whole life struggling directly or indirectly against Big Anna® and the neoliberal economic policies—"slavery by another name"— according to which that company justified its stranglehold on his island home.

This was, at the very least, an excruciatingly embarrassing moment, but the president handled it with aplomb. Without missing a beat or giving any sign of displeasure, she explained that it was for all these reasons that Professor Kabaka had been invited to Tripoli. She had hoped he might function as the "conscience" of the institution at this moment of crisis. She herself was deeply conflicted over the Big Anna® question, as indeed who wouldn't be? But the truth was inescapable: We could not afford to fill the soap dispensers in the bathrooms. Big Anna® had offered us a lifeline and we would have to take it.

The president's use of the word "conscience" seemed to convey an unpleasant impression, at least to the secretary, but Professor Kabaka said nothing.

There followed various items of no doubt great local importance, but the secretary paid them little attention. There was, to the best of his recollection, some discussion of the Library Digitization Project and then of the rec center, which had been renovated thanks to the generosity of an anonymous donor. The president's own office had been relocated to the fourth floor of the rec center.

Meanwhile, Professor Kabaka continued to sit quietly in his little chair, his face impassive, his arms crossed. No one paid any attention to him. It was as if nothing had happened.

The president now called upon Maura Riesling, professor of biology, who was heading up Tripoli's new Sustainability Initiative, a program administered by the Office of Environmental Health and Safety. Could Professor Riesling give us an update?

She could and did, but she limited her remarks to a single sentence, half grim prognostication and half expression of despair. She said, "Sustainability is not possible as long as there are humans on earth."

The president, now visibly frustrated, turned the meeting over to Antoine Benmarcus, professor of anthropology and dean of the faculty, who had a few items of his own. Dean Benmarcus wanted to remind us that we would be making no new hires this year. That, he said, is what "hiring freeze" meant. He then gazed meaningfully around the room, but there were no comments, not even from the economics department, which had lately been pursuing a policy of aggressive expansion.

The dean had a great deal more to say, but it grieves the secretary to report that he allowed his attention to wander once again. There was a game of Ultimate Frisbee in progress out on the quad. It was only the beginning of September, after all, and there was still a distinct summertime vibe on campus.

When the dean had finished, the president had a word to say about the Vocational Writing Program (VWP). As of this fall, the VWP was fully integrated: It would administer all introductory composition and professional writing classes—formerly the purview of the English department. The president was aware that many of us had objected to the creation of an independent and autonomous writing program, and in principle she agreed with us, but the VWP—which was also privately endowed—was important for our reputation as a school that catered to the needs of low- as well as mid- and high-ability students. Given the state of our finances, it was more important than ever to appeal to a wide range of students.

The president then introduced Bish Pinkman III, associate director of the VWP, who wanted to remind all faculty members teaching a VWP-sponsored course that the biweekly Curriculum and Pedagogy Symposia were mandatory. "These meetings," said Mr. Pinkman III, "are indispensable in that they afford you with the resources, outcome assessments, and degree of technicality for the relevant VWP writing outcomes, and any absence on your part means that your students will not have access to the level of pedagogy we expect you to produce."

There was a prolonged silence as faculty members, stunned and saddened by this announcement, attempted to gauge its relevance to themselves. Then Jennifer Wilson, professor of biology, said that the VWP was "one in the eye for anyone who bothered about the liberal arts" and moved that Mr. Pinkman III be locked up. The president treated this motion as a joke, but when several professors rose to second it, she explained that the VWP was too important to the trustees—its importance was political and not intellectual—and we would have to table the question of what to do to Mr. Pinkman III.

Wearing an expression of profound disgust, Professor Kabaka now rose and left the room. Because he was seated close to the door and because he moved swiftly and silently, his departure went entirely unremarked. The secretary noticed it only because he happened to be gazing longingly at the beautiful and corrupt Malinka West, professor of sociology, who was seated to Professor Kabaka's left.

But there was no time to consider what this may have meant: It was time to hear fall reports from standing committees.

The president now called on Pierce Reynolds, professor of computer science and chair of the Committee on Committees (CC), who explained that he and his fellow committee members had been unable to proceed with their work because they had discovered that the CC was the only committee not subject to its (the CC's) own review process. They had discussed evaluating themselves, but that solution was impracticable—it would, Professor Reynolds said, be like trying to lift one's own person off the ground and hold oneself suspended in the air. Better that the college form another committee, the so-called Committee on the Committee on Committees (CCC), whose purpose would be to evaluate the CC.

This motion was treated as a joke and met with good-natured laughter. Then, in a surprising turn, it was seconded by Professor Beckford, who volunteered to head the new committee.

Richard Carlyle, professor of English, who had only just arrived and whose disordered clothing and wild eyes suggested a prolonged debauch, wondered who or what would have authority over the CCC. Surely we were establishing a dangerous precedent, one that would inevitably lead to the creation of additional committees—the Committee on the Committee on the Committee on Committees (CCCC), the Committee on the Committee on the Committee on the Committee on Committees (CCCCC), and so on—each one holding review power over the previous one. But Hanson Brokovitch, professor of religion, explained that there was no reason the CC could not evaluate the CCC. The only committee it could not evaluate was itself. Did Professor Reynolds agree? He did, and yet Professor Carlyle worried that this arrangement, too, was problematic. Surely it would create a situation in which conflict would escalate indefinitely, perhaps terminating in violence, since each committee would be able to challenge the essential legitimacy of the other. Professor Beckford took issue with this "doomsday scenario," explaining that we would be sure to establish clear routes of appeal in the event that either committee should object to the suggestions of the other.

A vote was taken and the motion passed by an easy margin, with only Professor Beckford's enemies dissenting. Professor Carlyle, who was now busy pouring Gatorade powder into the mouth of a canned energy drink, was the only abstention.

Meanwhile, the president had grown impatient, and she moved that we skip over any remaining committee business, which was, in any case, detailed in a sequence of reports that the faculty had received by e-mail. A second was found, there was no discussion, a vote was taken, and the motion passed.

It was now time for the Athletic Association's report. Glenn Forrest, assistant to the deputy director of the Athletic Association, rose and was greeted with enthusiastic applause and cheers of "Go Tyrants!" Mr. Forrest thanked everyone for coming, evidently under the impression that he himself had called the meeting, and said that we had an exciting year ahead of us. He expressed his conviction—a conviction he shared with John Bacon, director of the Athletic Association, who sent his greetings and regretted that a prior engagement had prevented him from being here today—that the football team was poised to have a breakout season.

Attempting, as always, to curry favor with the wealthy and autonomous Athletic Association, the faculty reacted to this news with more applause and additional cheers of "Go Tyrants!" But Mr. Forrest was not finished. In fact, he had considerably more to say. He spoke and gestured for perhaps ten minutes, no doubt encouraged by the fervent and continuous cheering of the faculty, although the secretary cannot have been alone in tuning him out and gazing instead at the restful scene out on the quad, where the Ultimate Frisbee game was winding to a close but where there were still plenty of students lounging in the sweet grass or moving about in small, lazy groups.

At last Mr. Forrest paused for a drink of water and apologized: He was losing his voice. Luckily, he had only one item left on his agenda. He would now read a statement suggested by remarks said to have been made by Coach Kingman.

"Dear professors: Thanks for all your hard work!"

Were there any questions? There were not. Mr. Forrest thanked everyone and said that the Athletic Association would be "in touch." With that, he took his leave.

When he was gone, the president expressed her hope that we had been appropriately enthusiastic in our applause and in our cheers of "Go Tyrants!" She could appreciate that the effort of shamming enthusiasm probably left us feeling the "world exhaustion of a prostitute," but, as we knew, she had no direct authority over the disposition of Athletic Association funds. Those funds would continue to "trickle down" only as long as the Athletic Association felt that we admired what they did. At least we would no longer have to worry about the football players themselves: As of this fall, they were "academic exempt."

She then asked if there were any questions or announcements. In fact, she had one of her own. She had received a text message from Dean Brees, which she would read aloud:

"Dining halls must improve offerings. Very important! Greetings all."

Francis Amundsen, professor of English, observed that this was a very articulate text message, and he wondered why young people could not follow the dean's example. Professor Brokovitch suggested that maybe it was because they were undernourished.

Once again: Were there any more announcements?

There were not, and on this note the meeting moved into executive session, which is beyond the scope of these minutes. The dispassionate secretary slid his chair back and rose, his wrist aching and his stomach rumbling. There were a few pleasantries to be dispensed with—a good-night here, a see-you-tomorrow there—and then he slipped into the hall and descended the ringing marble steps, wondering where Dean Brees was that evening.

ENVIRONMENTAL SUSTAINABILITY INITIATIVE

Invasive Species Alert: African Walking Ape (Homo sapiens)

From its original home in central East Africa, this tropical creature has spread to every continent except Antarctica and has caused habitat destruction and the displacement or eradication of native species on an unprecedented scale. It threatens organisms across all ecological niches and has done irreparable environmental harm, destroying soil fertility, draining wetlands, contaminating waterways and groundwater supplies, causing deforestation and desertification, and initiating an irreversible process of climate warming that threatens to shift seasonal patterns even further.

The African Walking Ape is a large-bodied social mammal with a hypertrophic brain and extremely dexterous forepaws, or hands. Adults range from about one hundred to three hundred pounds, although larger and smaller individuals have been observed. Its skin may be anywhere from a sandy cream color to a dark brown, and it is hairless except for a large tuft on the top of the cranium and smaller tufts beneath the arms and between the legs of mature animals. It exhibits marked sexual dimorphism, with males of the species typically larger, more aggressive, and more heavily muscled. Females have proportionally wider hips, narrower shoulders, and two prominent mammary glands on the upper thorax. It is easily distinguished from other apes and monkeys by its distinctive upright posture and enormous cranial capacity.

The Walking Ape is omnivorous and can subsist for long periods on vegetable matter, but it is also a tenacious and irresistible predator. It has decimated fisheries in every ocean and eradicated megafauna in Australia, most of the Americas, and isolated islands across the globe. It also functions as a vector for other invasive species, clearing ground so that imported edible vegetation can flourish in traumatized areas. In addition, it "husbands" a number of animal species, including several birds, a number of other large-bodied mammals, and at least one species of social insect. The deliberate introduction of these species to virgin ecosystems is a further threat to native flora and fauna.

Although the Walking Ape reproduces slowly, it is adaptable, aggressive, and long-lived. It is also unique among other large predators and omnivores in that it forms very large communities, sometimes consisting of several million individuals. It has learned to construct dwellings and body coverings which effectively reproduce the warm conditions of its original tropical home, and this has enabled it to establish a lasting presence in environments as hostile as the high arctic.

Although the Walking Ape lacks claws and other obvious defenses, experience teaches that it should be regarded as extremely dangerous and approached, if at all, with great caution.

From: "Maggie Bell" <mbell1990@tripoli.edu>
To: "Chris Bell" <cfb456@mercurylink.net>
Date: September 19, 2009, at 12:15 AM
Subject: (no subject)

Mister C,

I woke up this morning one minute before the alarm on my phone was supposed to go off, and the alarm tone (bell tower) was already running through my head. It's terrible how the brain spends its time.

Last night I got a little drunk with the dean of students! He's living in a freshman dorm under an assumed name. Nobody seemed particularly bothered by this. He was wearing a tie-dyed shirt under his sport coat and he'd dyed his hair this weird rich creamy Nutella color. I told him all kinds of embarrassing stuff. I kept saying that I was turning over a new leaf. Am I?

Lonely, yeah. Or I don't know. I haven't seen Becca or Francoise more than once or twice all year. I've just been wandering around by myself. But actually I kind of like it. I'm not depressed or anything but I'm more thoughtful. When I saw Becca she yelled at me for not calling her. Like that's supposed to make me want to call her? I'd rather just hang out with the Chloes.

Do you still think you're going to tell Dad at Christmas? I guess I don't have any idea what you should do. I've just been assuming he'll be a jerk about it but who knows, right? Have I told you about my friend Big Ben? I hope someday you'll meet him. He was on the football team and then one day during halftime of some big game he told everyone he was gay and he hated football. He walked right out of the locker room and all the way back to campus in full uniform. Then he had to reapply to Tripoli because football credits don't count toward a bachelor's degree, and now he's a lit major and he smokes cloves. Not bad, right? I've been going to freshman parties with him and it's good because it reminds me of a more innocent time. Do you get nostalgic for freshman year? I know it's only been two years but I really feel like things are different now. Freshmen are so excited about everything!

Ben showed me a video of one of the Tripoli kickers falling down when he tried to kick a field goal. He fell twice in one game. Then the other kicker came in to replace him, but the other guy, I mean the backup, took his helmet off at midfield and started crying. I'll send you the link. That is some troubling shit, man! Like actual unabashed weeping on the football field. But Ben says some of the players are part of a mandatory drug trial and it's fucking them up. They use these poor guys like guinea pigs, I think. And anyway, college football is a pretty grim setup even if Genutrex or whatever isn't sticking needles in them all the time. Think about it: The players are mostly black and they work really hard and a crucial condition of their employment, according to the NCAA, is that they don't get paid! They go up and down a field in all kinds of weather while white men yell at them from the sidelines. And also there's this whole idea that they're so well cared for, the college gives them food and clothes and housing, everybody admires them, yeah yeah yeah. The white coach knows best. Then the players end up with injuries and multiple concussions and maybe they blow their brains out. Go Tyrants!

This is Professor Kabaka talking. I think he's really gotten into my head. I told you about him? My Atlantic history professor. He says things like this: He says, "Slavery is the rule in human history." He has a loud voice and he's beautiful and he makes these statements that you can't argue with. "Human enterprises naturally tend toward exploitative arrangements." Governments, businesses, civic organizations—everything tends toward slavery, he says, and in order to prevent slavery from coming back and reestablishing itself, you have to *actively* resist it. He says that good intentions are not enough. You have to actively avoid the sweatshop shoes and the cheap electronics and the plantation bananas. It's kind of an incredible way to think about daily life, you know? The idea that our choices are what make economic systems work one way or another way or not at all. The problem is that it's exhausting and miserable to live this way! You spend all day sweating over these choices and then you think, "I'll just sit down here and take a load off and watch a little college football . . ." And there's Big Ben, or someone like him, struggling up the green field while the overseer screams himself hoarse on the sideline. Do we just accept the impossibility of ever doing anything that doesn't harm at least someone?

Ugh! Sorry. I'm trying to think of something more lighthearted. Do you know the story of how Europeans started eating potatoes? At first no one would touch them because they were said to be Indian food, but then this French or German aristocrat planted a potato patch and fenced it in and put up a Keep Out sign. And *immediately* people started breaking in and stealing the potatoes.

The other day in my abnormal psychology class, I was sitting next to a girl who fell asleep right in the middle of writing her notes, but she kept on going. Her handwriting was still perfectly legible, so it was like, "PTSD: soldiers, accidents, terrorism, watermelon beep beep."

Oh! And they're selling the college to a snack-food company! We're all going to have the logo tattooed on our asses!

Watermelon beep beep,
Maggie

ENGLISH DEPARTMENT COURSE LISTINGS
Fall 2009

ENGL 150 / *Toward Good and Evil*
HERMAN

An analysis of Professor Beckford's character. We will focus on cloth-ing, mode of speech, characteristic gestures, tacit assumptions, personal hygiene, mental hygiene, and short-term memory loss. We will discuss the professor's embattled relationship to good and evil, with particular reference to his three failed marriages, his recent excommunication, the various plots and gambits for which he has been called to account in our nation's courts of law, and his involve-ment in weapons technology. We ask: Which of his crimes are excus-able on the basis of his extraordinarily advanced age? How did he obtain a heavy-gauge amphibious motor scooter with shotgun rack and mount? Are those his original eyes? We want to be generous. We are willing to accept any number of explanations.

ENGL 187 / *Encountering the Contemporary: Speed, Light, and Color*
CARLYLE

Students will participate in the excitement of the professor's rapid mood swings! On good days, we'll have raffles and fashion shows! The less said about the bad days, the better! The professor once spent two weeks in a dog crate!!! Raise your hand if you want to learn how to steam open an envelope! Let's slash Professor Amundsen's tires!!!

How much simple syrup can you drink!? A gallon? *Two* gallons??? Assessments will involve rum and drag racing!!!!!

ENGL 410a / *Senior Seminar: What Is to Be Done?*
BECKFORD

An hour appointed by destiny has struck in the heavens above our beloved Tripoli. The declaration of war has already been delivered, and all students should pay heed: This semester we go to battle against the parasitic bureaucrats and check-licking administrators who, at every moment, have hindered our advance and have often endangered our very existence. Recent events can be summarized in the following phrases: promises, threats, blackmail, and finally, to crown the edifice, an ignoble siege by those who would refuse the gracious charity of that corporation which offers its hand in friendship. There is no required reading for this course. The time for reading and writing is at an end. Inactivity is death.

ENGL 411a / *Senior Seminar: Reading Literature*
LONGMAN

Sterling R. Loman Distinguished Professor of English Language and Literature, forty-nine, seeks twelve undergraduate English majors for weekly discussions of the modern British novel, including works by Lawrence, Conrad, Ford, Joyce, West, Woolf, Forster, Rhys, and others. Enthusiasm a must!

UNDERCOVER DEAN: BLOG POST #2

I had originally thought that my undercover mission would last one week (two weeks at the most), but here I am in my fourth week as a Tripoli freshman, and I still have so much to learn! That's why I plan to stay undercover as long as it takes.

It's no surprise that dorm life has been a major adjustment: In Hogbender Hall, I sleep in a bunk bed, so my sleeping patterns depend in part on Akash, my roommate, a much younger (and much more romantically active) man. My room is too hot, my bed is too soft, and there's always someone talking to me. The building itself hasn't been renovated since I myself was a Tripoli student! Plus, it seems as if anything could happen at any time, whether it's Lehman practicing with a small gong in the middle of the night or a lacrosse player discharging a fire extinguisher in the hallway outside.

At the same time, I find that I welcome the noise and distractions. My wife and I ate breakfast together every morning for years and years. We'd make steel-cut oatmeal and read the paper and we wouldn't say a word, but after she died the silence was different. The silence was so loud that I couldn't read at all. It's nice to live in a place where there's always something going on.

TRIPOLI AT THE TROUGH: NOTES ON DINING SERVICES

I want to talk first about one aspect of student life that arguably has an effect on every other aspect, and that's the question of what our students eat.

Tripoli has gotten a lot of attention recently because of what's been called our "old-fashioned" (and sometimes, less generously, our "reactionary") approach to dining services, and it's true that we haven't responded as quickly as some institutions to new and changing ideas about diet and nutrition. Part of the reason that some members of the community welcome the partnership with Big Anna® is that the company markets a lot of low-calorie foods. Professor Amundsen has even proposed that we source all of our food and food products from Big Anna®.

In the past, I ate in the dining halls once or twice a week, but I usually had other things on my mind and I rarely ate more than a salad, a piece of fruit, and maybe some bread and butter. My appetite isn't what it used to be! Now, however, in order to get a better sense of how our students eat, I pledged to have the regular entrée and two sides at each meal. Little did I know how difficult it would be to keep that promise. At both lunch and dinner, Tripoli's dining halls typically offer a choice of three entrées, not including the vegetarian option, but I've found that often there isn't much to choose. On an average night, options might include old favorites like *Drippy Wrap w/Fish*, *Bacon Blast Pizza*, or *Soused Mackerel*, plus a vegetarian alternative like *Crushed Legume Patty*. Students ordering the *Legume Patty* can choose to have it "fully loaded"—i.e., served on a bun with pickles, pickle relish, mayonnaise, onion rings, barbecue sauce, garlic aioli, and ketchup—or they can eat it plain off a piece of wax paper. Side dishes might include *Potato Salad* or *Poached Green Beans*, but more often there are less nutritious items such as *Mini Tacos*, *Candy Apple Slices in Jell-O* (which is not considered a dessert), or *Deep-Fried Pasta*. Dessert options might include the popular *Nut Ball in Chocolate Sauce*—a frozen ball of peanut butter dipped in hot fudge—or a bowl of *Chilled Water Matrix with Flavor Compound*, our only low-calorie dessert option.

But as you can tell from reading any number of editorials in the Tripoli *Telegraph*, the real controversy has to do with our famous self-serve pudding bars (c.f. "The Problem Is in the Pudding," *Tripoli College Telegraph*, September 4, 2009). Made possible by a generous gift from the Walker family, Tripoli's pudding bars have always struck me as a fun diversion from the rigors of college life, but I soon discovered that the reality was different. At lunch one day during my first week, I was taking a breather before heading into the servery when Lehman sat down across from me with a full tray. He was wearing a suit coat with mesh gym shorts.

"You know the best thing about college?" he said. "I can have as much pudding as I like, or none at all."

I thought this was a joke, since there was no pudding on his tray, but later he returned to the servery and came back with a bowl of *Butterychocolate Home-Style Comfort Pudding* topped with peanut butter pieces, whipped cream, and gummy worms. He dug in with a soup spoon and said to me, "Live a little, Grandpa."

It's one thing to say "live a little" before enjoying a small piece of chocolate cake after a nutritious dinner. After all, "live a little" is another way of saying "indulge yourself just this once." But Lehman has a large bowl of pudding every day, and often twice a day. He is, you might say, living quite a lot. He told me that he's gained six pounds since arriving at Tripoli, and I would guess that he's by no means exceptional in that regard. Yesterday I saw a young man holding his stomach and resting his forehead on the table. There was a half-finished bowl of pudding on his tray and some pudding and whipped cream in his hair. Later I saw him licking the bowl clean.

The pudding bars have become so much a part of Tripoli's identity that criticizing them is thought to be in bad taste, and it's only the rare student (Akash is one) who seems inclined to give them a pass. But it's worth considering what happens when an occasional indulgence becomes a daily habit. It's worth asking, too, whether there are foods one should probably never eat, under any circumstances. We don't say "live a little" in order to justify using hard drugs.

I hadn't spent much time thinking about the consequences, as much psychological as physical, of eating in the Tripoli dining halls every day, but I quickly discovered that most of our menu items left me feeling sick and confused rather than fortified. I actually vomited after trying the *Mini Tacos*! I'd venture the argument that this is more than just a public health issue. Our students can't hope to do their best work if they're not well nourished. I've seen Burke and Lehman taking long naps after dinner, and sometimes after lunch as well. One night I heard Burke observe matter-of-factly, "Sometimes my vision goes all wonky after I eat."

NIGHTLIFE

Let me shift gears now and turn to a topic that anyone concerned about the character of student life is going to be interested in—the elephant in the room, so to speak.

Ask a few Tripoli grads how they spent their college years, and inevitably a large percentage will say "partying."

Obviously, alcohol abuse is one of our major concerns in the dean's office. We don't mind if students have a drink now and then, as long as they do so in moderation and in a safe environment, but how much is too much? When, and why, does good fun become no fun?

It's almost impossible for us in the dean's office to get a good idea of how much the average Tripoli student drinks on a night out. I had seen Lehman drinking rum most nights, but I didn't know whether he was representative and I was eager for the opportunity to get an insider's look at a typical party. It wasn't long before I got my chance.

One night I was having trouble sleeping, so I went out to take a short walk and smoke a cigar. When I got back to the room, Lehman and Burke had a case of beer open on the table and they were taking turns rolling a pair of dice and drinking from red plastic cups. They explained that they were playing a game, the rules of which they quickly outlined. I decided not to ask how they'd gotten the beer (they are both underage) and instead asked if I could join them.

I've never been much of a drinker. Usually, when I begin to feel "buzzed," as my suitemates would say, I decide that I've had enough. But tonight was different. I couldn't beg off and head to my room, because that would have been a violation of etiquette and it might also have jeopardized the trust my suitemates had placed in me. Plus, I needed to stay up and observe. So I continued to roll the dice, drink the watery beer (I promised myself that if I did this again, I'd spring for something better!), and listen to the loud music Lehman was playing on his stereo. As I did so, I began to feel a sense of ease and comfort that I hadn't expected. Maybe readers will tell me that it was only the alcohol, but I think it was something more: It was a sudden realization of what was important, and what was not important, at that particular moment.

I looked around at my dorm room. Here was the old fireplace, its brick darkened by years of smoke (the flue was now blocked). Here was the bay window, with its blue curtains that moved in the cool night breeze. Here was the scuffed hardwood floor and dirty rug, and here was the desk lamp that shed a dim yellow light and left most of the room in shadow. Here were the old desks, the old chairs, the old black molding and door frames and window frames. And here *we* were: three college freshmen, content in one another's company and excited about the possibilities of this September night. I remember thinking, What does it matter, what *could* it matter, that one of us is fifty years older than the other two?

Soon we were sitting on the window seat, laughing and drinking our beers and talking about all kinds of interesting things. They asked me about the Vietnam War, and I told them a little about it. I hadn't seen much fighting, but I'd been stationed in Saigon in the late sixties. It was nice to speak freely with people who were amazed by stories that someone my own age would have heard thousands of times.

"Hey, man, listen, hold on," said Burke, suddenly growing very serious. "It's really cool that you made the decision to come to school and finally get your degree."

Lehman nodded, and continued nodding, and took a sip from his beer. I knew that sometimes he simply ignored most of what we said, but I didn't mind. I understood that this was "just his thing."

"I don't care if I get my identity stolen," he said. "What I say is take it."

Lehman wanted to go to a party his friend was throwing over at Farrier Hall. At this, the dean in me shook himself awake: Here was an opportunity to see more of the real Tripoli. I was feeling so comfortable at that point that I didn't even worry about running into someone who might recognize me. We put some beers into our coat pockets and headed down into the courtyard, where there were lots of students laughing and talking and rushing off in large groups.

Although Farrier Hall was just across the street, it seemed to take an enormously long time to get there. We had to stop every few feet to talk to some people Lehman knew, and then we ran into Akash, who had a beautiful young woman on his arm. He said a quick hello as the two of them hurried away.

"He gets all the girls," Burke said as we watched them go. "I've got to ask him what's his trick."

"Step one," Lehman said. "Be about a million times more handsome than you are."

"Well, he's also pretty unscrupulous. He'll say anything. He's like, 'Oh, okay, I'm Akash, I was born in a flapjack restaurant at the top of a runaway-truck ramp. I failed the drug test at the National Spelling Bee.' "

"Step two," Lehman continued. "Be another maybe fifty thousand times more handsome."

Then we were at the convenience store, where Lehman bought some cigarettes and I bought a few cigars. For some reason, I chose the cheapest I could find. Don't ask me why! They tasted like coal dust and stove polish, and later Burke remembered me saying that I enjoyed the "heightened reality" of their flavor.

"Am I really so much less handsome than Akash?" he asked me when Lehman was distracted.

I told him that his features were just a little small for his head. They weren't so bad on their own.

Everything seemed to be happening at once. One moment, someone was saying very earnestly that he preferred Mickey Mouse to T. S. Eliot, and when I turned to ask him what he meant, I discovered that I was standing arm in arm with two other students and we were all singing "Old Man River." I wondered what my wife would have said if she could have seen me then!

Then we were at a party in a small, hot room, where we drank warm wine and liquor from plastic cups. It was incredibly dark (much of the undergraduate experience takes place in darkness), and disembodied faces seemed to wobble toward me in the gloom. The conversations were incredible and sometimes almost meaningless. Students spoke in a flippant, ironic, highly abstract style. Even so, I soon felt that I was getting the hang of it. For example, one student asked, "What's the ingredients of happiness?" Another began to chant his answer, "Sex money fame . . ." But I startled myself by cutting him short and saying, "Power." I spoke in a leaden, portentous voice. And I didn't mean it!

Later, a member of the Tripoli police department showed up. He identified himself as Officer Crenshaw and he was not interested to know why I, an old man, was up here drinking with these kids. At first, his presence made everyone very agitated, but when it became clear that he wasn't going to stop the party or check anyone's identification, nobody paid any attention to him. After all, everything was under control. But then he asked me if I knew Malinka West—by coincidence, one of my professors this semester, as well as a colleague—and when I said yes, he walked me into the bedroom and started asking me questions.

"Can you state whether she's mentioned my name?" he said. "When and where did you see her last?"

I decided not to answer truthfully. I guess I heard a worrisome note in his voice. I told him that I hadn't seen her in a few months.

"Neither have I."

Then he began to walk in small circles, clenching and unclenching his fists. I asked if I could help in any way and he said he'd like a beer, if it wasn't too much trouble. Then he said he wouldn't like one and that he shouldn't be drinking, especially on duty, and then he said he wanted a beer.

I was having trouble following these reversals, but at that moment a few students bustled into the room and began passing around a bottle of white rum. Officer Crenshaw announced that he was going to "secure" the bottle, by which he apparently just meant grab it, which is what he did. Then he climbed into the tight crack between the bed and the wall and began sucking on it like a baby. Lots of students at Tripoli drink white rum because the most popular brand is manufactured on the island of St. Renard, which is where our branch campus is located.

At the end of the night, I was talking to a young African-American woman whom I will call "Megan." She was very angry about the proposed agreement with Big Anna® Brands. One of the arguments against the partnership, which Megan articulated in no uncertain terms, was that the company was frequently in the news in connection with possible labor violations on St. Renard, where it maintained large factories and farms. I myself was also concerned about a potential conflict of interest: I knew that at least one Tripoli professor was a major Big Anna® shareholder.

"You want to let these businessmen tell you what happens on campus?" she said. "You'll see how it goes: 'Assignment for Monday is kidnap a Guatemalan boy. Assignment for Tuesday is poison his mother.' "

I lost no time in expressing my own reservations about the partnership. What I didn't say was that I had actually opposed it in a meeting with trustees. At the same time, I tried to help her see the other side of the argument. I explained that it was sometimes necessary to make concessions in order to preserve other features of college life. The Vocational Writing Program, which is a distinct departure from our traditional liberal arts curriculum, was an example of this. Many professors had objected to the creation of the VWP, but it did leave the English department free to offer a wider range of classes.

I thought I was handling myself pretty well, but now she said something that caught me off guard.

"I've got this friend who had to take a VWP class with Professor P——. He showed her his penis."

I was shocked, and more than shocked. If Megan's friend had reported this incident, I definitely would have heard about it.

"So that's what you get," she said casually. "You get perverts."

I asked her to clarify. Had this professor actually exposed himself?

"Maybe. She was pretty drunk when it happened."

This was troubling not just because Professor P——'s transgression, if substantiated, was very serious in itself, but also because the student in question had not decided to report it. Why? This was just the kind of question I'd gone undercover to answer. Unfortunately, now was not the time to press the point.

"Let's put a pin in that," I said. "Let's make sure to come back to it."

She crossed her arms and leaned casually against the wall. She was a very striking young woman.

"Anyway," she said, "I'm taking this class with Professor Kabaka. Have you heard of him?"

I was having some trouble moving past the incident with Professor P——, but I was indeed anxious to know how John Kabaka was settling in. I was worried that he wouldn't feel comfortable here at Tripoli.

"He says he doesn't feel comfortable here at Tripoli," Megan said, "but it's no matter. He says the revolution can start anywhere, even here."

I asked her if she was enjoying his class, but she said it wasn't about enjoyment; it was about injustice. She said she was fed up.

"Did you know that the white sailors on slave ships sometimes died at greater rates than the slaves? They were practically slaves themselves. So ultimately it was just the old story. It was businessmen with soft hands getting rich on someone else's misery. And it's the same today with Big Anna®."

I nodded and finished my beer. She was really very beautiful.

"Anyway," she said, "what it gets me thinking is that I've got to make radical changes in my way of living."

I told her that it was always good to make positive changes. I admitted that I'd recently made a few changes of my own.

"*Radical* changes," she said.

I waited a beat, but she didn't seem inclined to continue, so I asked her if she was changing anything in particular.

"No more Twitter. No more eating paninis out of the microwave. I'm just going to go for it, you know? No more lingering in doorways."

This seemed to accord with my own resolutions as well. After all, I myself had begun to feel that I was just hanging around at the margins of things, growing older and lonelier each year.

"I'm going to learn how to garden. So the global climate is ruined? I'll learn to grow manioc in New Hampshire. No more excuses. I'm never wearing these wedges again."

She kicked off her shoes and stuffed them into the trash. Then she thought better of it and put them back on again.

"No more unreasonable things," she said. "From now on, it's a sense of proportion or nothing at all."

I was enjoying this conversation. My heart was beating like crazy, but I didn't worry because I've always had the heart of a much younger man.

Suddenly her eyes widened.

"I'm not always so brave, though. Sometimes I just sit there and say to myself, 'Oh no oh no oh no.' I've practically stopped talking to my old friends. I practically don't even have friends anymore!"

She had gone from self-confidence to self-doubt in the space of an instant. I wanted to ask how she'd come to lose her friends, but in another moment she just laughed and shook her head. Then someone changed the music, and someone else knocked a table over, and Megan wandered away to get another drink. I stood there grinning from ear to ear.

That was my first experience of nightlife at Tripoli, and what an experience! Even though I was exhausted and, to be honest, I'd had a little too much to drink, I had trouble falling asleep. It had been exhilarating to talk with Megan, hashing out basic questions of right and wrong. I hadn't felt so alive in years, and certainly not since my wife died. I felt like I was a young man again!

From
THE TELEGRAPH SUNDAY MAGAZINE
October 8, 2009

What Are They Thinking?
Each month, we ask two Tripoli professors to weigh in on a controversial issue. This month, we hear from William Beckford, professor and acting chancellor of the English Department, and John Kabaka, visiting professor of history. The question: At times of great financial pressure, are institutions of higher learning justified in seeking support from for-profit corporations like Big Anna®?

In favor: William Beckford
The whole world, which is rapidly coming into neighborhood relations, is recognizing as never before the real needs of mankind, and is ready to approve and strengthen all the moral forces which stand for the uplift of humanity. Everyone agrees that there must be education for the orderly and permanent development of society, but so too must there be intercourse among peoples in the interests of commerce and economic growth. Every aspect of human endeavor is strengthened by exposure to the rigors of the free market, which is the great innovation of our time, and education is surely no exception. The upright and farseeing businessman and the honest and capable professor represent the combined forces which are to change the Tripoli of today into the greater and better Tripoli of the future.

There are those on campus who argue that Big Anna® is not a worthy ally in this cause. They say that corporations like Big Anna® have retarded the political development of fledgling nations like St. Renard, that globalization has kept these nations in a postcolonial limbo. To these people I will say that globalization, far from being a late-twentieth-century bogeyman, can be said to have begun in 1492, or even before, with the settlement and cultivation of island groups like the Canaries, and that it must therefore be considered a fundamental feature of our society, the wellspring from which all good things come. Indeed, our very presence on American shores is an aspect of globalization.

Additionally, when it comes to the island of St. Renard, it must be argued that the fine people at Big Anna® have as much right to the land as do any of the locals, who are themselves migrants. The indigenous population is extinct, and there no longer exist any people with an ancient claim to the land.

Opposed: John Kabaka

I am not interested in what Tripoli is or is not justified in doing, nor am I interested in the long-term viability of American higher education, but I will use this platform to remind readers of an important fact.

Corporations like Big Anna® are guilty—there is no doubt about this—of extravagant human rights abuses. You read about the vicious exploitation of workers in a Big Anna® snack factory, you learn that the company sells muffins that contain a known carcinogen, and

you say to yourself, "What gives them the right?"

Here is what gives them the right: the Fourteenth Amendment to the U.S. Constitution.

The Fourteenth Amendment was meant to guarantee all Americans equal protection under the law, but an 1886 Supreme Court decision extended this protection to corporations as well. Other decisions have reinforced the court's initial ruling. Cynical politicians tell you that corporations are people too, and in the eyes of the U.S. Supreme Court, it's the truth.

I will note only the sharpest irony. The Fourteenth Amendment was intended to give full citizenship to recently emancipated slaves. It was meant to guarantee *them* equal protection under the law. The carnival of cause and effect is of course very complicated, but in essence the doctrine of corporate personhood denied them this right, and in granting American corporations the freedom to operate without the burden of accountability, it makes possible the enslavement, today, of garment workers and agricultural laborers all over the world.

From: "Maggie Bell" <mbell1990@tripoli.edu>
To: "Chris Bell" <cfb456@mercurylink.net>
Date: October 13, 2009, at 8:30 AM
Subject: (no subject)

I'm fine! Don't worry! I'm just thinking about some of these things for the first time. I feel like I'm realizing every day that all these familiar things are not quite what I thought they were, like how in a dream you walk through your own house but there's a door where it shouldn't be and you think, Uh-oh. (And also, give me some credit, I'm not one of those narcissist creeps who bang their professors. Kabaka is good-looking but that's not the main thing.)

I *know* the football players aren't slaves, but race is part of it. No one talks about it but race is there. And anyway, who are you sticking up for? You hate football. But never mind. I've got a moral trump card for you! A few days ago there was an article in the Tripoli paper saying that a football player named Depatrickson White is descended from a runaway slave owned by the great-grandfather of the guy who runs Tripoli's remedial writing program. A guy called Bish Pinkman III. I know this doesn't prove my point, but it's pretty weird, isn't it? They're calling it the Pinkman Scandal. It's not really a scandal but it's a strange coincidence. I think the real problem is that the Pinkman family has given money to the college and now everyone thinks it's blood money. Like Big Anna isn't giving us blood money too? For me the consequence is that now everyone wants to prove to me that they're not racist. I'm everyone's only black acquaintance. You're lucky you're at NYU and you don't have to deal with this stuff. Why did I insist on going to a small college?

Dad actually wrote to me about it. Think of that! It's the first I've heard from him since coming back to school. He said he'd "have Pinkman's head." He is apparently very upset. Do we believe him? Dad with his polo shirts and his Republican shoes.

Everybody asked Kabaka about it in class, but he wouldn't even acknowledge it at first. He said, "Every American story is a slave narrative." But on Wednesday, Professor Amundsen came to evaluate his teaching. Professor Amundsen is this soft faceless guy, sort of squiffy and blurred at the edges, and Kabaka was so angry that he was there. He stared at Amundsen for like two minutes in total silence. Then he gave this astonishing speech about how if Amundsen raped your sister and your sister gave birth then the child would be the child of a rapist just as much as he'd be the child of a person who'd been raped. He asked if it made sense to say that the child inherited some of the father's guilt. He said (I wrote it down): "What is inheritance? If you fertilize your cabbage plants with horse dung, do your cabbages turn into horses?" He kept using phrases like "the rapist Amundsen." We didn't have the faintest idea what he was getting at until he said that Depatrickson White and Bish Pinkman III are probably cousins and if one was guilty, the other was guilty too. His point was that most black Americans have white ancestors, so how can you talk about inherited guilt? Then he said, "There is only now."

I don't want to ramble about this any longer. Also I'm worried you'll think I'm giving you a hard time about the football thing. Also I don't want you to think I'm going nuts. It's just that all of this demands to be thought about! (Ask Max what he thinks about football. He'll back me up. How *is* Max?)

Anyway, I was trying to tell you that the reason I'm so fixated on Kabaka is that he does these things. He calls this man a rapist in front of everyone. Crazy! And he doesn't give a damn. It's part of his whole philosophy: Why should we observe the proprieties? Why should we pretend that we want to bring about change within the context of the system that already exists? What we really want to do is change the system.

I need you to understand what I'm talking about! If you don't understand, then I really *am* lonely and isolated. Okay? So listen to me. I'm talking about the difference between a liberal status-quo American and someone like Kabaka. There's a big difference. Some of my other professors, maybe they have the right opinions, maybe they support gay marriage and they're pro-choice, maybe a lot of them are even people Dad would call pinko nutjobs. Fine. Good. But their lives are soft and simple. They think what a tragedy it is that we have so much racial inequality, but meanwhile they're the ones who benefit. So it means that hypocrisy is the only political position available to them. They write a little book and then afterward it's like, Oh no, I'm an idiot, I forgot about black people again! Or else they do think about slavery but they think of it as an "institution," a subject for scholarship, and meanwhile they're wearing jeans made in Guatemala by a kid paid thirty cents a day. These are nice people who use the phrase "African-American" because they're trying to be respectful, and they don't even think about how insulting it is. How long has it been since our own family lived in Africa? We've been here a lot longer than most white Americans. Kabaka says that basically all white Americans arrived after 1850 and before that it was mostly just black slaves and Indians.

You understand what I'm saying? Kabaka is something *else*. He's not just a professor who looks good in a suit and teaches us interesting things. He's like an alternative way of living in the world. I feel like I've woken up from the weird dream of upper-middle-class black America and now here I am, in History, which is an even weirder and less plausible dream.

Let's not argue about anything, okay? Not now. Sorry to be so serious. Does it help if I say I'm sitting here with my jeans around my ankles? I was checking the label and I was right: made in Guatemala. Should I take a picture of myself like this and send it to Kabaka?

Love to you and Max,
M

From

The Narrative of William White, a Fugitive Slave, Who Lived Twenty-Five Years in Hopeless Bondage, Containing Some Remarks on the Practice of Slavery in America and an Account of His Miraculous Escape (1845)

CHAPTER IX

WHEN I was about fifteen years old, I was sold to Mr. Theophilus Pinkman, who was known, according to the custom in that part of the country, as "Colonel," although he held no military rank, and, indeed, a coward's heart beat within his breast. The Colonel was as cruel a slaveholder as Almighty God ever suffered to draw breath, and he used to whip his slaves savagely and indiscriminately, usually where no particle of fault existed, in the belief that frequent application of the tyrant's lash was beneficial to the body and soul of his chattel.

The Colonel was a most intemperate man, and, for want of other amusements, being as we were almost completely isolated in that feverish and pestilential swamp, he used to become intoxicated most nights, and in this condition walk among the slave cabins. The Colonel was himself a slave to licentiousness, and many was the poor son, brother, husband, and father who was forced to bite his tongue, and check every impulse of love and fidelity, while his mother, sister, wife, or daughter was compelled to submit to the grossest and vilest indignity.

I knew of one slave, called "Platt," of pure African descent, considered one of the most loyal slaves on the plantation, and so strong he could do in three weeks the work another slave could do only in six weeks of the most backbreaking labor. Platt had a young wife named Milly, as virtuous as she was beautiful, and together they had a son. But this happy family was born into bondage, and every slave knows that his happiness may be taken from him at any moment, and sold to the next slave trader who happens by, because his wife and child, and indeed his very self, withal the blood and the sinews of his body, are not his own. And so it was with Platt, who was sleeping together with his wife and infant son in their cabin, when he heard the Colonel approaching, almost helpless with intoxication, whispering the most foul and base indecencies.

In the months of July and August, when the heat becomes so intense in that place that the dew never falls for months at a time, the Colonel was in the habit of wearing only a sort of cloak or loose robe, soaked in cider vinegar to keep off the mosquitoes, and woe to the helpless bondsman and bondswoman who smelled that astringent vapor on the night air! The Colonel stumbled into the cabin and began shouting, saying that Platt had not finished with some piece of work or another, although there was no justice in the accusation, and, indeed, Platt knew very well what the Colonel intended and for what purpose he wished to be left alone with poor Milly.

Reader! Can you imagine the feelings of this young husband and father, as he listened with bowed head to his oppressor, who was wrapped in a winding-sheet and stank like all the dogs of blackest Hell? Platt did not move to leave, and the Colonel, maddened by the frustration of his licentious passions, produced a knife from his boot, and lunged at his slave, intending to kill him. Platt was more than a match for this villain, and he stepped aside and caught the Colonel's arm, twisting it as he did so, in order to bring the soft-bellied man to his knees with pain, and then dealing him such a blow with his hardened fist that the white man's life was nearly extinct.

A slave knows that the penalty for defending his honor and protecting his beloved spouse is death, and accordingly Platt fled to the swamp, where he lived for three weeks in the most wretched conditions. Another man might have run for the Free States, but he was reluctant to do so while his wife and child yet remained in bondage, and so, for want of an alternative, at the end of this time he returned to his work.

At first the Colonel seemed to have forgotten the events of that night, and Platt supposed that he had been saved by the workings of that very demon, corn liquor, which had brought on the attack of licentiousness in the first place. But, O Reader, he was wrong! One day while he was working in the field, he saw three white men approaching with pistols and shotguns at the ready. Platt knew that he could not run, lest he be shot down in the field, never again to see his wife and infant son in the light of this world, although, in truth, he had little hope of seeing them again if he should allow himself to be taken. But he put his faith in Almighty God and suffered himself to be led to the barn.

The manner of whipping on Colonel Pinkman's plantation was to bind the victim by his hands to a high branch or roof beam, pulling the rope tight so that only the toes scraped the dusty earth. Then a rawhide whip was used, this weapon being favored over the bullwhip, with which a careless or drunken man might whip the life out of his victim after only a few strokes, thereby preserving the slave from hours, and perhaps years, of anguish, which was considered to be his due, and this for no crime other than that of his birth.

The Colonel was too cowardly to administer the punishment himself, and still fancied himself enfeebled by the blow dealt him by the husband and father whom he had sought to defraud of the rights that every white man knows to be his by natural law. These three men, contract laborers who would be considered mercenaries in any Christian country, undertook the responsibility, and Platt was whipped from morning until noon, when the men charged with executing this punishment, taking it in turns so that two might rest while one plied the whip, were exhausted by the heat. They cut Platt down and left him to bleed in the dust, and I saw him there, as the blood, which was the same bright red as the blood of any white man, turned the dust of the barn to mud. His back was lacerated so deeply that the flesh could have been turned back to expose the living entrails beneath. Platt was washed in brine, which was thought to prevent the lacerations from festering, but he survived only until about three o'clock in the afternoon, when he died of his wounds. If there is any justice in this world, he waits in heaven for Milly and his son.

All of this was common practice among the slaveholders in that part of the country. Platt was the only slave I ever saw challenge the Colonel's right to commit outrages so vile that they offend against every sacred principle of Christian society, and he paid for it with his life.

This, then, dear Reader, is the price of your cotton shirt, and of your wife's Sunday dress.

MINUTES / OCTOBER 2009
FACULTY MEETING

The president called the meeting to order and wished everyone a happy Halloween. Before we got started, we should all help ourselves to a Big Anna® brand Banana Bran Muffin®. As we already knew, Tripoli had concluded its partnership agreement with Big Anna® Brands, a corporation that had been "revolutionizing food products and services" for over a hundred years, and together we hoped to do great things. The president wanted to thank William Beckford, professor and acting chancellor of the English Department, for his role in facilitating our discussions with Big Anna®.

John Kabaka, visiting professor of history and self-styled "enemy of globalization," looked as impassive as a chess piece, but the secretary had not forgotten his passionate rebuke at the first faculty meeting, and he was interested to see what fresh mischief the professor had up his sleeve.

Most of the faculty, at least 80 percent, had retrieved a packaged muffin from the table by the door, and for a moment the crinkling and tearing of wrappers was the only sound. Then the president once again expressed her enthusiasm about this new partnership and observed, with the expressionless equanimity of one fulfilling a contractual obligation, that Big Anna® brand baked food products retained their glisten and freshness for months and months, even when they were removed from the package.

It pains the secretary to admit that he failed to take any notes during the first part of the meeting. All that remains to him are impressionistic memories: a monstrous image of Professor Beckford, who seemed, like an iguana, to blink without closing his eyes; Malinka West in a low-cut green blouse; Dean Benmarcus congratulating Hugo Ortega, who had just been named the first Big Anna® brand Professor of Arts of Sciences™; Matilda Yu choking on her Banana Bran Muffin; Malinka West again; Malinka West with her bright white teeth.

Indeed, the secretary had a dark moment as he sat gazing at Malinka West, unattainably beautiful as she was, and reflecting on the tawdry circumstances of his own life. For context, he had been fleeced by a car salesman just that morning.

But there was no time to worry about this. It was time to discuss the Pinkman Scandal.

Most of us were familiar with the details of the case, but the president gave a brief summary for anyone who hadn't been paying attention. Following the death of Bish Pinkman Jr.—father of our own Bish Pinkman III and one of our most generous benefactors—Greeley Baker, professor of history, who did not seem to be present today, had written an article revealing not only that the Pinkman fortune derived from cotton plantations in Mississippi, but also that Tyrants wide receiver Depatrickson White was descended from a slave—a man called "Ned," later William White, who subsequently escaped to the North—once owned by the Pinkman family.

All eyes were on Bish Pinkman III, who remained motionless, staring at his hands with a fixed watery glare.

Obviously, the president said, this was not a matter we needed to resolve on our own. The trustees and the senior administrators were already discussing it, and the Public Relations Office had issued the first of several press releases.

What we needed to decide here was what action, if any, the faculty itself would take.

David Herring, professor of physics, laughed cheerfully and moved that we "stage a demonstration." Perhaps Depatrickson White could strike Mr. Pinkman III with a bullwhip! He could do it on the lawn in front of Pinkman Hall.

The president treated this motion as a joke, although Richard Carlyle, professor of English, had risen to second it. Mr. Pinkman III did not react at all. He sat with his soft hands clasped, his head inclined, his rounded belly rising and falling at regular intervals.

Broward Chamberlain, professor of religion, wanted to explain that there was extensive justification for such a punishment in biblical law. The phrase "an eye for an eye, a tooth for a tooth," which was usually dismissed as an ancient barbarity, was actually quoted out of context. The biblical passage was a revision of contemporary Near Eastern laws, which stipulated that perpetrators of violent offenses would be punished in kind (an eye for an eye) only if the victim was of an equal social class. Under biblical law, the idea was expanded to protect victims of a lower social class as well. It was actually a progressive measure, and one that obviously had a particular resonance here, where questions of slave and master were at issue. There was also a lengthy biblical precedent for the punishment of an individual for the crimes of his ancestors.

There followed a period of tense silence. The president frowned and looked at her hands. Was Professor Chamberlain joking?

Professor Herring was joking. He laughed again and asked us to consider how "cathartic" it would be to watch Mr.

Pinkman III whipped savagely in front of the building that bore his name.

Professor Kabaka, on the other hand—the so-called conscience of Tripoli College—was not joking, nor perhaps did he ever joke. He summarized his own position as follows: He was furious. We were making a show of outrage over a trivial coincidence. More importantly, however, we were behaving as though slavery were a matter of individual rather than societal guilt—a crime that could be avenged by calling responsible individuals to account. Slavery was in fact only one expression of an ethos of exploitation that had preceded the invention of the plantation complex and the creation of distinct racial categories. That ethos persisted to this day, and companies like Big Anna® were only one of its present manifestations. We could not pretend to condemn slavery at the moment we allied ourselves with such a corporation.

The president, an honest person in an impossible position, thanked him for his remarks. She agreed with him. Unfortunately, we were not in a position to change the world, nor was ancient Near Eastern law "germane to the case." Once again, all we had to decide this afternoon was whether the faculty would take any action. She thought it would be good if we could be seen to act in concert with the Athletic Association, which had its own interest in the matter, and toward that end she now called on Glenn Forrest, assistant to the deputy director of the Athletic Association, whom the faculty greeted with scattered applause and subdued murmurs of "Go Tyrants."

"Obviously," Mr. Forrest began, "we all want what's best for the Tyrants." He then expressed his hope that the whole problem would "just vanish," adding that the Tyrants were a "postracial" football organization.

Jennifer Wilson, professor of biology, slapped the table and rose to her feet. "Here is the problem," she said, and now she addressed herself directly to Mr. Pinkman III: "Your sinecure was paid for in blood."

Mr. Pinkman III, rubicund under normal circumstances, turned beet red. "I cannot disavow," he said, "the beliefs, principles, and convictions of my great-great-great-grandfather. It is feasible that it could be disputed that the strategies, procedures, and manner of the implementation of those beliefs and convictions were unobjectionable in some respects. However, I believe in heritage, not hate."

This was understood as an endorsement of slavery, and Professor Wilson nodded sharply and said, "Case in point." Perhaps we remembered her suggestion, at an earlier meeting, that we lock him up?

But now Professor Kabaka stood up once again. As he did so, there was at least one audible groan. The faculty had grown weary of hearing from its conscience.

Professor Kabaka had removed his Banana Bran Muffin® from its package. Now he lifted it above his head and solemnly crushed it in his fist. Bits of glistening muffin were squeezed out between his fingers. With his fist still raised, he said that he would like to resign his position, effective immediately. He meant to return to St. Renard and take up arms against the corporation that had degraded his countrymen and despoiled his island home. That was all. He let the muffin fall to the table and left the room.

This was a troubling development, to be sure, but the meeting had acquired a fiendish momentum, and the embarrassment occasioned by Professor Kabaka's abrupt departure only reinforced the general feeling that something had to be done.

And yet what could be done, now, this afternoon, about the legacy of American slavery? It was impracticable to dissolve our partnership with Big Anna®, which was conceivably the responsible thing to do. We were thus prevented by economic necessity from addressing the problem—whatever the problem was, for indeed the whole thing had become nebulous and obscure, and even supposing that the problem, whatever it was, could ever be addressed by anyone—in its larger dimensions. In all that followed, therefore, we proved Professor Kabaka correct and justified his criticism of us. There was no alternative. Our hands were tied.

Professor Beckford stood up and said that he agreed with Professor Wilson: It would be advisable to remove Mr. Pinkman III from public life until a solution to the problem of his existence could be found.

The president, looking glassy-eyed and sick, rose and remained standing for some time without saying anything. Then she sat down.

Professor Wilson said that there was a vacant office in Ulster Hall where Mr. Pinkman III could be imprisoned. What did we think of that?

Mr. Pinkman III rose and was no doubt on the point of uttering another abstruse formulation when Fitzgerald Simon, professor of francophone language and literature and himself the descendant of Afro-Caribbean slaves, came unexpectedly to his defense. Professor Simon reminded us that Mr. Pinkman III had not, himself, ever owned slaves, nor was there reason to believe that he had ambitions in that respect. He also wished to point out that in robbing Mr. Pinkman III of his natural rights, we were ourselves guilty of the very crime for which we were trying to atone. Perhaps we could distinguish the issues of reparation and revenge from the more practical questions of how Tripoli should deal with 1) the bad publicity, and 2) the gifts we had received from the Pinkman family?

This was very reasonable, and the secretary was sorry that in all the confusion we had managed to forget about Professor Simon. Surely he would have made a better conscience than the troublesome Professor Kabaka?

Professor Wilson agreed with him in principle, but she insisted that he was being idealistic. The issue was not whether or not Mr. Pinkman III was himself a slaveholder—she was willing to concede that, in all likelihood, he was not. The problem was that he was now perceived as a symbol of American slavery. The "publicity problem," in short, was inseparable from the problem of Mr. Pinkman III's existence.

Professor Herring asked if he had missed something. Had we decided that Depatrickson White would not be allowed to whip Mr. Pinkman III in a "cathartic public spectacle"?

The secretary, at least, could appreciate the appeal of this suggestion. He had been thinking again of his humiliation at the hands of the car salesman. He now recalled an argument he'd had with his wife the day before. Nothing in his life had turned out the way he'd once hoped it would. Someone—and why not Mr. Pinkman III?—ought to pay.

The president had begun to respond, but she was shouted down by Pierce Reynolds, professor of computer science. Professor Reynolds was incredulous. "I can't believe we're thinking of locking this man up," he said. He cited the prohibitive cost of food, water, and basic chamber-pot service. There were also the bribes we'd have to pay to maintenance workers—"the cost of silence." He reminded us that this was a time of financial hardship and proposed that we simply kill Mr.

Pinkman III and dispense with the whole problem that way. He even had a knife in his boot.

This provoked a flurry of discussion: Professor Carlyle, though hastening to explain that he was "no fascist" and apologizing for his "protofascist aesthetic declarations," was in agreement, saying that this was even better than whipping him or locking him up. Monica Fletcher, professor of economics, wondered if there might be legal repercussions associated with killing a member of the Tripoli community, "even if he *is* a slaveholder." But Professor West was confident that there wouldn't be any problem—she "knew some people" at the Tripoli Police Department. And indeed she did. The secretary had read her salacious memoir.

The president, who looked more disaffected by the moment, said that probably this was going too far. She was sorry that she had allowed the discussion to get so out of hand. The truth was that she had not slept more than a few hours in the last three days. She was feeling, she said, "deranged." She then echoed Professor Fletcher: Murdering a member of the Tripoli community might have unwelcome consequences. Did the faculty not understand this?

The faculty did not, or would not, understand this, and ignored the president's remarks. Professor Beckford then proposed a comprehensive solution: Mr. Pinkman III would be imprisoned in Ulster Hall. Additionally, Professor Beckford's own committee, the Committee on the Committee on Committees (CCC), would undertake an investigation of the VWP, which was partly endowed by the Pinkman family, and it would also draft a provisional statement indicating the position of the college viz. slavery. It might be a good idea to change the committee's name in order to reflect these new obligations. He proposed the following: the Committee on Curriculum and Core Programming (CCCP).

Francis Amundsen, professor of English, leapt to his feet in order to second the motion, commending Professor Beckford for his decisive leadership. But Michael Herman, yet another professor of English, and indeed one whose hatred for Professor Beckford was proverbial, demanded that we "repudiate" Professor Beckford before it was too late. He cautioned us against a policy of appeasement. We didn't want today's meeting to be "our Munich."

To the surprise of the secretary, at least, who kept forgetting that he was in the room, Mr. Pinkman III now declared that he wished to speak in his own defense. He was not permitted to do so.

The president asked for a vote on Professor Beckford's proposal, adding that she herself was "beyond caring" and that she would simply cast her vote and let the chips fall where they might. A vote was therefore taken and the motion passed almost unanimously, with no one except Professor Herman and Mr. Pinkman III dissenting, not even Professor Beckford's many additional enemies. Despite her claim, the president herself did not vote.

Only now did Dev Gupta, professor of computer science, ask if we were empowered to make such a decision. Was the original idea not simply to make a recommendation?

The president shrugged and declined to answer. The provost, Alexander Kosta, recognizing that she had come to the end of her strength, took the reins: He said that he did not know— in fact, nobody knew—which cast the whole meeting, and all previous meetings, into suspicion.

"And yet there can be no precedent," he said, "unless a precedent is first established."

The faculty seemed pleased, but the president remained impassive. She sat with her hands folded in her lap, doing nothing and saying nothing. Her face was expressionless and pale.

The provost, who had now assumed command of the meeting, asked if there were any more announcements. There were not. Time was running short, after all. Many of us would have to hurry if we wanted to be home in time for dinner.

With an expertise that could only have derived from experience, Professor Carlyle seized Mr. Pinkman III and bound his wrists with an extension cord. The secretary found himself shouting encouragement. It seemed that the misfortune of another was indeed some consolation for his own disappointments.

Then Professors Carlyle and Reynolds dragged the prisoner away, and although the secretary would have liked to go with them, if only to make sure that there was nothing in the designated Ulster Hall office with which Mr. Pinkman III might contrive to kill himself, his duties were at an end. He said his good-byes, grabbed a Big Anna® brand Banana Bran Muffin® for the road, and skipped down the stairs and out into the dark. It was a cool night; it was good to be at liberty.

From: "Maggie Bell" <mbell1990@tripoli.edu>
To: "Chris Bell" <cfb456@mercurylink.net>
Date: November 5, 2009, at 4:15 AM
Subject: (no subject)

C,

Kabaka is gone! Apparently he left everything in his office, coat
and hat and books and everything. He took his laptop and that's all.
What this amounts to is that he talks and talks and then, instead of
just talking some more, he does something about it, which is why I
admire him, I guess, but it's also kind of an insult, like we're not
worth his time and effort. But it's not our fault that we were born
American, is it? Should we really feel so guilty and awful all the
time?

I got drunk and played basketball with Big Ben last night, and
this morning I feel like a squashed bug. I've just been sitting here
groaning and drinking tomato juice. Sometime today I have to do
laundry. I did that thing yesterday of going to the store and buying
underwear instead of just washing my clothes.

So: You're right. I am not doing so great. I admit it. Big Ben is
practically the only person I've been hanging out with. I don't know
why. Nothing really happened with Becca and Francoise or anyone
else, but it's just that I suddenly feel like I can't talk to anyone. I've
actually been talking sometimes to the dean! I told you I hung out
with him at a party? He's a very sweet old guy. I think maybe he
loves me but at the same time I'm totally positive that he cares
about me as a person. Maybe it's just nice to talk to someone a lot
older. He's a grandfather figure. Also, he understands loneliness.
He's very lonely too.

You don't have to come up here. It's okay. I'll see you pretty soon anyway. I've just got to work through some stuff on my own. My eating thing is under control, don't worry about that.

Maybe I was expecting an *answer* from Kabaka? When I got home last night I spent twenty minutes looking at lynching photographs online. I know what you're going to say and it isn't what you think, it isn't like I was crying and cutting myself and flipping through these things. It just seemed like if I only concentrated really hard I could figure out what makes people do these terrible things. But either there's nothing to figure out or the explanation is so awful that it's better not to think about it. Those white southerners bringing their kids to watch a lynching. The whole thing escapes me. I can't get to the end of it. Going to the lynching and then coming home refreshed and eating dinner and sleeping soundly. Professor Kabaka says the devil is real. The devil lives in the human heart.

Chris! What's happening to me! All I talk about is myself but I think about you all the time. I'm really glad everything is okay with Max. I started to worry something had happened. Obviously it wouldn't be the end of the world, but I like Max.

I had a dream last night that I peed in my dresser drawer. In the dream it seemed like a perfectly acceptable place. I was telling one of the Chloes, "This is one of the places you're allowed to pee." When I woke up I had to check.

Love,

M

From

THE TRIPOLI COLLEGE TELEGRAPH
November 6, 2009

THE SPORTING LIFE

Tyrants' Woes Continue

This season, the Tripoli Tyrants are contending with more than just the legacy of American slavery.

Tyrants kicker Ernst Blovitch was arrested Saturday night following a dismal performance in the Tyrants' 31–24 loss at Barnum College.

Blovitch, who missed two extra points and a 25-yard field goal in the game, allegedly parked his car at the intersection of Main St. and Sycamore Ave., where police officers discovered him lying on the hood.

"It was a cold fall night," Blovitch said later, "and the hood of the car was warm. I was gazing up at the night sky. I was haunted and bewitched by the sweet moonlight."

Alcohol does not seem to have been a factor, and Blovitch was released later that night.

The incident is just the latest in a series of bizarre events involving Tyrants kickers, who have missed 13 consecutive field goals and all but one extra point this season.

Giles Saint-Paul, who missed two field goals and two extra points in Saturday's game, explained the problem this way: "When you watch from the stands, you can't hear what the football is saying."

The news isn't all bad for Tripoli. Depatrickson White and Teshawnus Marchampton didn't seem at all distracted by the Pinkman slavery scandal. The two freshmen combined for 220 yards and four touchdowns last week, and quarterback Tom Hoffman went 16 for 22 in another efficient performance. If the Tyrants could make their field goals, their offense would easily be the most dangerous in the conference.

———————

The other day I ran into Megan in the dining hall. I waved and asked if I could sit with her. She shoved her backpack aside.

"Did you know that Pacific Islanders made it all the way to the coast of South America?" she said. "Way before Columbus crossed the Atlantic."

I told her that people said they were the greatest navigators in history.

"They brought sweet potatoes back with them. In some parts of the Pacific, sweet potatoes are still known by their Quechua name."

She sighed and looked down at her empty plate.

"I just ate a muffin and pudding sandwich," she said. "Pretty gross. Do I look fatter to you?"

To me she was almost inconceivably beautiful, although I couldn't think of a way to say it without embarrassing her. I told her she looked very healthy and fit.

She shook her head. "Did you know that Professor Kabaka left?"

"He what?" I said. "He left? Who left?"

"Kabaka left. He said he was going back to St. Renard. To fight against neoliberalism, he said."

I told her I was sorry to hear it, and I *was* sorry, but from the tone of her voice and the way she looked down at her plate, I could also tell that she must have had feelings for him. I'd been starving just a moment before, but now I didn't even want to look at my *Drippy Wrap w/Fish*.

POETIC EXCURSIONS

I went back to Hogbender Hall and took a nap. I didn't know what else to do. Luckily, college is full of distractions. Sometimes it seems to consist of little else. While I was sleeping, Lehman pinned a poem to my shirt. He'd written it just for me.

ON THE OCCASION OF HIS BIRTHDAY

My suitemate has a bad hip
From crossing the Bering Sea land bridge.
He has a scar on his cheek
From the first Punic War.
He says dodo tasted great
But mastodon was better.
My suitemate smells like a urinal cake,
Like an old papaya, like a musk ox
Running from a wolf running from death
Through the long tunnel of the years.
My suitemate is one year older today—
A college freshman
On his last legs.

It wasn't even my birthday!

Burke had also been trying his hand at a little verse. He was reluctant to share his work, but Lehman was able to make him understand that we were all friends here, and we'd give him the most balanced and well-intentioned critique we could.

Darkness at Nightfall

I peeled myself off my bored bed,
Aching to confront another day.
It's 2 AM in my soul

And it's midnight in my heart
And it's too late,
It's been too long,
(How can I go on?),

Since I saw her in lecture yesterday.
Cold days, long nights,
And the hardest thing is knowing
That Akash banged her.

Every night in this nightmare of love,
I put a dagger in my
Imaginary
Heart.

I was thinking of Megan. The truth is that I felt jealous of Professor Kabaka, so I could certainly relate to the thematic content of Burke's poem, but I think I was prejudiced against it for that reason. Its poor execution made me worry that my own feelings were cheap. As a result, I'm afraid I was a little too hard on this unhappy young man. I tried to explain that his work was perhaps too honest, but all I ended up saying was that I preferred Lehman's poem. The comparison was unfair and unwarranted, and immediately I felt bad about it.

Burke looked at me with misty eyes and said, "How can a poem be superior if it isn't sincere?" His features, already very small, looked smaller still. His eyes were like two currants in a big ball of rising dough.

I told him that I wasn't discounting the importance of sincerity. Or at least I didn't mean to.

Lehman said, "Should the work of art always be conceived and executed in a spirit of deadly earnest?"

"I just think you should try to say true things," Burke said.

"In my poem, I address themes of history, mortality, and the migration of peoples. I resent the suggestion that there's anything insincere about it."

THE DEAN IN DEEP COVER:
SCENES FROM UNDERGRADUATE LIFE

Who can believe that we're already more than halfway through our first semester? College life seems to move quickly and slowly at the same time, and the last few weeks come back to me in flashes:

Here I am in the common room with Akash. It's a somber moment. He's describing a feeling of despair and emptiness in the face of mortality. I'm saying to him, "Everybody gets old, Akash. It's a part of life. Everybody dies." He nods sadly, but then Lehman shouts from the other room, "Whoa! Spoiler alert!"

Here I am with Megan at a protest rally, carrying a sign that says *A Vote for Big Anna Is a Vote for Slavery*. We're marching in solidarity with the workers on Big Anna®'s Renardenne plantations. We're also calling for more detailed nutritional information on Big Anna® product labels, because they tell you there are only 120 calories in a Banana Bran Muffin®, but when you eat one, all the sugar makes your eyes ache. So I'm also holding a sign that says *What's in My Muffin?*

Here I am staring into the mirror.

Here I am standing on my chair, risky business for a man my age, reciting Tennyson's "Ulysses."

Here we are at "Pub Night" in the dining hall. I've eaten *Fried Cheese Bollocks*, *Fish and Chips*, *British Buffalo Wings*, and a *Scotch Egg*, which is a hard-boiled egg wrapped in Italian sausage and deep-fried. I feel like I've swallowed a meteorite.

Here I am at a party, where a student wearing a bathing suit and a shiny toreador's blouse is telling me how surprised everyone was when he threw his turtle into the pool earlier that day. He holds a beer in one hand and a Gatorade in the other. He says, "So he starts swimming, my turtle, and everyone's like, 'Holy shit!' And I just say to them, 'He's a turtle, man. Of course he can swim.' "

Here I am washing my socks and underwear in the bathroom sink while Lehman shows me that you can get a little drunk from swallowing mouthwash. The dean in me is alarmed, but in the mirror I see that my face is stony and expressionless.

Here we are at Casino Night!

Here we are at the Battle of the Bands. Our favorites are the Singing Waxworks, Free Pat Down, and Benign Neglect.

Here's another bright crisp fall day, and I can hardly see for the storm of yellow leaves. I'm wearing a coat and scarf and I'm walking up the hill to the science library, even though I've stopped attending classes and I don't really have anything to do up there. I'm listening to the Velvet Underground on my new iPod.

And I'm remembering the fall days of my youth. That first breath of cold, the leaves gathering against walls and fences, a foretaste of nostalgia that comes paired with a wild excitement. I remember it—the strength and pain of youth—and now, miraculously, I feel it again.

THE MAN IN ME MIGHT BE ALMOST ANYONE

To blow off some steam, we thought we'd have a party. In an e-mail invitation, Lehman called it the "First Annual Autumn Antislavery Bash."

By now I'd gotten used to these events, but I still marveled at the way excited college kids spoke to one another.

"I tried to start my thesis last night," one student announced, "but it just came out gibberish."

I heard another student saying to his friend, "You know Pete? I figured out Pete isn't a Hasid. The side-locks are an affectation."

At the beginning of the night, while Lehman was polishing off his third or fourth beer, I reminded him not to drink too much. He'd made me promise to remind him, because just that morning he'd been so hungover that he brushed his teeth with exfoliating facial cleanser. But now, only eight hours later, he shrugged the episode off.

"It's a way of life," he said, "like being a galley slave or an Alpine skier. There are highs and lows. Sometimes the routine is difficult to bear."

Soon Lehman was sick again, and Burke dragged me into the bathroom to check on him. He was pale and wall-eyed, hugging the bowl of the toilet and gesturing madly with his fingers. There were four or five people watching him. Tripoli bathrooms are spacious, even if the fixtures are older than I am. Ours has three sinks, two showers, two toilets, and lots of room for spectators.

"Problem in a secular world," Lehman was explaining, "is no point of reference. How far to go? Which books to consult? Where to find the correct solutions?"

All good questions, I thought, but I was a little frustrated that Lehman had put himself in this position for the second night in a row. I was turning to leave when he caught sight of me and called me over.

"Who are you really?" he whispered.

"I'm Bill Dean," I whispered back, "mature freshman."

"I only had one beer," he said. "One glass of wine. One liter of scotch. Ask the demented foreigner Volokhonsky. He'll give you the exact tally."

He spoke with a hoarse clarity, exactly to the point. The trouble was that we didn't know anyone named Volokhonsky.

"What should we do?" said Burke.

I suggested that we call the health center. He just cocked an eyebrow. Students who end up at the health center for alcohol-related problems are required to attend substance-abuse work-shops afterward, so everyone thinks of it as a last resort. It seems that students would rather risk death than attend substance-abuse workshops. This is something we ought to address. We don't want to be in a position where students are declining essential medical care simply in order to avoid a week's worth of alcohol counseling. I myself have come to believe that mandatory workshops are largely ineffective in any case. I'm thinking of my friend and long-time colleague Richard Carlyle, who has been in and out of manda-tory rehabilitation programs for years, and always to no effect.

"What's the alternative?" I said. "Should we leave you to die, Lehman?"

"Of course."

Burke frowned and shook his head. "That's no good. This is a terrible place to die."

Then Lehman began to weep, and I heard him whisper incredulously, "A gentleman *and* a scholar?"

I went to the window and looked out at the dark rainy street. Exasperating as all of this was, I realized that I felt wonderfully privileged to be a part of it. I peered down at the slate roofs, which were sparkling in the rain, and at the cars swishing by under the yellow streetlights, and at the piles of yellow leaves. My life seemed rich in a way it hadn't in a long time.

Then I turned from the window and saw Megan, who had just come in from the hall. She had high cheekbones and madwoman's eyes, and she was laughing with an animation that seemed to overcome her. The choice is the same whether you're seventy or seventeen: You can knuckle under and let life pass you by, or you can put up a fight. I said to myself, Who cares if she loves John Kabaka? I've got nothing to lose by giving it a shot.

And it was then, just then, that the whole thing seemed to swing out of my control. The whole giddy semester, I mean. The project and the mission and the enterprise. I felt it. One moment and I was lost.

Later, Megan and I were drinking white wine and sitting by an open window in the common room. Lehman was asleep in a shower stall and the party was getting loud.

"Who are you really?" she said.

"I used to be the dean of students."

"Well, sure. I knew that. I wanted to hear you say it. And you gave it up to come back to school?"

"Sort of."

"You're like me. You're turning over a new leaf." But then she shook her head. "Some new leaf!"

I could see that she was a little down, so I asked her if she needed someone to talk to. I tried to explain that my door was always open, although I wasn't sure if I was speaking as her friend or as the dean.

"I'm not feeling so good, but it'll pass. I try to stay positive and energetic."

She took an enormous swallow of wine. She winced and frowned and shook her head.

"I feel like my face is sort of loose and baggy," she said, "like meat hung on a corpse. Too much pudding. Look at me!"

I did look at her. She was lovely. And sitting there, sipping cold wine in that hot room while the first breath of winter rattled the window frame, I could hardly believe that any of this had happened.

"You look beautiful," I said.

"Sometimes I feel like nobody really listens to me. Do you know my dad sometimes forgets the name of the college I go to? He calls it Tivoli. Once he called it Monopoly."

She finished her wine and leaned back.

"It's just that the twenty-first century is getting me down."

"Is it?" I said. "I haven't really gotten a feel for it yet."

"Look at this country! Everyone's a sicko. Something goes wrong and they send poor kids off to die in the desert. And nobody cares. And *I* hardly care."

I'd heard other students articulate the same feelings, and I realized that I felt bad for these kids. The hopelessness! Was it their fault? A lack of spirit, maybe? I hadn't been a radical or anything in my own youth, but I did participate in a few protests and I always felt like we were making a difference. We thought we were winning.

"I marched with Dr. King in Washington," I said. "Maybe it doesn't seem like it, but it's a different world now. Trust me. Things are better."

Of course, I'd only gone to Washington in order to impress my wife, who wasn't my wife yet. I'd just gotten back from Vietnam and I'd met her at a friend's apartment in New York. I still couldn't believe she was gone.

"But in Professor Kabaka's class," Megan was saying, "I did care! I cared about everything. I sort of came alive. And now he's gone, and what am I supposed to do? I've been reading slave narratives for two months and I can't see the world without seeing the ghosts. They're up and moving around, like Professor Kabaka says. They don't know what century they're in."

Two students came crashing by, both of them in pirate costumes, and one of them shouted across the room:

"Hey, Pete, you faux-Hasid freak, say something in Jewish!"

"*Sh'ma, Yisroel . . .*" Pete shouted back.

"Don't say it as a mockery, you son of a bitch. My friend Jack knows your sister at UMass. You're a Methodist!"

"I have a twin brother," Megan said. "Chris. He's gay and he keeps saying he's going to come out to Mom and Dad, and part of me just wants to tell him, 'Chris! Don't ever tell them!' Because Dad's never going to accept it. And part of me knows that when Chris *does* tell him and Dad *does* get angry, that'll be it. My relationship with Dad will be over. I'll never forgive him. I'll have to grow up all at once in that moment because after that I won't have even the half father I have now."

I could think of nothing to say to this. And I was having trouble concentrating as well. I was having a very strange feeling, a kind of déjà vu.

Megan grabbed my hand. "You're an adult! Tell me it's going to be okay! Just say it and I'll feel better."

"It's going to be okay," I said.

But now I realized what it was. There was something about Megan's eyes, her cheekbones, her teeth. There was something about her energy. It was nothing I could put my finger on, and maybe it was my imagination, and maybe it was a trick of the dim light, but except for the difference in skin tone, this young woman looked just like my wife on that long-ago Monday when I met her for the first time. How else to say it? I could hardly breathe.

Letter from
ISRAEL FRAMINGHAM TRIPOLI
to
ZEPHANIAH FITCH

———

November 10, 1788

Dear Sir,

Yesterday afternoon, as I stood frowning into the twilight
of our descending winter and reflecting that it is near five
months now before the sun shall supply us with anything like
a hint of summer's balmy warmth, I found myself longing for
the heat and light of Saint Reynard. Is it not comical, Sir,
when in my last letter I represented the island as a place of
exile and condemnation? Yet such is the operation of the
mnemonic faculty, that we forget what we wish to forget, &
invent what we wish to remember.

I was standing at my window thinking of these things
when, as chance would have it, there came a knock upon my
door, & Mary, my housemaid, handed me a letter just arrived
that moment from Mr. Sturge, who was my host when I was in
the island. I wonder if I failed to give you some account of this
fellow? He is in the habit of reading his children a sermon
each afternoon before those little wretches are permitted to
eat. They must sit perfectly composed in their flannel and
wool as their father raves and gestures like a Bedlamite for
whole hours at a time. These sermons are thorough-stitched
nonsense such as never got vent through the keyhole of a

street door, but Mr. Sturge thinks highly of them and frequently affects to weep from what I believe he supposes an ebullition of feeling. An ebullition of spirits is more likely. He is a man of low character, a shuttlecock of a fellow, apoplectic with rage one moment and the next a smiling, Supplicating Fool.

But I dodge my subject, Sir, which is this, viz. that not three weeks after I departed, some of the slaves upon Mr. Sturge's Binghamshire plantation rose up and Murdered the clerk, a blameless & callow youth named Mr. Claibourne. The conspirators had armed themselves with cane knives and were it seems intending to flee to the island's uncultivated interior, but their organization was poor and their intentions betrayed by one of their own number, a cowardly fellow named Virgil, whom I remember meeting and of whom I formed a disagreeable impression. This Virgil had hidden the silverware and sent to a neighboring plantation for aid, and thus the rebellion was swiftly crushed (and, I am sure you will rejoice to learn, the silverware preserved). There followed a species of trial, tho one can imagine its theatrical absurdity, and then the slaves, three young men and one woman, were broken alive upon the rack and decapitated, their heads displayed afterward at a crossroads near the plantation.

My emotions upon receiving this news were such as I could only confide to you, dear Friend, for while I do lament the effusion of so much blood, and while I feel that Mr. Claibourne cannot be said to have deserved his violent death, being a harmless fellow with a brain like wet tinder, yet I am not surprised, and I could almost wish for a bloodier outcome still, if only to bring this great injustice of slavery to a point of crisis. As long as the slaves are so wretched, and the planters so intractable, such events will be commonplace, and it is folly indeed to hope for peace when the best one can expect are periods of fearful respite.

I have, as you know, striven all my life to be unoffending in my course and unambitious in my views, and yet the bloody current of the times turns me radical. Intimations and apprehensions crowd upon me thick and threefold. It is a war, Sir, and the crisis upon Mr. Sturge's plantation only a skirmish in that war, and the matter at stake is precisely that for which we ourselves so recently fought: freedom from tyranny. Indeed it may be that this matter of slavery is the greater cause, for until the world is cured of that vast and terrible pestilence, and the balance of nature restored, how can one speak with any confidence or sincerity those now immortal words, "We hold these truths to be self-evident . . ."? As long as our sable brethren toil beneath the lash, whether it be in our own Southern states or in the islands of the West Indies or indeed anywhere upon the globe, our Great Declaration is a lie.

I am troubled to-day, Sir, but I remain, with great fondness and humility, your servant and Friend,

Israel Framingham Tripoli

HISTORY OF THE BRANDS, HISTORY OF THE AMERICAS
A Big Anna® Heritage Timeline

Prehistory: Delicious bananas evolve in South or Southeast Asia.

600 B.C.: Greeks build the slave-powered Diolkos wagon-way, thought to be the world's first railway.

500 B.C.–
1492 A.D.: Polynesians carry the banana as far east as Hawaii, while Arab traders are responsible for the fruit's westward migration. Europeans first encounter the banana in West Africa, probably in the early 1400s.

1492: Columbus, miscalculating the circumference of the earth, which he believes is shaped like a pear, discovers America. Unfortunately, so do European epidemic diseases, which kill almost all of the New World's indigenous peoples over the next hundred and fifty years. Big Anna® honors them (the people) and celebrates their heritage yearly during its Amerindian Festival™.

1516: Friar Tomás de Berlanga brings the banana from the Canary Islands to the "undiscovered country" of the Caribbean, after which it spreads through Latin America like the epidemic diseases already blazing a path.

1519: Hernán Cortés arrives at the court of Aztec king Moctezuma II, where he learns that the monarch consumes more than fifty cups of chocolate a day. Aztec chocolate isn't the delicious treat that Europeans will come to know and love. It's a spicy unsweetened beverage. Gross!

1520: Moctezuma II is killed.

1520–1600: The banana serves as a nutritious treat for early colonists and slave laborers alike.

1600s: Ditto.

1692: The city of Port Royal, Jamaica, is completely destroyed in an earthquake!

c. 1700: After trying to start a mutiny on the merchant ship *Tatterdemalion*, John Morehead Tripoli is marooned on the Caribbean island of St. Renard. He lives among the Carawak Indians for a full year before being rescued, and he's the first European to taste the fruit of the Carawak Apple Tree, which will later prove to have important medical applications.

1769: After making some improvements to preexisting steam engines, James Watt becomes the man we think of as the inventor of the steam engine.

1776: Theodor Rubella declares independence from bland snack treats with his delicious biscuit thins, which he sells from the back of his stable in Philadelphia. Hard work! Because of a misunderstanding, he is later hanged as a traitor. Theodor Jr. takes over the business, and his father's legacy lives on to this day in Rubella Crackers™, one of Big Anna®'s oldest and most beloved snack items.

1819: Keith M. Cheek, railroad mogul and uncle of Andrew Cheek, the great father of Big Anna®, is born in New York City on the same day as Herman Melville.

c. 1839: Adolphus K. Mortonton begins selling cheese from a cart in Manhattan.

1842: Jakov Fleischman takes over Mortonton Cheese Co. when Adolphus K. Mortonton is hanged as a traitor.

1846: The Rubella Cracker Company introduces Horse Liver Crisps, precursor of Big Anna®'s beloved Equestrian Classic® crackers.

1847: Englishman Joseph Fry manufactures what everybody now thinks of as the first chocolate bar. The truth is that chocolate bars already existed, although Fry may have been the first to introduce factory methods of production to the industry. Where do inventions really come from?

1871: Keith M. Cheek signs a contract with the government of Nicaragua to construct a railroad connecting the capital city of Managua, situated close to the country's Pacific coast, with several Caribbean ports. In the first three years of the

project, an estimated two thousand laborers, or
about 60 percent of the total workforce, die
from tropical diseases like yellow fever and
malaria. After laying only sixty miles of track
through dense jungle, Cheek declares that the
trans-Nicaraguan railroad can't be built.

1875: Andrew Cheek, nephew of Keith M. Cheek,
takes over the trans-Nicaraguan railroad project.
He imports thousands of Afro-Caribbean laborers, who prove more resistant to tropical diseases
than his uncle's predominately Irish workforce,
and sets up banana plantations to provide freight
for the railroad and offset skyrocketing costs.

1880: The Nicaraguan government defaults on its
payments to Andrew Cheek, who raises money
from private investors and continues the project
himself. In gratitude, the government offers
Cheek an "eternal lease" on the operation of the
railroad, as well as significant territorial concessions and tax exemptions.

1882: Mortonton Cheese Co. acquires the Rubella
Cracker Company. The new company is christened Mortonton Foods.

1883: Facing bankruptcy, Andrew Cheek halts
construction of the trans-Nicaraguan railroad to
concentrate on improving the infrastructure of
his banana plantations on the country's
Caribbean coast. Construction never resumes,
although Cheek's banana business, soon

christened the Tropical Fruit and Rail Company, begins to expand rapidly and soon establishes plantations in many Central and South American countries.

c. 1885: In Columbus, Georgia, John Pemberton formulates a coca wine that he calls Pemberton's French Wine Coca, an imitation of another coca wine called Vin Mariani, which had appeared in 1863. He sells the concoction as a patent medicine for the treatment of morphine addiction, irregularities of the stomach, and neurasthenia.

1886: Fulton County passes prohibition legislation, forcing John Pemberton to develop a nonalcoholic version of his French Wine Coca. The result is Coca-Cola, a watery nerve tonic that goes on sale that year. Gerald Whiteman steals the recipe for the authentic, alcoholic beverage and begins manufacturing it in his basement and selling it as Whiteman's Wine Coca.

1887: Police raid Whiteman's Atlanta home. He is able to escape to Charleston, South Carolina, where he stows away on a ship bound for Central America. Later that year, he meets Andrew Cheek in Santa Marta, Colombia, and persuades the railroad and banana mogul to invest in his new company, South America Coca and Wine, which he founds at that very moment in the waterfront brothel where the two men are spending the siesta hour.

1888: John Pemberton dies. He has been a morphine addict since his first exposure to the drug in a Civil War field hospital, and he's been struggling to find a remedy for his addiction for more than twenty years. Coca-Cola is just one result of his experimentation. Even if it's a tale of Gilded Age quackery, Pemberton's story is very sad, and Big Anna® pays tribute to him by including a short bio and photograph on its Coconut Wine™ beverage, which is enjoyed today throughout the Caribbean.

1892: John "James" Otto comes to New York with $13 in his pocket and starts selling insecticide powder. As an incentive, he offers a free stick of Otto Chew Gum with each can. Later discovering that the gum is more popular than the insecticide powder, he discontinues the gum incentive and resumes selling insecticide powder on its own.

1893: Andrew Cheek's Tropical Fruit and Rail Company acquires South America Coca and Wine from the now-destitute morphine addict Gerald Whiteman.

1894: John Otto goes bankrupt and commits suicide. His brother, James "Tex" Otto, arrives in New York to collect his effects and discovers several unopened crates of Otto Chew Gum. Tex Otto has $11 in his pocket. He begins selling the gum from a cart outside his brother's building.

1895: Andrew Cheek states publicly that he has observed Anna Worthington, wife of rival banana mogul Christian Worthington, consume two full bunches of unripe bananas in one day. Cheek tells the *New York Times* that "Big Anna" is his greatest ally and that he believes she will eat his competitor out of house, home, and business. Continuing the good-natured joke, he names a Colombian plantation after her.

1896: Christian Worthington challenges Andrew Cheek to a duel. Cheek accepts, but before the two men can settle their score, Worthington dies of a heart attack probably caused by coca wine poisoning. Tropical Fruit and Rail acquires Worthington Fruit.

1898: Bayer begins marketing diacetylmorphine under the trademark name "Heroin." The new product is intended for use as a cough suppressant, although it proves to have other applications.

1899: Tex Otto enjoys his first banana. Astonished by the sweet and delicious fruit, he develops Otto Banana Chew Gum. It soon replaces clove-flavored Otto Chew Gum as Otto Co.'s most successful product. Tropical Fruit and Rail supplies bananas to Otto's factory.

1900: Andrew Cheek marries the widow Anna Worthington.

1902: St. Pierre, Martinique, which is known as "the Paris of the Caribbean," is completely destroyed by a volcano!

1906: Otto Co. introduces its first chocolate confection, the Otto Bar, made from rich, thigh-tremblingly sweet West African chocolate.

c. 1908: Gerald Whiteman stops using morphine! He'll be clean for the rest of his life, proving that there's hope for all of us.

1909: Joan of Arc is beatified.

1910: Andrew Cheek gets too big for his britches and decides it's time to expand, first organizing an unsuccessful coup in Nicaragua and then declaring himself king of the so-called Big Anna Republic, a sovereign nation comprised of several Colombian banana plantations, including the notorious Big Anna plantation. That same year, he begins construction of "Big Anna by the Sea," a lavish three-hundred-room palace.

1912: There were no bananas on the RMS *Titanic*, which could have been one reason for the fatal mishap that sent that ship to the bottom of the ocean, since bananas are proven to increase wakefulness and improve concentration. Second-class passengers did enjoy something called a "Coconut Sandwich."

1913: "King" Andrew Cheek hosts a banquet to celebrate the completion of his new palace, Big Anna by the Sea. Guests include Hapsburg archduke Franz Ferdinand, J. P. Morgan, and Tex Otto. Cheek is reportedly dressed in a light, loosely fitting suit made from vampire-bat wool. Otto stays on for two months after the event, enchanted by the natural beauty, stimulating coca wine, and furnace-fire heat for which Cheek's tiny Caribbean nation is known. J. P. Morgan dies of unrelated natural causes later that year.

1914: Archduke Franz Ferdinand dies in Sarajevo of causes unrelated to his experience with the Tropical Fruit and Rail Company or with Cheek's Big Anna Republic.

1914–1918: The Big Anna Republic enjoys consistent prosperity, although Tropical Fruit and Rail struggles during this period.

1920: Andrew Cheek dispatches a small expeditionary force to the Caribbean island of St. Renard, where the Big Anna Republic intends to establish a colony. The enterprise is threatened when 80 percent of the colonists die in a yellow fever epidemic later that year, one of the last such outbreaks in modern times.

1922: Andrew Cheek agrees to recognize Colombia's territorial claims and dissolves the Big Anna Republic, although the change is only nominal and Tropical Fruit and Rail continues to rule efficiently over the region.

1924: Mortonton Foods acquires Otto Co.

1925: Mortonton Foods introduces Moctezuma Chew Chocolate, the precursor of Big Anna®'s Authentic Aztec® Sweet Chocolate Chew™.

1926: Tropical Fruit and Rail merges with Mortonton Foods. The new company is christened Big Anna Foods.

1927: Andrew Cheek dies peacefully of natural causes and suspected coca wine poisoning at Big Anna by the Sea. Control of Big Anna Foods passes to his son, Ricardo Furenza de la Santidad Cheek.

1931: Big Anna Foods acquires Cafélisto, an exciting new company that produces a coffee-flavored soluble drinking powder.

1932: Big Anna Foods maintains profitability without laying off a single worker. Nevertheless, thousands of Big Anna workers go on strike, forcing the company to train and dispatch elite security personnel, the precursors of its heroic Big Anna® Shock Troops™.

1933: The Dietetic Muffin Company introduces its Banana Bran Muffin at Chicago's Century of Progress World's Fair. Originally marketed as a cathartic, Banana Bran Muffins are soon beloved by more than just costive snackers.

1941–1945: Big Anna Foods enjoys profitability and expands into new niche markets.

1946: When Gerhard von Papenburg, president of the Dietetic Muffin Company, is hanged as a traitor, Big Anna Foods acquires the company. Afterward, Big Anna Foods changes its name to Big Anna® Brands, the name by which the company is known today.

1947: Big Anna® brand Banana Bran Muffins®, a reformulation of the Dietetic Muffin Company's original muffin, are introduced in order to satisfy the continuing demand for semisweet high-fiber snacks like those Big Anna® had produced during a period of ingredient unavailability lasting from 1941 to 1945. To this day, Banana Bran Muffins® have the most fiber per unit volume of any snack cake or muffin, making them arguably the most dietetic snack product currently available without a prescription.

1955: Big Anna® Coconut Wine™ is introduced throughout Latin America and the Caribbean. The new beverage is a sweeter, carbonated version of Whiteman's Wine Coca, itself a reformulation of John Pemberton's French Wine Coca, which was in turn an imitation of Vin Mariani. The popular drink isn't made with coconuts, however. It gets its name from Coconut Key, the tiny island in the Eastern Caribbean where Gerald Whiteman spent his last years.

1961: Intrigued by the continuing success of Banana
Bran Muffins®, Big Anna® science associates
begin to experiment with other ways of processing unsold bananas, research that bears fruit, as
it were, in the form of Banana Baby Pap™,
Banana Bran Flakes™, leather polish, ointment,
teeth whitener, and several varieties of banana
wine.

1973: Radical communist Marville Guajiro, newly
elected president of St. Renard, announces that
he's going to expel Big Anna® from the island
and nationalize the banana farms and sugarcane
fields. Fortunately, Big Anna® Democracy
Technicians™ expose electoral fraud and help
reinstate former president Torrington McKay.
Big Anna® Shock Troops™ remain on the island
to keep the peace.

1975: In response to continuing challenges within the
banana industry, and in order to ensure reliable
sources of top-quality bananas for its Banana
Bran Muffins® and other products, Big Anna®
decides to stop producing bananas for export to
the United States and instead to reserve that fruit
for its own use. In a revolutionary move, the
company transfers the majority of its snack
production business directly to the Latin
American and West Indian plantations that
produce the necessary raw ingredients, thus
maintaining an efficient and environmentally
friendly vertical-integration production model.

Big Anna®'s facilities and plantations on St. Renard remain the cornerstone of its Caribbean business to this day.

1978: Big Anna® acquires Whig Vegipaste, a New Zealand–based sandwich spread company; Top Hole, a Canadian nautical equipment manufacturer; and Paramount Food and Drug, a used-medicament reprocessing company.

1982: Big Anna® acquires the Polynesian island of Moahu.

1990: Big Anna® acquires Genutrex® Nutrition, a vitamin and supplement manufacturer.

1991: Working closely with technicians from Paramount Food and Drug, Big Anna® Science Associates™ develop Moisture Seal™ technology, which enables Big Anna® products to retain their glisten and freshness for months and months, even when they're removed from the package.

1992: Expanding quickly into newly opened Central and Eastern European markets, Big Anna® Brands purchases the Croatian arms manufacturer Obradovic, plus three Kazakh television stations.

1999: Big Anna® demonstrates its continuing sensitivity to the struggles of non-optimal-weight Americans by introducing new Waistshaper® snacks like Bottle Brush™ crackers and Cherry

Explosion™ snack treats. Both products are 100
percent isotonic. Big Anna® also introduces
individual-serving Microwavable Toast Slices™,
Diet Fruit Pieces™, and Zero-Calorie Wigglers®,
a gelatin-based No Guilt™ snack treat.

2007: Big Anna® "goes green" with its LoCarbon™
initiative on St. Renard, which includes the
introduction of clean Human Power™ plow
technology, arguably the company's most
sustainable innovation to date.

2009: Following a decade of significant, business-
friendly tax legislation, Big Anna® gives back by
increasing its involvement in higher education.
The company cosponsors the Caribbean Field
Studies Program with Tripoli College.

Now: Big Anna® remains a company committed to
unceasing technological modernization while
maintaining an emphasis on traditional heritage
brands, dietetic and isotonic foods, "green" business, and vertical integration, with lots of new
prospects and opportunities on the horizon.

From: "Maggie Bell" <mbell1990@tripoli.edu>
To: "Chris Bell" <cfb456@mercurylink.net>
Date: November 18, 2009, at 12:26 PM
Subject: (no subject)

Hi, Chris,

I have some news! I know this is coming out of nowhere and I'm sorry I didn't talk to you about it, but it was practically just an impulse. I applied to study abroad on St. Renard next semester. I think it'll be really good. It'll be good just to do and see something different. It's not like a desperate plan to make Kabaka my husband. It's just that I'm really in a rut here. I'm lonely and angry and worked up all the time about all kinds of stuff. I applied yesterday after I had lunch with Becca and Francoise. We went to get Thai food and we just sat there for an hour. It was terrible. We didn't have anything to say! Freshman and sophomore year it was like everybody was in it together, but now I think we're all growing into our differences, you know? I felt this high moral righteousness too. I wanted to say, Hey, Becca, you don't know how easy you've got it! Stop complaining! (Not like you and I have had it so bad, but still.)

Dad will pay for it, I guess. He didn't give me a hard time about it and that's nice. The only thing is I'm not entirely comfortable going down there under the umbrella of Big Anna, but if I do some good I do some good, right? I don't really understand in what way Big Anna is involved. There's botany and oceanography but there's also this program of service for locals. We help with some kind of agricultural work, I think. It will all be explained.

I've been hanging out a little more with Dean Brees. Not a ton, you know, not so it's weird, or weirder than it already is . . . Anyway he's just a really sweet guy and it's made a difference for me this semester to have him to talk to. It's a pretty unlikely friendship I guess. The other day I had lunch with him and he shot milk through his nose! It was totally spontaneous. We were eating in silence, reading our papers or books or whatever, and then suddenly he took a drink of milk and bam! Both barrels. Now I'm pretty sure he has feelings for me, but part of the reason I like spending time with him is that he's a real adult and he can keep those feelings in check. He treats me like a human being.

I don't want you to feel like I'm abandoning you for a semester. I have to get out of my rut, that's all.

I feel like a lawn that needs mowing. See you next week!
Love,
M

From
THE TRIPOLI COLLEGE TELEGRAPH
November 20, 2009

More Revelations of Fiscal Mismanagement

Investment officer Tom Haley is facing disciplinary action and possible criminal charges after admitting this week to losing "a large hunk" of Tripoli's endowment in Las Vegas over the summer.

Haley claims that he was engaged in a form of speculation known as "short selling." Typically, short selling means borrowing stock, securities, or commodities, selling them, and then buying them back at a lower price and returning them to the lender. In this way, an investor can bet on the devaluation of that financial product.

Haley, who admits that he "didn't understand it very well," simply "invested" a large sum of money, perhaps as much as $1.2 million, in chips at Caesars Palace. He then stayed up for 48 hours playing roulette, during which time he lost everything.

In a press conference yesterday afternoon, Haley explained, "I was trying to sell myself short, in econ terms. I borrowed a loan, sold it for poker chips, then bought the loan back for less than what it was originally worth. I was engaged in a high-risk venture, i.e., gambling, and I knew it was virtually certain that I'd lose that money, which is why I was betting on the decrease in the value of the sum of money I'd originally borrowed. It's a classic financial gambit."

Asked why he thought the strategy didn't work, Haley was stumped: "That's where I lose my grip on the whole thing. The idea is you buy one thing, exchange it for another thing at a certain rate, then exchange it for the first thing again when the rate is favorable. That's the whole principle of finance. I can't understand where I went wrong."

It is not clear whether Mr. Haley was acting alone, in which case the lack of oversight in this respect is cause for serious concern, or whether he was acting with the tacit approval of administrators. In any case, the incident could have serious consequences for President Richmond, who has also been criticized for what many feel is an unsatisfactory response to the Pinkman-White slavery scandal.

The president has been slow to defend herself, and her erratic behavior has been cause for comment in recent weeks. She appeared at yesterday's press conference in sweatpants and a hooded sweatshirt.

"I'm kind of losing faith here," she said." Asked to clarify, she explained: "Since very little of this can be construed as my fault, my only role in this situation is that of a scapegoat. It doesn't matter what I say in my defense. I could say anything."

This remark did not win the president any friends, and her position is more tenuous than ever. Several members of the faculty, as well as a number of prominent alumni, have already called for her resignation.

Professor Francis Amundsen has been particularly vocal in his condemnation of the president, citing many instances of financial and personal irresponsibility. Professor Amundsen has not been able to substantiate his allegations and he is also an outspoken supporter of Professor William Beckford, who is considered one of President Richmond's possible successors, but it is a mark of the growing feeling against the president that one so obviously partisan has gained an audience.

The board of trustees will meet next week to discuss the situation.

SCANDAL VULNERABILITY ASSESSMENT

ORIGINAL DRAFT PREPARED FOR THE BOARD OF TRUSTEES
OF TRIPOLI COLLEGE BY DR. FRANCIS AMUNDSEN,
NOVEMBER 28, 2009

Investigation of potential areas of legal, behavioral, and/or financial issues associated with President Lillian Richmond have yielded the following allegations, areas of potential vulnerability, and possible grounds for removal:

- She has been moonlighting as a phone-sex dominatrix.

- Each morning, according to reports, an attendant prepares a solution of crushed pearls and absinthe, which the president drinks as an elixir of invulnerability. The expense is borne by the college.

- She drinks palm wine all day out of a giant, heraldically decorated ceremonial mug, which she purchased with college funds.

- She wears tailored underwear made from vampire-bat wool.

- She has a live-in servant whose only duty is to remove one half of the "stuf" in her "Double Stuf" Oreos.

- Each morning, she covers herself in gold dust and takes a ceremonial bath in the Tripoli River. She purchases the gold dust with college funds.

- She attacked Professor Amundsen with a sawfish rostrum as he was walking home from class.

- With college funds, she purchased three pounds of psychoactive Hopewell tobacco, which she smokes out of a hollow jaguar-head sculpture, also purchased with college funds.

- She reportedly commissioned a set of manatee-bone vomiting sticks from an Indian craftsman in Guyana, the cost of which is to be borne by the college.

- She maintains a stable of three horses at college expense. She reportedly said that the stable is her "walking meat locker of horse meat."

- She allegedly told a student reporter that cannibalism is "an ecologically efficient means of disposing of a corpse."

- She reportedly told student reporters that she "just can't start the day" without a hummingbird-egg omelet, which a live-in chef prepares for her each morning. The great expense associated with maintaining the necessary hummingbird aviary is borne by the college.

- She allegedly destroyed her laptop computer, which was college property, when she had difficulty buying a human head on Amazon.com.

- Another indication of cannibalistic tendencies is that she asked Health Center employees to bring her "some of that good hot blood" donated by students during Tripoli's recent "Blood for Our Heroes" initiative.

- In the basement of the presidential mansion, there is a pool filled with Polaroid pictures of disgraced investment officer Tom Haley.

- According to reports, she spends at least two nights a week snorting hallucinogenic cohoba powder.

- In a secret memo to department chairs and senior administrators, she reportedly demanded the following in tribute: jade figurines, jaguar skins, Jesuit's bark, and tunics made from hummingbird feathers.

- In her desk, there is a draft of an erotic novel allegedly called *Sentiment and Sensuality*.

- At a banquet honoring scholarship recipients, she reportedly offered students handfuls of dried ants, spirulina loaves, mosquito larvae, and tamales made from red worms, adding that the last-named were "good enough for Huitzilopochtli."

- Another creature she has threatened to eat is Lucien, Professor Amundsen's King Charles spaniel.

- She opposed Tripoli's partnership agreement with Big Anna® Brands.

———————

I spent Thanksgiving by myself, just puttering around the empty dorm. My daughters were celebrating the holiday with their in-laws, and I wanted a bit of solitude after the long, crowded months. There were a few international students around, but I didn't talk to anyone. I did my laundry, read a book or two, listened to the Pixies and the Kinks on my iPod, and took long walks in the cold. In the knock and clamor of the breathless year, this was a nice moment of calm.

Then everyone came back to wait out this strange intoxicating moment between Thanksgiving and Christmas. In some ways I've settled back into the old routine—I fool around on the Internet, go to parties, and eat slab after slab of *Bacon Blast Pizza*—but I'm afraid I'm just whistling in the dark. Things are not the same and they won't be the same. In early December, I ran into President Richmond in the science library. She was wearing sweatpants and eating ice cream with a fork. I thought, This is a woman who has given up. She hasn't even bothered to deny any of the wild stories that people are telling about her. I have no doubt that she'll announce her resignation soon and that William Beckford will be named her successor. This is particularly troubling because, as I have already hinted, Professor Beckford is a shareholder in the Big Anna® corporation (though I should say I have trouble believing that he's motivated by anything so simple as financial considerations).

The students don't care who the president is, and why should they? But they notice other changes. One day Burke came home and told me a bizarre story. A football player named Jamari Hall had been sitting in on his "Colonial America" lecture. Everyone knows that football players aren't supposed to take classes—they are "academic exempt"—and apparently someone had called the Athletic Association to complain. In the middle of class, two men in Tyrants polo shirts crept in and tried to get Mr. Hall to leave.

"So then he started to shout," Burke told me. "He's like, 'I'm just sitting here! I'm just listening!' Professor Coleman stops talking. We're all just sitting there watching this thing. So now Hall is shouting, and one of the men is telling us that everything's under control, they'll be out of our hair in just a second, and the other guy is taking something out of his pocket and fiddling around with it. I couldn't see what happened, but I heard a click or like a thunk, almost, and Hall goes quiet and sort of sits back. Then both guys take him under the arms and help him walk out, and all the time we're just watching this terrible thing happen and no one does anything."

The football team has been a sensitive subject this fall. First there was the trumped-up and now mostly forgotten Pinkman Scandal. Then they lost four straight games. Now two of their kickers are said to be in locked wards at Tripoli Regional Hospital. The Athletic Association has adopted a "no tolerance" policy with respect to its players.

"What I'm saying," Burke said, "is I think this guy shot Jamari Hall with a *tranquilizer dart*."

What about Mr. Pinkman himself? He is supposed to have taken a leave of absence, but I saw him standing in a dark seminar room in Ulster Hall. He was dressed in a lab coat and he didn't have any shoes on. He tried to get my attention when he saw me peeping in at him, but I pretended not to notice. The door was padlocked from the outside.

So that's the world we're living in here at Tripoli. It's the end of an era. But my own mood is in the toilet for another reason: Megan recently told me that she's going to enroll in the Field Studies Program on St. Renard next semester.

"Actually," she said, "I don't really know why I want to go. To fight against neoliberalism? I'm not sure what neoliberalism is. Maybe I'm chasing after Professor Kabaka? I think it's mostly just that I need a change. And maybe I can also exorcise some guilt by helping the Renardennes in a small way. I can say, 'Hey, Big Anna® will nail your ears to the doorpost, but use a condom and you won't get AIDS.' "

My stated mission, at the beginning of this semester, was to discover what student life was really like. I had been a little concerned that my personal feelings and relationships had come to interfere with that mission, but now, as I reflected on the surprise and unhappiness that Megan's announcement had caused me, I realized that I was simply experiencing the great truth of student life: Student life is about personal relationships. Student life is about other students. I don't know why I never understood it before.

As for Megan herself, I still haven't told her how I feel about her, and in some respects I find my feelings hard to put into words. Sometimes I think I've fallen in love with her, but at other times I'm concerned about her as any responsible adult is concerned for a young person in distress. In any case, she has come to mean a great deal to me, and I don't like to think of life without her. I don't think I could bear any more loss.

I told her that she would have a wonderful time on St. Renard, but I didn't want to talk about it. In fact, I felt desolate. I especially didn't want to talk about Professor Kabaka. His name was enough to give me a queasy feeling. It was like all those years ago when I'd first met my wife and she was still engaged to Tom Hassock. She used to complain about him to me, Tom this and Tom that, and I'd feel like throwing up. In addition, I was a little uneasy about Professor Kabaka. I worried that his allegiance was ultimately to ideas and not to human beings.

I went back to the dorm and stood peering out the window into the icy black night. I could smell heating oil in the air. It had been fifty years since I graduated from college and I felt like I still didn't know who I was or what I wanted. I thought about calling one of my daughters, but I didn't want to bother my children with these concerns. In the end I called Richard Carlyle, but he was having problems of his own. He said he'd realized that he was an "Ezra Pound fascist lunatic" and now he was trying to atone for this crime of outlook. He was concerned to distance himself from Beckford, whose own fascist ideas, Carlyle said, were procedural and not simply aesthetic.

Meanwhile, Burke was trying his hand at a new poem in the common room. Both he and Lehman had gained weight this semester, and Burke's whole head seemed to have gotten larger and softer. I knew he was self-conscious about it, so I never gave him a hard time, like Lehman did, but it was true: His forehead was enormous, like the forehead of a sperm whale. It seemed to press down on his tiny eyes and give him a peevish look.

"She's in love with Professor Kabaka!" I said, although I hadn't meant to say it out loud.

"Yeah," he said. "Jeez, man. Who is?"

I said, "Maybe I'll go to St. Renard myself."

"Sure, man. Yeah. You owe that much to yourself."

I was practically muttering. I said, "What's stopping me?"

He nodded vigorously, although he had no idea what I was talking about. Then he and I had a shot of white rum. The lights seemed to flicker and I had to sit down. Students always want to take shots. I can hardly stand it.

"Want to hear some of my new poem?" he said. And he began to recite:

> My ancestors fought for freedom,
> On distant shores, in unfamiliar climes
> The bondsman's chains were strong,
> But stronger was his heart and mind.
> And all so that one day, in lecture class,
> They shoot you with a tranquilizing dart.
> My lips of steel between your ribs,
> My poison in your heart . . .

"Has anyone explained to you about perspective or point of view?" I said.

"It's like Carlyle says: My poetry is to be a poetry of revolt. I mean to leave the old devices behind."

"It's just that the point of view shifts a few times. You have to think about what's happening in your poem. There are rules you have to follow or the reader gets confused."

"It's called 'The Dart of History.' "

"Sure. That's a pretty good title."

"I always start with the title and go from there. Want to take another shot?"

Then it occurred to me that there was no reason I couldn't

go to St. Renard. I had plenty of money. I'd all but quit my job. I could do whatever I wanted. How had I managed to forget these things? And suddenly I was very excited. I could go there to be on hand in case Megan needed help. I could prove to her that I was a man of action like Professor Kabaka.

"I feel like I'm really coming into my own as a poet," Burke said.

"But you have to think about who the speaker is. Is it the man or the dart? Is it an omniscient third person?"

He shook his head and smiled. "It's art, man. You've got to leave these preconceptions behind." Then he pointed to the window and said in astonishment, "It's snowing!"

And it was. A few dusty flakes of snow came wheeling out of the dark sky. We had another shot, and then another.

Maybe it was the time of year or the time of night, but I found myself thinking of my wife. I remembered how she used to make up funny songs when she was doing housework. She used to walk around the house singing in a high piping voice about watering the plants or rearranging the books. Sometimes she sang about me. She sang with great feeling. I thought it was the most wonderful thing in the world.

Rather than filling me with longing and sadness, this memory brought me a deep sense of calm. I had lived a rich, full life with someone whom I had loved and who had loved me. Of course I missed her, but as long as I had those memories of her, it seemed like nothing could touch me. I was safe. And I thought maybe this was what revolutionaries like Professor Kabaka must feel like: so solid in their hearts that they were untouchable.

I cast my mind back over the events of the last few months. Undergraduate life can be so innocent and beautiful! Everything happens now and now and now, but at the same time there's a poignant quality, a sense of time passing, and a sort of nostal-gia for things that haven't even happened yet. When I thought of all the things that added up to that incredible fall—the wine and the music, the sight of Lehman drinking mouthwash, the young man in the toreador's blouse, the yellow leaves, the smell of an old fireplace, a hustle across wet cobblestones in a dark rain—they all added up to a uniform thing. They were all part of the beautiful idea of that time and that place. Maybe my feelings for Megan were just part of a desire to experience it all more intensely, but who cared if they were?

From: "William Beckford" <wbeckford1898@tripoli.edu>
To: tripoli@lists-tc-fall.edu
Date: December 15, 2009, at 3:50 AM
Subject: Memo to Tripoli Community

"Everything in the College, Nothing Outside the College, Nothing Against the College."

Students and faculty of Tripoli College, brothers and sisters of St. Renard, generous benefactors, executives of the Big Anna® corporation, alumni all over the world—beyond the mountains, beyond the seas—listen!

For many months, the wheel of destiny has moved toward the goal. In these last hours, the rhythm has increased and nothing can stop it now. A solemn hour is about to strike.

I have been asked today to serve as acting president of Tripoli College. My name has been put forward by students, by faculty, by alumni, by trustees.

Comrades, I accept.

The enemies of progress oppose my candidacy, but developments in academia, which sometimes are speeded up, cannot be halted any more than the fleeting moment of Faust could be halted. History takes one by the throat and forces a decision. This is not the first time this has occurred in the history of Tripoli!

If this institution does not wish to die—or, worse still, commit suicide—it must provide itself with a new doctrine. This shall not and must not be a robe of Nessus, clinging to us for all eternity, for tomorrow is something mysterious and unforeseen. Nor shall the new course taken by Tripoli in any way diminish the fighting spirit of this institution. To furnish the college with doctrines and creeds does not mean to disarm; rather, it means to strengthen our power of action and make us ever more conscious of our work. Tripoli shall take for its own the twofold device of Mazzini: Thought and Action.

But we stand today at a great moment in our history, and with great moments come great challenges and responsibilities.

For some time, the attention of our administration has been focused on St. Renard. All the work of the program directors who succeeded each other on St. Renard was aimed at strengthening, economically and academically, and always in coordination with Big Anna® Brands, that tiny island—transforming the virgin forest and beaches into fecund land and a beautiful campus for our Proxy College.

Miracles! This word describes what has been done down there.

But liberalism, democracy, and plutocracy have declared and waged war against us and condemned our venture on St. Renard, spreading libelous reports and accusations of gross misconduct even when we were intent upon the work of national renovation which is, and will remain for centuries, the indestructible documentation of our creative will. These accusations must only accentuate that cold, conscious, implacable hate, hate in every dormitory and classroom, which is indispensable for our ultimate victory. But it is because we are certain regarding the grade of moral and intellectual maturity reached by the Tripoli community that we continue to follow the cult of truth and repudiate all falsification.

I do not attempt to hide the facts. My regime will be one of brutal frankness and I will not conceal even the most insignificant detail. On St. Renard this year, violence perpetrated by conspirators and anarchists has left ten wounded and one dead. Two houses have been completely destroyed by fire, three more have been damaged, and the Proxy College had to be evacuated after a gas leak thought to be the result of sabotage.

I supply these facts and figures in order to prove to our enemies that we do not deny the truth. We accept the truth, and we face these enemies with determination and hate in our hearts.

What of that fallen woman, our outgoing president, who accuses me of being the "mad architect" of the labor disputes on St. Renard?

It is said that this woman is the descendant of an aristocratic family and that she has a great deal of blue blood in her veins. In my veins, on the other hand, flows the pure and healthy blood of farriers and coopers and ironworkers, and at this moment I feel myself to be infinitely more cultivated and well mannered than this woman from whose mouth, fetid with alcohol and tobacco, comes forth such vile baseness.

But let me say no more about our Proxy College. Let me turn now to concerns of even greater moment.

Closer to home, the struggle is no less fiercely combated. I say to you now, in all frankness, that I do not believe there has ever been a crisis of such proportions as the present one, and we must make it plain that this crisis has to be faced, and faced not merely as a problem of funding and institutional policy, but as a spiritual and moral problem as well.

We must recognize this!

We have had gray days!

But think of the Punic Wars, when the Battle of Cannae threatened to crush Rome. At Zama, Rome destroyed Carthage and wiped it from geography and history forever.

Where Rome can wrest victory from the abyss of defeat, so too can Tripoli College.

But let me close this statement with a few words about Tripoli College in its spiritualized conception.

Tripoli is not only an academic institution. It is also the highest and most powerful form of personality. It is a force, but a spiritual force, which takes over all the forms of the moral and intellectual life of our young men and women. It is the form, the inner standard, and the discipline of the whole person; it saturates the will as well as the intelligence. Tripoli, in short, is not only a granter of degrees, but the educator and promoter of spiritual life. It wants to remake not the forms of human life, but its content: Man, Character, Faith.

We have created our myth. The myth is a faith. It is passion. It is not necessary that it should be a reality. It is a reality by the fact that it is a hope, a faith—that it is courage. And to this myth, to this grandeur that we wish to translate into a complete reality, we subordinate all the rest. Thus I pledge myself to this cause.

Signed,
William Beckford

RECOMMENDATION LETTER FOR BILL DEAN

December 18, 2009

Prof. Richard Carlyle
212 Dropsy Place
Tripoli, NH 03791

To Whom It May Concern,

I'm writing on behalf of Bill Dean, a student I've known for almost thirty years. He'd be a great addition to whatever program he's applying for. Is it the Field Studies Program? He didn't even bother to tell me! And did he mention that he's actually the dean of students? His real name is William Brees. That's just by way of saying that I have a personal relationship with him. I don't mean that we have an improper relationship. I've never even been with a man! Not that I'm ruling it out. The first thing I tell my students each semester is NEVER RULE THAT OUT!

If he'd been in my poetry class, I'm sure Bill would have done great work. But maybe he's not the kind of guy who goes in for literary art! At least I can be sure he'd have been a great addition to our classroom discussions, since he always does manage to keep the conversation going and make you feel at ease. He's a great guy—that is to say, student. More important, of course, is that he's gotten me out of some big-time serious no-joke TIGHT SPOTS in the twenty-eight years I've known him. There was this one time when I was up on the roof of Longman Hall with a potato gun! Another time I was living in one of the period rooms at the museum. I slept under the bed during the day. They have those fancy bed skirts, so it was no trouble keeping out of sight, and anyway the guards knew I was in there and they didn't mind.

And a few years ago—this one will blow your hairpiece off—I sort of kidnapped a student!

Dean Brees is a good kid, or man. And I wouldn't say that about just anyone! If I could be as steady as that, my God, you wouldn't believe the things I could do. All the good he's done for me, bailing me out of jail, etc., etc. It gives me the screaming meemies just to think about it, and then I feel the old familiar feeling, the high singing craziness, and off I go for another spree in toon town. If you end up accepting his application, TELL HIM I'M SORRY!

Best,
Richard Carlyle

FIRST PROCLAMATION
OF THE ANTILLIA LIBERATION ARMY / DECEMBER 21, 2009

To the people of St. Renard
Brothers and Sisters:

We are the product of five hundred years of pain and horror and humiliation. For five hundred years we have lived and died at the pleasure of men hardly fit to lick the dirt from our bare feet. For five hundred years we have shed our blood so that other people, white people, can have cheap sugar, cheap clothes, cheap bananas, cheap drugs. For five hundred years we have been the uncomfortable fact, the other side of sweetness, the dark surprise in the basement of world history. We have been the men and women outside the gates.

And we are still here. We have lived at the crossroads of empire and in the slums of empire, and we have never moved from this spot. We came to these shores against our will, we came in misery, but we came, and after five hundred years this island is our only home. We mean to claim our rights as free citizens of the world.

What has been happening all this time? What do these five hundred years have to teach us?

We watched Columbus's men rape and brutalize the indigenous population. And when the Indians were gone, when the Spaniards had moved west and south, compelled by their depraved passion for gold, we watched the British and the French tear each other to pieces for the right to these islands, the right to rape us and murder us and enslave our children.

We have watched fathers and mothers and brothers and sisters and aunts and uncles die for the sake of sugarcane, for the sake of a giant tropical grass. They died so that a woman in London could sweeten her tea.

Through the centuries we have watched the Europeans debarking from their filthy ships, setting up their houses and plantations, getting rich from the soil they fertilize with our blood. We have stumbled against them in the street and we have been beaten for it. We have seen them in the noonday heat, in their waistcoats and tails, arguing over the value of our flesh, buying us and selling us with the cattle and the hogs.

A traveler to the island two hundred years ago tells of a white child, the son of a sugar baron, who demanded an egg. Told that there were no eggs, the child said: "Then I want two."

We have lived through abolition—that fragile hope—and the degrading years of apprenticeship, only to see slavery return in the guise of "Free Trade."

We have cried out in pain as Marville Guajiro, the first democratically elected president of the free and sovereign nation of St. Renard, was ignominiously deposed, hog-tied, hauled from his bed by mercenaries in the employ of the Big Anna corporation and the government of the United States of America.

We have watched Big Anna creep like a rash over the skin of our island. We have watched our sisters and mothers work their hands to the bone in the factories of the St. Renard Free Zone. We have watched our fathers as they stumble up the road from the banana farms and the cane fields. We have seen the suppurating wounds on their arms. We have seen the yellow skin, the blue skin, the chemical burns. We have seen the hope go out of their eyes.

It has been the same everywhere. Globalization began with the conquest of the Canary Islands. It continued with the Spaniards on

Hispaniola, the Spaniards in Mexico, the Spaniards in Peru. Year by year the horror was renewed. The slave port of Whydah, the Portuguese East Indies, the Dutch East Indies, the British Raj, the plantation complex in Brazil and Cuba and the U.S. South, indentured "coolie" labor, Chinese peasants kidnapped and enslaved on the guano islands off South America, King Leopold in the Congo, the brutalization of Australia and the Pacific islands, the Amazonian rubber trade, the Germans terrorizing Namibia, the Germans terrorizing Europe, interned Japanese in the beet fields of the United States, apartheid, Ian Smith's Rhodesia. Millions dead for gold, silver, sugar, cotton, rubber, ivory, oil. The same thing in all places at all times. The merciless exploitation of the multitude by those whom arbitrary circumstances have made strong.

And now we say: Enough, enough, enough.

We—men and women, whole and free—declare war on the United States, on Big Anna, on the forces of neoliberalism. We ask for your support in this plan to expel the murderers and the rapists from our island, to claim for our people all the rights that have been denied us for five centuries, the rights to education, health care, justice, food, land, peace.

Our fathers were coachmen and cane cutters on St. Renard, but their fathers were kings in Africa. We have been slaves but we will be slaves no longer.

Join the insurgent forces of the Antillia Liberation Army
Commandant Kabaka, December 2009

WINTER
BREAK

WINTER GETTING YOU DOWN? TIRED OF THE COLD AND THE DARK? VISIT THE TROPICAL PARADISE OF ST. RENARD!

Imagine a place where fewer than 20 percent of visitors are mugged within three days. Imagine a place where hardly anyone reports yaws, piums, creeping eruption, white and black piedra, and chromomycosis. Imagine a place where the only tropical disease—besides typhoid, yellow fever, malaria, beriberi, filariasis, river blindness, and numerous unexplained fevers—is Relaxation. Imagine ST. RENARD. You won't be able to look away.

ABOUT US

Silky white sand, crystal-clear water, sizzling entertainment, inconceivable fruits, misty rain forests, beautiful locals, and all the white rum you can drink. Sound good? St. Renard is the island paradise you've been looking for all your life, a place literally throbbing and pulsing with a diverse and rich mingling of cultures and influences—France, England, Spain, Denmark, the Netherlands, and a shot of Africa for color.

Originally home to a large native population of Carawak Indians, St. Renard was unknown to Europeans until the early sixteenth

---

* This message has been approved by, or is distributed with the cynical approval of, Big Anna® Brands.

century, when it was discovered by Spanish conquistadors searching for El Dorado. Juan Hombre de Rosa claimed the island for Spain in 1511, and San Renard remained a Spanish possession until 1635, when it fell to a British expeditionary force under Captain Burroughs Hertfordshire, who rechristened the island St. Reynard. The British immediately traded the island to the Dutch, reportedly to settle a private debt, and the Dutch abandoned Sint Reinaert ten years later, when disease wiped out most of the early colonists. The island became a French colonial possession in the early eighteenth century and was sold shortly afterward to the Danes, who sold the island back to the Dutch, who resold the island to the French, who surrendered the island to the British after an afternoon of naval bombardment. St. Renard gained its independence from Great Britain in 1973, at which time—following an ill-starred attempt at self-government—the fledgling republic was obliged to sell itself to the United States (called, by Spanish-speaking Renardennes, "El Pulpo de Gran Maldad"), of which it is still an unincorporated insular possession.

This almost unbelievably rich and diverse cultural history makes St. Renard one of the most historic, diverse, and culturally rich places in the Caribbean. There's literally something for everyone. Whether you're into relaxation, sex tourism, snorkeling, gambling, psychoanalgesic tropical vegetation, or just eating and drinking as much as your body can tolerate, we've got you covered. And if none of those things appeal to you, don't worry about it! We'll find something that does. After all, your satisfaction is what keeps us out of the cane fields!

WHAT TO DO

If this is your first time on St. Renard, your first stop should be **Buzzard Point**, a bawdy shantytown abutting colonial San

Cristobal. There you'll find authentic thatch-roofed bars and gambling houses, colorful street vendors, and beautiful women. Enjoy a half pint of Renardenne white rum and make friends with locals who really know their island. You'll pick up the basics of Plantation Creole in no time, and by morning you'll feel like a Renardenne yourself.

MEET THE LOCALS

Huntington Flaneur has lived in Buzzard Point his whole life, but you wouldn't know it to talk to him. He's managed to cobble together a serviceable education by reading the textbooks that vacationing college students leave behind. "I am so desperate to learn," he says. If you see him in the bars around Buzzard Point, buy him a pint of sea grape brandy and maybe he'll quote you some Shakespeare! "For me there is no way out," he says. "But I read."

If you're a nature lover, you probably already know that St. Renard has one of the most unusual (and least diligently policed) national preserves in the Caribbean. Biddy Plimpton, a colorful local smuggler and biopirate, offers a new eco-adventure tour through **Raginherdsted National Forest**. All you need is a pair of boots, a handgun, great night vision, the ability to follow orders, and an appetite for tree frogs, orchids, and psychoanalgesic sap.

There are tons of charters and equipment rentals available for water-sports fanatics, whether you're into scuba diving, fishing, or just buzzing around the harbor on a Jet Ski. But whatever you do, don't miss our Ghost Reef, which, as of 2008, was the only fully bleached coral reef in the Caribbean.

> *Renardennes have always gone their own way. During the*
> *colonial period, our slave-labor system was one of the least*
> *coercive and vicious in the entire Caribbean. Not only that,*
> *but white planters sometimes left property to children they had*
> *fathered with their slave mistresses. Need another reason to*
> *visit? St. Renard managed the transition to a free labor system*
> *with substantially less bloodshed than neighboring islands.*

History buffs will love the ruins of our sugar mills and boiling houses. In colonial times, there were about thirty sugar estates on the island. They've all been consolidated into one operation under the stewardship of Big Anna® Brands, but most of the old haciendas and mills are still standing, some of which provide temporary shelter for descendants of the very slaves who worked in them long ago. Let **ignorance** be your guide as you stroll through the countryside, carried away by thoughts of a simpler time.

Finally, did somebody say beaches, beaches, beaches? St. Renard has more than twenty public beaches, and you're guaranteed to find the special place that's right for you. Whether you want a quiet spot where you can do some wading or a bustling cruising ground where you can pick up a **fancy boy** or a dusky **mulatta mama**, St. Renard has the beach for you. So get out the sunblock, fill your thermos with Big Anna® brand Coconut Wine™, and ease your plush, puckered body into the sand!

WHERE TO STAY

Adventurous visitors may want to check out **Colonia Tropical by Big Anna®**, a resort unlike any other in the Caribbean. You'll sign one-, two-, and three-week contracts promising to Work™ a few hours each day in Big Anna's beautiful sugarcane fields and lush banana plantations. In exchange, your room and board (hearty meals of salt cod, breadfruit, and cornmeal) are absolutely free. If you agree to a long-term stay, you may even find Big Anna® willing to cover your travel expenses. The décor ranges from Renardenne traditional to minimalist chic, but we guarantee that the décor is the last thing you'll be thinking about!

MEET THE LOCALS

Party animal Bryan "Bro" Desanty has residences in New York, Miami, Paris, and Rome, but he always comes home to his shore palace on St. Renard. What's so attractive about the island? "They say the geographical cure doesn't work," he says, "and they're right, but I don't know what else to do." Catch up with Bryan at the San Cristobal yacht club most afternoons. If you let him tell you his story, he might even buy you a drink! "Pills, crank, booze," he says. "It follows me like a demon. But I guess I'd just as soon die here as anywhere."

For visitors who prefer to take their leisure straight up, there's **Hertfordshire's Plantation Inn Resort and Spa**. This peaceful all-inclusive offers a heavy swallow of relaxation and water-centric fun served up with just a dash of history. Period cottages, many of them original structures, are tucked away beneath the glorious palms and majestic silk-cotton trees, while the great house is the inn's social hub. Activities include polo, trap and skeet shooting, lawn bowls, quoits, cribbage, croquet, and sundowners. But for innkeeper Maxwell Hertfordshire, a descendant of the plantation's founder, the beauty is in the details: elegant four-poster canopy beds dripping with mosquito netting, antique furnishings, curios, and hardwood floors as dark as the hotel staff. Says Hertfordshire, "We don't make sugar anymore, but literally nothing else has changed." All the luxury of a bygone era, all the convenience of the present, all included in one fixed price. Try a "Colonial Martini," a traditional cocktail made with pure cane juice and ether (sometimes called a "Postcolonial Martini").

If that doesn't make your left arm tingle, we've got something that will: St. Renard's most economical all-inclusive is definitely **United States Offshore Detention Facility (USODF)**, a 1,750-cell property in sleepy Sin Orgullo. The facility boasts Danish "showers," a huge dining room, and a fully appointed exercise yard. Except for a few folks who are advised to volunteer for voluntary scientific informational programs and optional discussions with staff, guests aren't required to do anything but kick back and wait for mealtimes. The USODF is perfect for anyone who needs to get some thinking done.

WHERE TO EAT

St. Renard has some of the best food in the Caribbean, and because of our rich colonial history, you can find cuisine from all around the world available at prices that even locals find competitive.

Start at **Pompey's**, where you can get traditional Renardenne slave food served up in American-size portions. Roasted breadfruit, plantains, salt cod, curry goat, and cornmeal porridge are just a few of the highlights, and everything is served on heavy platters, banana leaves, or wax paper. Wash it down with sea grape brandy, called "el consuelo de muerte" by the island's Spanish speakers. This hearty fare is traditionally eaten with the hands, so leave your hang-ups at home and bring your big American appetite!

A Mixed Tradition: Don't leave St. Renard without sampling the national drink, a Manchineel Martini. This cocktail contains no alcohol, but don't let that fool you. It's the drink of choice for locals who can't take it anymore. Fresh manchineel juice/lidocaine syrup/lots of ice. Stir gently, put your affairs in order, and swallow in one gulp.

For those visitors with continental tastes, the old Danish neighborhood of Mareridt Strand, just southwest of downtown San Cristobal, provides all kinds of great options. For breakfast, head to **Cafe Danske Hjerteanfald** for traditional Danish goodies like wienerbrød, horn, birkes, spanske, rundstykker, haandvaerker, and krydder. For lunch, track down a pølsevogn, and if you're in the mood for a longer sit-down meal in the evening, head to **Myokardieinfarkt** for frikadeller, hakkebøf, and medisterpølse. American eating habits don't always mix well with Danish cuisine, but there's a great "sygehus" in Mareridt Strand for anyone who overdoes it!

Finally, don't leave St. Renard without sampling the delicacies of our bright blue sea. Head down to the wharf in **Port Kingston**, or visit some of the **nearby alleyways**, for fresh-caught seafood. Some species of fish are so endangered, you could be the last person who ever tastes them!

NIGHTLIFE

First, head to **Tia Mamita's** in Buzzard Point, a repurposed waterfront brothel turned chic nighttime cruising ground for locals and yachties alike. Make sure to try all the signature cocktails. There's the "Ostenfeld," made with Renardenne white rum, acacia powder, sweet prune juice, sodium picosulfate, and tons of ice. Next up, a

"Pinker Shade of Pale": Big Anna® brand Coconut Wine™, pink gin, and sunblock (SPF 50). Chase that with the house specialty, a delicious and addictive "Ghost Appletini," made with St. Renard's own miracle fruit, the Carawak or "Ghost" Apple. Prices are reasonable, and sometimes the staff will even accept a little food or a pair of kids' shoes in lieu of payment.

Once you're good and liquored up, go watch the islanders dance for you at **Circe and Spice**, where local bands play all the soca standards, plus their own tropical versions of American pop hits. It's a charming, floor-show parody of Caribbean culture!

If you've got a morbid turn of mind, or even if you're just lost in boozy dreams of violence and desolation, head out to the **mass grave of the Carawak people**. The Old World meets the New at this uniquely historic Renardenne attraction. Make sure to bring a heavy crucifix and a thermos full of manchineel juice, and don't forget to bang on some pots and pans as you approach the central mound!

March 7 through March 13 is **Carnival** week, when locals pay tribute to the island's namesake, Saint Reynard of Antillia, whose feast day is March 13. This is a great time to let your hair down and blow off a little steam. There are parades, festival games, and plenty of authentic Renardenne friction dancing. In the riotous Port Kingston marketplace, there are even private stalls and enclosures for anyone with a taste for the rack and the screw, but don't stay away too long: The festival culminates in a bloody reenactment of the saint's life! Don't be surprised if you see locals engaging in some ecstatic prophesy, a Renardenne tradition that dates back to the early days, when new arrivals on the island would enter mystical trances in order to beg the great kings of Africa to intercede on their behalf!

DON'T EVEN THINK ABOUT IT! BUY YOUR TICKET TODAY!

Take a stroll down to any of our soft beaches, look out at the maddening beauty of the blue water, feel the sun on your sunburn, and just soak it in. There's no reason to be haunted by visions of the slave ships in which we suffered and died (10 to 15 percent of us!) on the voyage into bondage. In fact, hardly anyone knows anything about the history of the New World, and most people don't even care!

St. Renard is a quick flight from the North American mainland, or you can "stow away" on a container ship and enjoy a longer trip at sea. Why wait? For more information, give us a call today. We don't have a phone in the office yet, but our mobile numbers are on the website!

SPRING
SEMESTER

From: "Maggie Bell" <mbell1990@tripoli.edu>
To: wbrees@tripoli.edu
Date: January 5, 2010, at 3:05 PM
Subject: RE: Hi

Dear Bill,

Thank you so much for the kind words and the book of poetry. I've always wanted to read Professor Carlyle's work. I'm surprised by how, um, lucid it is, given what I know about him . . .

I'm feeling a little better, yes. I feel good about my decision to go away. I think it's the right thing. I had a really tough semester. I wish I could say why. It wasn't like I had a bad breakup or Becca turned out to be a racist or whatever. It wasn't so simple. I just kind of felt more and more alone. Partly I got frustrated because I felt like my old friends weren't really growing up, and partly it was just that I started to think about what it really meant to be a black person in America. Kabaka had a lot to do with it too. But it's good, it's a necessary process. I don't know. I hope that going to St. Renard will clarify things a little.

Right now I'm home with my brother and my parents. I think I told you that Chris is gay? He keeps telling me that he's going to come out to Mom and Dad. Right now he and Dad are sitting at the kitchen table and Dad's going on about how the recession was caused by "illegal Mexicans" buying houses, but he doesn't know anything, it's just a weird hectoring monologue like always, and Chris is sitting there listening to it and hoping there's going to be a moment to tell Dad this really big thing, and my heart just breaks for him.

Dad is one of those guys who hangs a big American flag out in front of the house and soaks the yard in pesticides so it looks like artificial turf. His way of communicating is that he repeats himself over and over and doesn't listen to a word anyone says. He doesn't even look at people when he talks to them. Also, I've been home for how long now? A few weeks? And he hasn't once asked me anything about my life at college. When I told him I was going abroad, he wanted to know how much it would cost. He didn't ask what the program was or why I wanted to go or anything. I wish he'd at least tell me to be careful so I knew he gave a damn.

I don't really know who Dad is, you know? And I don't know if *he* knows who he is. I remember how once, when he was in his lawn-mowing clothes in the front yard, a policeman stopped and demanded to know what he was doing. The policeman thought he was a homeless guy loitering in a rich man's yard! Pretty much the exact same thing happened to me when the laundry room was closed in our dorm last year and I had to go across to Farmar Hall. I forgot my key and nobody would let me in. But the thing is that I picked the incident apart and worried about it for weeks, and I can't imagine Dad doing that. He never talked about the lawn-mowing thing. We were pretty young but he didn't turn it into a lesson or anything. He never said a word. He's like a superhero of denial. Denial Man.

My poor mom just slips in and out of the kitchen without a word, tidying things up, smiling at everyone. She's almost transparent from years of self-effacement. Her life is kind of terrible and she's trying so hard! She's been a good mom to me and that makes me feel awful too, because the truth is that I don't like visiting. Every visit is harder than the last. I want to tell her to stick up for herself, have an affair, yell at someone once in a while. I know she's a smart thoughtful person deep down, but she won't acknowledge that anything is wrong. She asks me about school and I tell her I've been having a hard time and she just goes blank. She makes very general statements, like "Being young can be hard." We hardly communicate anymore. She won't listen to bad news. And when I told *her* about St. Renard, she was so worried that she could barely stand to talk about it. But I guess I prefer worry to indifference.

Thank God for Chris! But he's so worked up about his own things now that I don't like to bother him with my own problems, which I can hardly put into words anyway.

I'm beginning to rant. I apologize. When I think about it, I feel like I spent hours ranting at you this fall. But maybe that's because I actually felt like you were listening. Which is not a familiar experience for me.

Anyway, I'm glad to hear you might be on the island yourself in the next few months. Definitely send me an email. I don't know what my schedule will be like, but I'm sure I'll have plenty of time.

Thanks again for being such a good friend to me this fall.

Best,
Maggie

MINUTES / JANUARY 2010 FACULTY MEETING (EMERGENCY SESSION)

———————

The faculty secretary, invigorated after a short nap, was among the first to arrive. Although fundamentally disinterested—a keeper of records—he had been perversely curious about today's meeting. It would be the first at which William Beckford—professor and acting chancellor of the English Department; chair of the Committee on Curriculum and Core Programming (CCCP); executive director, or so the secretary had just been told, of Tripoli's Proxy College of the West Indies at St. Renard; and now acting president of Tripoli College—would preside.

The acting president was attended by Francis Amundsen, toady and professor of English, who was tasked with operating the gavel. Professor Amundsen did so now, feebly striking the old wooden table in a plea for silence.

Acting President Beckford rose and addressed the faculty, although it must be said that only about 40 percent of the faculty was in attendance. He was, as always, an arresting sight. His extreme old age, his electric blue eyes, his startling teeth, and the hypnotic character of his speech gave the impression of a vivid computer graphic rather than a human man.

His introductory monologue took in many important topics, including the weather, which was inclement; our partnership with Big Anna® Brands, which was proving advantageous; the Tripoli *Telegraph*, which he had "modernized" and which would publish only approved content this semester; and

Tripoli's Proxy College of the West Indies at St. Renard, which had undergone a change that he would describe, if there was time, later in the meeting.

Dining hall menus had been completely overhauled during the winter break. We would have to say good-bye to the old standards like "Drippy Wrap w/Fish" and Tripoli's famous pudding bars. The new dietary program, a product of the acting president's own imagination and research, was based on the principle of calorie restriction, which was proven to lengthen life and improve concentration. Now we would be able to enjoy dishes like "Shaved Manioc with Fresh Potato Greens." These fully rationalized meals were also much cheaper to produce, which would enable the college to cut redundant dining-services staff by almost 80 percent. Total savings would be at least eight million annually, and Tripoli would go from being an educational institution that consumed, notoriously, more pudding per capita than any other in the United States, to being "considerably more mobile" than rival institutions.

Ginnie Hampton, professor and chair of philosophy, asked whether this would affect our partnership with Big Anna®, no doubt assuming that Big Anna® brand food products were incompatible with such a diet.

The acting president had been anticipating this question, and he was happy to answer it. Big Anna® brand food products, particularly Chocolate Puff Pieces® and Banana Bran Muffins®, were actually an ideal component of his proposed "One Thousand Calorie" diet. They provided a large amount of insoluble fiber and essential heavy metals, but they were, more importantly, unique among similar food products in that they were especially rich in inert substrate. They would not tip the scales or compromise the mobility and awareness of our students, as substrate-poor food products and muffins were proven to do.

And what—asked Hanson Brokovitch, professor of religion—about the supplement tablets that students were being asked to take with each meal?

The acting president had been anticipating this question as well, and he was thrilled to answer it. In fact, why not refer that one to the experts? He indicated Tompkins Gerard, professor of biology and director of the pharmacology concentration, who rose unsteadily and made the following statement:

"Malpraxalin® is a comprehensive dietary and mood additive designed to sharpen concentration and increase productive thought volume when taken in coordination with a calorie-restricted diet. It's one hundred percent natural—made from the sap and fruit of the Carawak Apple Tree of St. Renard. Students are not technically compelled to take it, but we encourage them to give it a try."

The acting president thanked Professor Gerard, who was struggling to lower himself into his chair, and went on to explain that the supplement had been developed by trusted Big Anna® subsidiary Genutrex® and approved for use in humans by independent nutritional and science consultants. Conveniently, the FDA exercised almost no regulatory control over nutritional supplements of this kind. A statement on their website ran as follows: "Manufacturers do not need to register their products with FDA nor get FDA approval before producing or selling dietary supplements." Essentially, the acting president explained, market forces determined the safety of a given supplement. It was almost too good to be true.

At the risk of jeopardizing his reputation for objectivity and impartiality, the faculty secretary will note that he himself had been having great success with this new supplement. The ceiling in his bathroom had collapsed three days before, but after a few doses of Malpraxalin®, everything was different. It hadn't even seemed necessary to repair the damage. In fact, he had taken some just before the meeting, and he took another tablet now.

The acting president had one more item, which involved the location of his offices. He would be retaining his office in Ulster Hall, in which he would continue to function as a professor. When attending to his presidential duties, however, he could be found in a suite of offices on the top floor of Tripoli's Venezia Museum. He had been inspired by Richard Carlyle, professor of English, who had lived in the museum for a few weeks several years before.

The acting president now gave Professor Carlyle a little wave, but the professor was visibly outraged by the foregoing remark. Although he acknowledged that it had been "very restful" to live in the museum, he demanded that the acting president stop behaving as if the two of them were friends. "I am nothing like you," he said. He then placed his can of Bud Light and Clamato on top of the recycling bin, fastidiously buttoned his coat, and left the room. The acting president watched him go with an indulgent smile. "Thus," he said, "the poet laureate of a new and brighter Tripoli."

There was no time to dwell on this peculiar exchange. The acting president now introduced himself, William Beckford, professor and acting chancellor of the English Department and chair of the CCCP, in which capacity he had some remarks to make.

But Professor Beckford's remarks must go unrecorded—at this point, the secretary slipped into unconsciousness. When he came to himself, Professor Beckford was already wrapping up. "Thus," the professor concluded, "we demonstrate to our benefactors, alumni, and current students that we are committed to remaining an institution that does not condone slavery in word or deed, or even by proxy."

Then Professor Beckford sat down, only to stand up once again and assume the role of acting president. He then asked the faculty whether anyone had seen Bish Pinkman III recently. When there was no answer, he repeated his question in a louder voice. Several members of the faculty said, "No," and one or two went so far as to say, "Of course not." The acting president was pleased to hear it, and he said, "Correct."

With this, he sat down and immediately became, once again, Professor Beckford, in which capacity he wished to ask himself—William Beckford, acting president of Tripoli College—some questions. His questions were these: Had he, the acting president, decided how Tripoli should respond to the rumors of coercive labor practices, harassment of workers, and unsanitary conditions at Big Anna® plantations and factories on St. Renard? If these rumors were substantiated, would the acting president consider ending our relationship with Big Anna®?

Professor Beckford twirled slowly through a full three-hundred-and-sixty-degree rotation and underwent, while twirling, a miraculous and instantaneous change, once again becoming Acting President William Beckford. It was a good question, he said, and one that he was glad someone had the courage to ask. In fact, he had been on the point of addressing this issue when he—William Beckford, professor of

English—had spoken. But perhaps it was best to refer this matter to William Beckford, executive director of Tripoli's Proxy College of the West Indies at St. Renard?

The acting president sank to a crouch and then began to rise slowly, thus effecting the necessary transformation. When it was complete, he—William Beckford, executive director of the Proxy College—wished everyone a good evening.

There had been widespread allegations, he said, having to do with criminal labor practices on Big Anna® sugarcane and banana plantations. The riot on St. Renard last semester, though initiated by a few bad apples, had added fuel to the fire, and now the radical and unbalanced ex-professor Kabaka was stirring up more trouble. Obviously, the news from St. Renard was of particular concern not only because we had signed a partnership agreement with Big Anna®, but also because St. Renard was the location of our Proxy College. Indeed, the Field Studies Program in Tropical Agriculture—the largest program at the Proxy College, and now, he added parenthetically, the only program at the Proxy College—was now intimately associated with the Big Anna® operation. This semester, instead of simply "mapping the seafloor and pressing flowers," as they had in the past, students would get some hands-on experience in the cane fields and banana plantations, where they would help to make Big Anna® agriculture even more sustainable by following LoCarbon™ farming protocols like Human Power™ plow technology.

He appeared to have finished, although he remained standing. A short and restless silence intervened. Then Fitzgerald Simon, professor of francophone language and literature, rose and said that he—that is to say, William Beckford—had not answered his own questions. How should we respond to the horror stories we had been hearing? Should we demand accountability? Should we reconsider our agreement with Big Anna®? Should we express sympathy and support, as some of our students had already done, for Commandant Kabaka and his Antillia Liberation Army?

Executive Director Beckford snapped his fingers and emitted a vocalization not unlike a pig call, as a result of which he transformed himself back into Acting President Beckford. Then he crossed his arms and said that he'd wondered when we'd be hearing from Professor Simon. He explained that anyone who had been following the story would know that Big Anna® had long been the victim of absurd rumors and conspiracy theories.

The secretary was transfixed by the acting president's extraordinary teeth. They looked like porcelain, and this reminded him of his own upstairs bathroom. It was still, as noted, open to the winter winds.

Professor Simon asked for clarification. Could the acting president please just answer the questions?

Indeed he could. He would even give his answer in the form of a story:

He had spoken recently with two students—Johnny Singer and Bethany Page-Exley—who had gone to study on St. Renard last semester. Ms. Page-Exley had become romantically involved with a local man employed as a ditch digger for Big Anna®. Mr. Singer had become friends with some of the cane cutters. Both students had been drinking rum in a local restaurant when a "labor-related" disturbance had broken out . . .

And this, to be sure, was at least the beginning of a story, but the secretary can't have been alone in feeling that the acting president's narrative now began to shed significance as a snake sheds its skin. For instance, he pointed out that St. Renard had a small but significant Danish population. He then reminded us that the island nation had been, until Big Anna® saved the day, massively indebted to the International Monetary Fund (IMF). He said that he admired the Renardenne custom of not eating more than was necessary to sustain life, and sometimes not even that. He himself had eaten only three Chocolate Puff Pieces® that day, and there were some days when he consumed only a thimbleful of Big Anna® brand Coconut Wine™.

Here was a tip: Extend your life by chilling those parts of your body that were not in use. And who said humans couldn't photosynthesize? All it required was an act of will. Bristlecone pines lived five thousand years.

Plenty of labor disputes on St. Renard had been settled peacefully.

Don't grow new hair in the summertime. Why would you?

It was only in the celebration following the successful resolution of a labor dispute that some Big Anna® employees had been cut to ribbons.

Were there any questions?

There was a period of silence, perhaps almost ten seconds, while faculty members absorbed this information. Then Professor Hampton said that she still didn't understand how Big Anna® brand food products could possibly be low in calories. Were they low in sugar? If so, why did Big Anna® maintain such large sugar plantations?

The acting president began to recite the dates of significant slave revolts on St. Renard. February 1748. June 1791. April 1923. Then he said, "I imagine you can carry on from there."

Were there any other questions?

Perhaps there were, or perhaps not, but now was not to be the time to address them: Without waiting for an answer, the acting president strolled briskly out of the room, leaving the faculty deflated and discouraged. Professor Amundsen attempted to strike the table with his gavel and instead struck his own thumb. His cry of pain brought the meeting to a close.

It had not been an auspicious start to the semester. The secretary, who had been in a kind of trance since his midmeeting Malpraxalin® tablet, tossed his pen onto the table, wadded his notes into a coat pocket, and stumbled down the stairs and out into the wind.

———————

I'm writing from St. Renard, where I'm staying at a bed-and-breakfast called A Piece of the Indies. Not surprisingly, my application to the Field Studies Program in Tropical Agriculture was denied, so I ended up coming down on my own steam. But before I go any further, I have to describe the circumstances of my departure from Tripoli. Sensitive readers be warned: It's not a story for the faint of heart.

As of the new year, I'd moved my things out of the dorm and I was living in my own house once again. After the excitement and camaraderie of the fall, I could hardly bear to be alone with my memories. It was even harder than before.

I hadn't gone back to work and I doubted that I ever would, but I was still in contact with Burke and Lehman, and from them I heard some bizarre rumors: Beckford was living in the art museum, which he'd trashed. He'd put student-athletes to work cleaning bathrooms. He'd been pushing a drug called Malpraxalin.

One day I went back to campus to see for myself, but the place seemed quiet and serene. In the library, where I went to warm up, some students were discussing an article on the *Telegraph*'s website. The president of Keesy College had reportedly said that you could lock a young person in a closet for four years and they'd do as well on the job market as they would if they'd spent those four years at Tripoli.

"But it's absurd," one of the students was saying. "He doesn't even consider the psychological damage that being locked in a closet would do to someone. Trust me, you're not going to do well on the job market if you've been standing upright in the darkness for four years, eating whatever your captors allow you to eat and eliminating waste under who knows what circumstances."

I tightened my scarf and went outside thinking that nothing had changed. It was business as usual at Tripoli.

But as I walked east across the quad, I saw a crowd of students and professors that had gathered around the big bare oak in front of Pinkman Hall. Since there was a crust of ice on the flagstone paths, I was concentrating on my footing and at first I didn't see the pale stubby man under the oak, but there he was: Bish Pinkman III. He was stripped to the waist and his hands were tied to a low branch above his head. The rope was pulled so tight that his toes were only just touching the ground, and he rotated slowly as he struggled to free himself. He was much thinner than the last time I'd seen him, although you still wouldn't call him thin. His soft body looked sad and vulnerable in the frozen afternoon.

Acting President Beckford was standing on the steps a short distance away. He was wearing a black trench coat and sunglasses, although there was only a diffuse gray light in the southern sky. I marveled at how his teeth seemed to be getting bigger and stronger and whiter every year. How did he do it? I was at a point where I felt like my own teeth would shatter if I tried to eat a pecan.

Beckford was attended by his lackey, Professor Amundsen. Both of them were saying something to a tall student whom I recognized as the football player Depatrickson White.

At a signal from the acting president, Professor Amundsen clapped some wooden blocks together. Everyone fell abruptly silent, and for a moment the only sound was the whistling of the frozen wind. Depatrickson White looked up at Beckford, who nodded, and then, taking a deep breath, he drew a short rawhide whip from his coat pocket.

At first, I was struck most of all by the focused intensity with which he went about his work. He took short, efficient, powerful strokes, driving from his back foot and snapping his hips to get all of his weight behind each blow. His coordination was perfect. He was truly a gifted athlete.

But then, as the blood began to flow, poor Depatrickson White seemed to unravel. His strokes got sloppier and went wide of the mark. He looked suddenly like the college kid he was. And he began to cry. This was particularly affecting because he's such a large and imposing person. He looks like he's never cried in his life. The Tripoli Tyrants have turned out to be especially sensitive young men, although I suppose anyone might have wept in his place.

With each stroke, Mr. Pinkman III rotated about five degrees, and after a while he had rotated far enough that he was facing me and I could see his round face, pinched in agony and red as a tomato. It was a terrible moment. White struggled to muffle his sobs, and no one else said a word. You could hear the wind stirring the bare branches of the trees. The whip broke the silence with an indistinct, meaty thump, like a gun fired into a pillow.

After a while, Professor Amundsen began to clap the wooden blocks together again, and White took a few steps back, dropped the bloody whip, and began to vomit. Mr. Pinkman III was unconscious by now. Beckford cut his bonds and he collapsed in the pink snow beside the traumatized football player.

If I'd had any doubt about heading down to St. Renard, this incident helped me make up my mind. I went home, packed my duffel bag and carry-on, and bought a plane ticket that very night. I was going out of a sense of responsibility, to be sure— so that I could be on hand in case Megan needed me—but like her I was also going because I couldn't bear to remain at Tripoli any longer!

NEW FROM GENUTREX® NUTRITION

AMPLIFY YOUR LIFE™ WITH MALPRAXALIN®, A DIETARY AND MOOD ADDITIVE FOR THE MODERN WORLD

The research team at GENUTREX® Nutrition has done it again with MALPRAXALIN®, an all-natural dietary and mood additive designed to amplify productive thought volume, improve vasodilation, diminish political anxiety and moral fatigue, and restore the healthy functioning of emotions, metabolism, and feelings! Are you worried about so-called global warming? Do you grind your teeth at night? Has it occurred to you that you might be able to experience the sweetness of life only in retrospect? By using optimized, clinically authenticated herbal analogs of the actual chemicals found naturally in the sap of the Carawak or Ghost Apple Tree (*Hippomane renardennia*), which grows only on the Caribbean island of St. Renard, MALPRAXALIN® is guaranteed to provide you with an intense sensation of enhancement, disaffection, brio, clarity, and appetite suppression, with absolutely no "dread" or annoying tremors! But don't listen to us: Once you try MALPRAXALIN®, you'll immediately feel what it does!*

HISTORY

The Carawak people were the original inhabitants of St. Renard. They were a peace-loving tribe who flattened their skulls by tying pieces of

---

* These statements have not been evaluated by the Food and Drug Administration. This product is not intended to treat, diagnose, cure, or prevent any diseases.

wood to the foreheads of their infants. Having lived on the island for thousands of years, they knew all the secrets of the tropical forest, including the medicinal and supplement virtues of every tree, root, grub, fruit, and flower. For instance, the Carawak captured local parrots by burning dried Renardenne peppers beneath the trees where these clever birds were roosting. When the parrots fell to the ground, they were stupefied and drugged, enabling the Indians to tie them up and train and/or eat them. But when Spanish mariners first landed on these shores, the idyll came to an end, and the Carawak were forced to confront new and sometimes troubling situations and realities. Small wonder that they turned increasingly to the natural mood enhancement provided by the psychoanalgesic fruit and sap of the Carawak Apple Tree, which they brewed into a tea and drank from dried gourds whenever the stresses of the modern world were too much for them. John Morehead Tripoli, British adventurer, Indian sympathizer, and notorious troublemaker, was the first European to taste this revolutionary New World brew. Having led a mutiny on board the merchant vessel *Tatterdemalion*, Morehead Tripoli was put ashore on St. Renard in the year 1700 and lived among the Carawak for a year until British sailors returned. He would speak for the rest of his life about the magnificent properties of that beverage, and later he would even say that he regretted leaving the island!

WHY SHOULD IT WORK FOR YOU?

MALPRAXALIN® is bioequivalent to the active psychoanalgesic derived from the Carawak Apple Tree, which has been proven to interact with numerous biochemicals in the human body in order to relieve discomfort associated with nonoptimal levels of psychosensation and/or knowledge. MALPRAXALIN® is formulated to include highly bioavailable vitamin cofactors, making it even more effective than the Carawak's original tea beverage. Not only is it hypersilicum-free, but it deregulates kinetic pathways without mobilizing tropo-spheric pollutants, helping the body to harness the adrenaltropic power of the adaptogen Tryptosine™. It's even manufactured right on the island of St. Renard, close to the source of its original inspiration!

INDICATIONS

If you are experiencing any of the following symptoms, you may have a psychological and/or dietary problem. MALPRAXALIN® can help. Take MALPRAXALIN® if you

- Frequently say "Oh no!" first thing in the morning.
- Sometimes feel anxious or have neck aches.
- Long to feel your teeth rattled once again by the wind of youth.
- Are suffering from depression due to emotional disharmony, chest oppression, loin pain, alarming taste in mouth, painful wind, esophageal ulcers, sluggish Kidney Action™, dropsy, or phlegm entanglement.
- Can't find the television remote!
- Are experiencing difficulty swallowing and speaking due to cate-cholamine deficiencies.
- Are experiencing shifting political allegiance.
- Keep telling the mailman not to leave this junk mail in your box, but he doesn't listen.
- Have heard recently that pine blight is destroying the Rocky Mountain forests.
- Are experiencing intolerable zeolite bioburden.
- Come from the tropical third world.
- Are an indigenous person.

CAUTIONS

Side effects that may go away almost immediately, if they occur at all, include

- A lemon-yellow discoloration of the skin
- Retrograde ejaculation
- Synesthesia
- Syncopated mindbeat
- Anticlerical prejudice
- Psychogenic rash
- Transient combativeness
- Bioluminescence
- Anhedonia
- Chemical burns
- Keratoconjunctivitis
- Harlequin-type ichthyosis

DOSING STRATEGIES

MALPRAXALIN® has been specially formulated to increase in effectiveness the more you use it, so don't worry about dosage. We believe in a holistic approach to dosing: Let your body tell you how much MALPRAXALIN® it needs. Just take at least one with a jelly jar of milk or juice first thing in the morning, then take more whenever you want to. Easy! If an enhanced effect is desired, pulverize two tablets and inhale via the nose.

TESTIMONIALS

I used to drink three bags of wine PER DAY, and then I began taking MALPRAXALIN®.

—Greg, Michigan

I felt the effects of MALPRAXALIN® right away.

—Gary, Indiana

Since I began taking MALPRAXALIN®, there has literally been a revolution in my country!

—Anonymous

I've been taking MALPRAXALIN® for two weeks and I've already lost 19 pounds!

—Michelle, New Jersey

From: "Maggie Bell" <mbell1990@tripoli.edu>
To: "Chris Bell" <cfb456@mercurylink.net>
Date: January 18, 2010, at 1:00 PM
Subject: (no subject)

Chris!

They limit our internet time pretty severely for some reason, so I've only got a second. I wanted to tell you I've been having a good time so far. Last night we set fire to an old wooden cart that washed up on the beach, and this guy Henry tried to roast a chicken over the dirty flames. He speared it on a pitchfork, but he forgot to take the plastic wrapper off, so in the end we had this chicken that was charred on the outside, cold and raw on the inside, and stank of burnt plastic. Henry insisted on eating some of it anyway.

Later we met these three Renardenne guys on the beach and we drank something called coconut wine, which I think might have cocaine in it. It didn't taste like coconuts. It was good to meet some islanders, and at first I felt that familiar first-world feeling, like I wanted to prove I was one of them, or sympathetic to them, or whatever. But then one of them tried to grab my ass and I hit him in the mouth with a bottle of ketchup. It was only a plastic bottle. His friends laughed at him and nodded at me like I'd passed some test, and after that all three of them were perfectly fine. But the other kids, who I guess were operating with a heavier burden of guilt than I was, couldn't admit that these guys were acting like assholes, and they spent the rest of the night pretending this high-handed interest in their lives and trying to commiserate with them. The Renardennes knew what was going on and sort of played it up. They were saying things like, "It have a river come down from the mountains just so, but you get hot, let me tell you, you think you go swim, the white man go string you up. He don't want the black man in the river. He think the black go wash off and get on he white white skin." It was bullshit, and meanwhile the Renardenne guys were drinking all our beer and winking at me like I was in on their game, which I guess I was. The other Tripoli students didn't even notice. They just sat there nodding earnestly and saying, "Shit, man, yeah. That's capitalism."

Anyway, the director told us to write to family and say we're heading out tomorrow and we'll be away from the phone and the internet for a little while. Exciting! We've been living it up here in this swanky old house above the ocean, but it'll be good to see more of the island.

Be well, huh? Keep me updated? Just be a college kid and hang out with Max and don't worry so much about the rest. At least for now. And don't worry about me either. I'm having a good time. I feel better already. Maybe I'll write my own slave narrative when I get back! Like Professor Kabaka says—every American story is a slave narrative. Or should I say *Commandant* Kabaka? I don't know what to think about that . . .

Love,
M

FIELD STUDIES PROGRAM IN TROPICAL AGRICULTURE
Student Handbook 2009–2010

INTRODUCTION

Many and varied are the difficulties which will beset you when you first exchange your campus and its surroundings for the vicissitudes of life on St. Renard. Few students realize the sacrifices they will be called upon to make in taking such a decided step. This handbook will enable you not only to judge for yourself as to what things it may be necessary to take with you from home, but will also be useful as a small guide on points affecting your own health, and on matters connected with traveling, diet, and residence in the tropics.

BASIC SAFETY INFORMATION AND PREPAREDNESS

The habits of life in a temperate climate render one unfit for tropical life, and one must change them or break down.

Sun Protection

Panama hats and Renardenne straw hats afford inadequate protection for the head. When compelled to go in the sun, a black umbrella should be used, or better still, one should be provided with a broad-brimmed cork helmet which will not allow the actinic rays to penetrate. It has even been proposed that one make doubly sure and line the helmet with tinfoil, which is opaque to the sun's rays. It is surprising how transparent the scalp and skull are to light rays.

Protecting Yourself from Thieves

The thieves of St. Renard are renowned for their dexterity. Their usual method is to divest themselves of all clothing, oil or grease their bodies, and then, imitating the whine of a dog, prowl about on all fours until they find an opportunity of making off with your valuables. If you feel convinced that a thief is in your tent or cabin, do not make use of firearms. The safest weapon is a knife, but your movements must be so quietly performed as not to excite his attention, or your chance of catching him will be gone.

Understanding and Respecting Locals

Something that is perfectly acceptable to you may be unacceptable to a Renardenne, and vice versa. For instance, women should not smoke cigarettes in public areas. This is considered an intolerable provocation.

Fruit Safety

Mangoes are heating and stimulating, and are apt to produce a pustular eruption if freely indulged in. Pineapples should be eaten with great caution.

Water Safety

If you wish to enjoy the pleasure and benefit of bathing, choose a clean place in a river that is free from alligators and go into it very early in the morning, when you are free from every feverish symptom. By no means attempt to tamper with your constitution by plunging into a cold bath in the heat of the day, for thousands and thousands have by that means caused their own deaths.

Insanity

Nervous diseases are aggravated in the tropics. Insanity is much more prevalent on St. Renard than in the United States. Last year, the insanity rate among students per 1,000 for those at Tripoli was just 22, or 2.2 percent, while on St. Renard it was 16 percent.

HINTS FOR MAINTAINING HEALTH IN THE TROPICS

People from temperate regions have sweeter and richer blood than those who reside in the torrid zone, and until it becomes diluted or weakened by sickness, frequent perspirations, and other evacuations, they seldom enjoy a robust state of health.

Prickly Heat

The prickly heat is an irritating affection of the skin that manifests itself in a red, pimply eruption, usually on those parts of the body that come into contact with clothing. To ameliorate this condition, rub the body all over with the juice of fresh limes. Stimulants should be avoided; the bowels should be relaxed and the kidney made to act freely. A mixture of three drachms of acetate of potash, about half a drachm of sweet spirits of nitre, and eight ounces of decoction of broom will answer this purpose.

Cholera Belt

It is most essential for the preservation of health that a double fold of flannel, made in the form of a broad belt, should be worn round the abdomen night and day. Such an article can be obtained ready-made from all outfitters, and two or three should be included in a student's kit. When the waistband of the drawers is lined with flannel, this belt will only be required for night wear.

Spasms

There is great susceptibility to spasms across all populations on St. Renard. Frictions with olive oil is the popular remedy, and the expressed juice of the garlic taken by the teaspoon may also provide some relief.

Fever

Quotidian, tertian, and quartan fever are common afflictions in the tropics, and one must learn how to bring the temperature down. Quinine, or Jesuit's bark, is effective in most cases. If no quinine is available, the best method is to spread out two thick blankets on the floor or bed, with a couple of pillows under them at the head. Upon these blankets place a large sheet soaked in cold water. Let the patient lie down at full length upon the sheet, the arms placed against the sides. An attendant is then to rapidly fold the wet sheet round the body, from the chin to the feet. The blankets are similarly to be tightly folded.

Dysentery

Dysentery is very common on St. Renard, and its effects are frequently most disastrous. Even when the disease is not immediately fatal, it is apt, if neglected in its earlier stages, to pass into chronic dysentery, a condition which renders life a veritable burden. Abuse of stimulants, immoderate indulgence in fruit, or the habit of constantly eating highly spiced or peppery dishes are all indirect causes of the disease. Luckily, we have in ipecacuanha a remedy specific to dysentery. Even in the most advanced and hopeless forms of the malady, this invaluable drug often arrests and obviates the fatal termination which appears so near. The next-best remedy will be pills of lead and opium, of which two or three may be taken in a day. Hot stupes or poultices will also be found grateful, and will relieve the colic and the nausea.

The Black Vomit

The black vomit, also called yellow jack or yellow fever, is the most feared of tropical afflictions and remains the single greatest impediment to our educational endeavors in the tropics. Some success has been seen in patients treated with mercury, and venesection may offer relief, but when it comes to this most horrific of all maladies, it may be that "prevention is the best medicine," for there exists no surefire remedy. We may thank Dr. John James Hayes for his discovery that inoculation with either Lachesus or Crotalus venom does much to prevent an attack. All students should receive one of these inoculations before departing for the island.

ALCOHOL POLICY

There is a great difference of opinion in regard to the effect of alcohol in the tropics. Woodruff states that "statistics of about 2,800 soldiers show that the damage done to these vigorous men by the small amount of excessive drinking they indulged in was not so great as the damage done by the climate to the total abstainers. Approximately 11 percent of the abstainers died, while about 3.5 percent of the moderate drinkers, and less than 2 percent of the excessive drinkers. About 15 percent of abstainers were invalided home, about 9 percent of the moderate drinkers, and about 8 percent of the excessive drinkers." Other observers give a directly opposite opinion—that nowhere are the effects of alcohol so detrimental as in the tropics.

FREQUENTLY ASKED QUESTIONS

Q: What are the bathroom facilities like?
A: Many students are surprised by how little time it takes to get used to unfamiliar sanitary arrangements.

Q: For religious reasons, I have to wear a special woolen undergarment. Will I be okay on St. Renard?
A: Be sure that the climate will revenge itself for this folly.

Q: I'm really worried about my weight. Will there be healthy dining options?
A: After a short sojourn on the island, want of appetite will suffice to guard students against the dangers of overeating.

Q: I feel like there's something you're not telling me.
A: Occasionally an active and special stimulus to the liver will be necessary. For example: two or three of Cockle's Pills, or a few grains of rhubarb, calomel, and ipecacuanha. A dose of Lamplough's Pyretic Saline, with the juice of a lime, is also a very safe aperient, and will assist the action of the pills should they fail to operate satisfactorily of themselves.

Q: I've heard that one remedy for intermittent fever is to tie your hair to a tree and run forward.
A: This will leave the fever, as well as the hair, attached to the tree. The shortcoming of this remedy is that it may only be performed once in a period of several months, for it leaves the sufferer hairless.

Q: How will I know when I've taken enough quinine?
A: The drug has produced its effect on the system when you experience a singing in the ears, deafness, and throbbing in the temple arteries.

Q: Now I've got a headache!
A: The juice of fifty limes may be rubbed into the hair, and a jug of cold water poured over the head.

Q: Okay, I'm on the island and I've just eaten a bucket of uncooked mangrove oysters. What happens next?
A: When vomiting or nausea begins, apply a mustard poultice to the pit of the stomach, below the breastbone and a little to the left. Then take two drops of chloroform, or thirty drops of chloric ether, with a little lime juice.

Q: Jeez, man. Now I've got diarrhea.
A: The best and hardiest remedy is Dr. Collis Browne's "Chlorodyne." If the evacuations are large, it may be well to allow two or three motions to pass away before attempting to arrest the discharge.

Q: How can I distinguish dysentery from simple diarrhea?
A: Almost invariably, with dysentery, there is a very distressing sensation of weight and an apparent want of unloading about the fundament and lower bowel.

Q: Now I'm suffering from sunstroke. What should I do?
A: The bowels should be made to act, but not too violently, by castor oil given internally, or by purgative enemata. Injections of warm soap and water can be used, and to these turpentine may be added.

Q: *These physical problems are one thing, but what about my mind?*
I'm going crazy in this place.
A: From prolonged exertion in a climate which is naturally enervat-
ing, or it may be simply from the climatic influence itself, a student
often falls into a state of weakness and languor which, if it does not
absolutely incapacitate him, certainly makes him disinclined for active
work, and renders his life more or less a burden to him.

Q: *Something's wrong with my eye!*
A: A watch-glass should be obtained and used to cover the healthy
eye. This will prevent its infection with purulent material from the
affected eye.

Q: *Maybe it's not my eye. I can't tell what's real and what's not!*
A: An overdistended state of the stomach, flatulence, and indigestion
may often produce palpitations, shortness of breath, and a sensation
of giddiness. Study of the scriptures will afford some comfort.

Q: *I think I'm just going to sit down.*
A: Great care must be taken when sitting down, as parasites and
biting insects abound in the tropics.

Q: *I don't care. My feet are swollen.*
A: Oedema is a common affection and often develops as a hypertro-
phied heart subsides into a dilated one.

Q: *My feet feel like they're going to burst. I'll just make an incision and*
allow the fluid to drain.
A: Careful study of the scriptures will be found more grateful in this
case.

Q: Oh no, now I've cut myself!

A: If the bleeding is from an artery, the blood will be scarlet in hue, and will come out in jets.

A MODEST PROPOSAL / JANUARY 21, 2010
A MESSAGE FROM COMMANDANT KABAKA
OF THE ANTILLIA LIBERATION ARMY

To the shareholders, executives, and employees of Big Anna:
To the people of the United States:

We have been asked what we are fighting for. It's all very well, you tell us, that history has not been kind to us, but history is history. Don't we have televisions in our rum shops? Don't we have our steel drums and our homemade soccer balls? Don't we have plantains and curry goat when we're hungry? Don't we live in paradise? Don't we see the sun rise over the luminous tropic sea every day of our lives?

We will tell you what we want.

We want the same chance you have. We want to live like middle-class Americans. Who are you that you should profit by our misery? Who are we that we should be miserable?

Here is our first demand:

The federal minimum wage is set at $7.25 per hour in the United States. The same rate applies to the U.S. Virgin Islands and to some industries in Puerto Rico.

St. Renard, like those islands, is a vassal state, its economy swallowed up by the monster in the north. But workers on St. Renard are paid only a fraction of what workers on neighboring islands are paid. Big Anna® banana workers on St. Renard make $6 per day.

If we are to live at the mercy of the United States and Big Anna®, if the United States and Big Anna® mean to tell us how our democracy should operate, then let Big Anna® compensate us at rates equivalent to the legal minimum wage for U.S. employees.

Let's do the math:

Say a Renardenne man works three hundred days a year on the banana farm. This is a conservative estimate.

If he earns $6 per day, in one year he will make $1,800.

If he works for fifteen years at this rate, he will earn $27,000.

Can a man live on $1,800 a year? Can he support a family? It will be said that the cost of living is lower on St. Renard, but so is the standard of living. Can a man earning so little expect to give his children a better life than the one he has had?

Twenty-seven thousand dollars in fifteen years. It isn't enough to pay for one year at a good private college in the United States.

Now consider how much this man would earn if he were paid at the minimum rate required by U.S. law. Say he works three hundred days a year for an average of ten hours per day. He could expect to earn $21,750 per year.

It isn't a princely sum. A Big Anna® executive thinks nothing of spending three and four times as much for another car to add to the enormous fleet in his garage.

This, then, is our first demand.

Our second demand is that Big Anna® make restitution to all current employees, according to the following formula:

Total payment = (years of employment × 300 days per year × 10 hours per day × $7.25) − (years of employment × $1,800)

The Renardenne who has worked for one year on a Big Anna® plantation, and who earned $1,800 during that time, is owed $19,950.

The man who has given fifteen years of his life to this company is owed $299,250.

Are these demands unreasonable? Is it unreasonable to demand a sum of money that the U.S. government regards as minimally sufficient for its own citizens? Upon what is the concept of minimum wage based if not on the belief that human beings are entitled to some minimum amount of dignity? Why should that dignity not be available to us as well? Are we not human beings? Does Big Anna get to decide who is human and who is not?

A prisoner on work detail in the U.S. is given room and board. In essence, he is paid a subsistence wage. He is paid what a Big Anna® banana worker is paid.

We are prisoners of neoliberal economics. We are being held without trial. What have we done to deserve it?

UNDERCOVER DEAN: BLOG POST #6

It took me a week or two to get used to the heat here on St. Renard. At first, I thought the sticky tropical air would be nice, a relief from the cold, but almost as soon as I stepped off the plane, I was dizzy and I felt like my underpants were too small. I was already sweating heavily as I stood at the airport taxi stand, though lately I'd begun to think I was past the age of sweating. In addition, the image of Bish Pinkman's face kept flashing through my mind, and in this tropical setting it mingled bizarrely with memories from my days in Vietnam.

I'd reserved my room at A Piece of the Indies the night before, and now I gave the address to the cab driver. At first, he didn't seem inclined to go anywhere. He said something dismissive and fluttered his hands in a gesture I couldn't understand. I just sat there. Eventually he sighed and put the car in gear, although I almost wished he hadn't. He drove with stunned incompetence, as if he'd just been slugged in the face. It was a terrifying experience, and it reminded me of riding with my daughters when they were first learning to drive. He drifted through intersections without looking right or left, he never signaled, and sometimes, when he was turning, he let the car drift in one direction before cutting the wheel and turning sharply in the other. He had the windows rolled down and his cigarette smoke kept blowing into my face. In the hot wind, with a face full of smoke and a head full of gruesome images, I thought I'd be sick.

Luckily it was a short ride, and in about five minutes we came to a prosperous neighborhood full of big white houses and tall mahogany trees. Other travelers—at least those inclined to write online reviews—seemed to like A Piece of the Indies, and my own first impression was favorable. It was a beautiful old house with a wide verandah on the first and second floors, a few guava trees in the front yard, and a tidy tea service laid out at a small table in the shade of the garden.

I got out of the cab and fumbled with some Renardenne currency I'd gotten at the airport, but the driver asked for American dollars. With a mischievous smile, he said, "Give me five dollars now, sir." I could tell he thought he was trying to cheat me, but the attempt was so pathetic that I gave him twenty.

I stood looking up and down the street for a moment before I went up the walkway. I recognized some of the trees from my time in Vietnam. There were traveler's trees, royal poincianas, a few tropical fig trees with their amazing aerial roots, and lots of different palms. Bright pink bougainvillea poured abundantly over the low stone walls. In some respects, it was a beautiful scene. Steep wooded hills were visible in the east, and I could hear the ocean just down the road.

But it was too hot, and it was too quiet, and it was too still. Stupefied tourists walked by without a sound. I had a terrible sense of foreboding.

I went inside and registered with the owner and proprietor, an inscrutable British expat named George Codrington. He gave me a glass of champagne and led me around the house and grounds, explaining this or that feature of the establishment in pedantic tones. Somehow he managed to communicate the feeling that he himself took no pride in any of this but that it was better than I deserved. There was a long narrow pool in the courtyard, a mango tree, and a sophisticated vending machine filled with bottles of fancy wine.

When he finally let me go, I was puffing and sweating in the heat, and he left me with this advice about adjusting to the climate:

"Let the sun scorch the skin and blister it until it peels, and scorches and peels again, and scorches and peels alternately until, having no more dominion over the flesh, it tinctures the very blood and transmutes mere ruddiness to bronze."

What a way of talking! I went up to my room and turned the air-conditioning up as high as it would go. My accommodations were very comfortable, which was a relief. There was a large wicker ceiling fan, white drapes, white sheets, and a general sense of light and comfort. But I couldn't enjoy it just yet. I fell asleep before I got my shoes off and dreamed that I was playing badminton with Mr. Pinkman III, who kept slipping on the long folds of bloody skin that hung down his back. I woke up screaming and it took me a full minute to remember where I was.

It seemed clear that I wasn't meant for the tropics. I hadn't enjoyed Saigon as a young man, and I wasn't any better adjusted at this stage of life. I wondered whether it was even worth the trouble. Shouldn't I just get on a plane and head back to Tripoli? But then I thought once again of Pinkman, and I thought about Megan, and I promised myself that I'd stick it out.

I think I was just exhausted, because the next morning everything was different. The world seemed full of possibility and excitement. I woke up a little before dawn and witnessed, for the first time in almost fifty years, the abrupt, explosive radiance of sunrise in the tropics. By the time I got out of bed, it seemed like the sun was already high in the sky.

When I'd eaten my breakfast and enjoyed my coffee, I thought I'd head to the beach. It was only a short walk down the hill at the end of the street, and it turned out to be just what I needed. The water was a delirious Listerine blue, a color you could lose yourself in forever. Everything was still and warm and soft. The palm trees were motionless and picturesque in the deep golden light, and I saw a cruise ship pressed like an ornament between the sea and sky. It was perfect. The Caribbean morning looked just like a Caribbean morning, and I thought suddenly of John Morehead Tripoli, grandfather of Tripoli's founder, who had been marooned on this island three hundred years before and who'd written a compelling narrative about his experience. If you were going to be marooned somewhere, you could do a lot worse.

I sat looking out over the clear water to the reef, where the waves broke. The sand was bright white—actually it was mostly crushed shells—and there was a large heron standing in the surf. With its long legs, its upright posture, and its air of deadly patience, it looked just human enough to be strikingly alien.

Then another tourist came strolling down the path. He paused beside me and gestured casually at the beach, the water, the gauzy morning clouds. He said, "Postcard."

When I was coming back up the hill a short time later, I noticed a scrubby little tree with a faded sign nailed to its trunk. The sign warned visitors that it was a manchineel tree: Its bark, sap, and fruit were poisonous. The sign was hand-lettered, and "poisonous" was spelled "poisonus." This detail, and the sense it gave of a person without resources earnestly trying to do some good, endeared the place to me more than anything else so far.

I didn't have any plans. I'd been reading the dispatches that Professor Kabaka had been posting online and I found them extremely compelling and persuasive—they made me want to do something, to get out there and stir things up, to show Megan I was a man of action like her beloved professor—but I knew I was no revolutionary. I was just trying to relax, at least for the time being. It was nice to be somewhere different.

Soon I settled into a comfortable routine. Each morning, I woke up early and watched the sunrise from the balcony outside my room. I had a little coffee and a roll or croissant, and then I went down to the beach for an early swim. Every day, I was shocked and delighted by the whiteness of the sand and the luminous blue of the water. Sometimes I stayed down at the beach the whole morning. One day I went on a chartered snorkeling trip. I think the reef itself is mostly dead, but I saw a few big schools of yellowtail snapper and angelfish, I watched parrotfish chomp at the algae on the dead coral, and I saw a few turtles and one shark. I was fascinated by the dark depths of the water on the other side of the reef, where the sea floor drops away into nothingness. One moment you can stand, the next you're in a thousand feet of water.

After I'd been on the island about a week, I received a dinner invitation from a Big Anna® vice president named Johnson Price. It was a simple courtesy—I was still nominally a senior administrator at an institution with which his own company had formed a partnership. I was a little put out by this, because it meant that Acting President Beckford wasn't tracking my activities, or at least that he hadn't repudiated me or even bothered to tell Mr. Price that I'd all but left my position. Did Beckford have such a low opinion of me? Did he really think I was so ineffectual that my trip to St. Renard didn't warrant any suspicion?

No matter. Maybe I could dig up some dirt on the company when I attended the dinner.

For the moment, it seemed like it was all business as usual on St. Renard: sunshine, surf, tourists, mellow sunsets. But I knew that things on the island were not as quiet as they seemed. Commandant Kabaka was in the mountains, where he and his "Antillia Liberation Army" were threatening violence. Somewhere out there were the Big Anna® banana farms and cane fields—places of misery and hardship—and one day, as I was walking in town, someone pointed out a man named Cudjoe, "the maroon," who was said to have burned down a Big Anna® storehouse. He was a sturdy little fellow with a kind of hump on his back, and he wore a red coat, red pants, and a feathered hat. He looked like he had just stepped out of the eighteenth century, and I thought to myself, Well, the prevailing winds blow from the opposite direction down here—maybe time moves in the opposite direction as well!

from

THE TRIPOLI COLLEGE TELEGRAPH
(APPROVED CONTENT)
February 3, 2010

THE SPORTING LIFE

Tyrants to Hew Wood, Draw Water

Over the winter break, the Tripoli Tyrants wrapped up a disappointing season with a loss to Wampanoag College of the Arts in this year's Genutrex® Palmetto Bowl in Lawtey, Florida. But those who think that it's back to the gym and better luck next year should think again.

Volunteerism and service have long been important priorities for Tripoli sports teams, and the football team is no exception. Next week, the Tyrants are off to beautiful St. Renard, where they'll give back to Big Anna®, Tripoli's generous corporate benefactor, by helping out with the company's many progressive initiatives on the island.

Some players will learn about home construction in Big Anna®'s new Port Kingston Executive Village, while others will provide invaluable domestic assistance to Big Anna® wives, help out on LoCarbon™ plantations, or just keep things running smoothly by providing security in snack factories.

As Acting President Beckford explains, "What better way to atone for dismal failure and cowardice on the gridiron than by the sweat of one's brow?"

The acting president mentioned several advantages to this program. In the first place, football players will provide an excellent reservoir of labor should local laborers decide to shirk their duties and take to the hills. More important, however, is the particular fitness of those players for service on the island.

"Most of our football players belong to the sable race," said the acting president, "and are therefore better able to withstand the ravages of the climate than those of us whose ancestors hail from temperate zones."

The acting president went on to put the proposal into a historical perspective:

"Napoleon's great failure was to send white Frenchmen to fight the black Jacobins in St. Domingue. Of the 65,000 French troops dispatched to the island during the Haitian revolution, perhaps 50,000 died of disease, and thus the diminutive Corsican lost the most valuable colonial possession in the New World."

The acting president has also championed a plan to employ student athletes in maintenance positions here at Tripoli. The question of "what is to be done" with student athletes is one that has preoccupied him for many years.

AN OPEN LETTER FROM THE
ANTILLIA LIBERATION ARMY / FEBRUARY 10, 2010

To the managers and directors of Big Anna:

We explain again and again what we're fighting for, and again and again our pleas are met with incomprehension. You say you don't understand what we want. You tell us to be "reasonable."

How many times do we have to explain ourselves? For five hundred years we have been fighting for the same thing. The past wells up and jumps its banks. History skips over whole lives, whole centuries, and nothing changes. Two hundred years ago John Stedman quoted a maroon leader complaining to a Dutch colonial commissioner in Suriname:

"We desire you to tell your Governor and your court, that in case they want to raise no new gangs of rebels, they ought to take care that the planters keep a more watchful eye over their own property, and not to trust them so frequently in the hands of drunken managers and overseers, who by wrongfully and severely chastising the negroes, debauching their wives and children, neglecting the sick, &c. are the ruin of the colony, and wilfully drive to the woods such numbers of stout active people, who by their sweat earn your subsistence, without whose hands your colony must drop to nothing; and to whom at last, in this disgraceful manner, you are glad to come and sue for friendship."

It's all the same, always the same, never anything but the same. With one or two emendations, his complaints are our complaints:

We want you to tell your CEO that in case he wants to raise no new gangs of rebels, he should attend more carefully to the needs of the banana workers and cane cutters. He should not simply abandon them to the drunken overseers, who—by abusing these laborers, debauching their wives and children, and neglecting the sick among them—are the ruin of the company, and willfully drive to the jungle those strong young workers who by their sweat earn his subsistence, without whose hands his company must drop to nothing, and to whom at last, in a disgraceful manner, he will be glad to come and sue for friendship.

Commandant Kabaka, the Antillia Liberation Army

From: "William Brees" <wbrees@tripoli.edu>
To: "Maggie Bell" <mbell1990@tripoli.edu>
Date: February 15, 2010, at 11:05 AM
Subject: RE: RE: Hi

Hi, Maggie,

I'm sorry to bother you. I know you're probably extremely busy. I just wanted to make sure that everything's going well. Have you gone to the interior already? I'm actually in San Cristobal right now. I also thought you'd like to know that I've arranged an invitation to a banquet at the home of one of Big Anna's vice presidents. Maybe I'll learn something compromising about the company. If I can, I'd like to be of some help to Professor Kabaka in his liberation struggle.

Send me a line or two if you have the chance, and maybe we can meet up when you get back to San Cristobal. I've been enjoying myself very well here. There's a café near my bed-and-breakfast where they serve sea grape brandy. Apparently the slaves would brew it in their cabins. It tastes like poison fruit juice, which I suppose is what brandy is. I've also been enjoying Renardenne food—spicy curry goat, ackee, cornmeal porridge with a cinnamon leaf. I suppose you're probably a much more informed tourist than I am. In any case, I look forward to hearing from you and I hope you're well.

Your friend,
William "Bill Dean" Brees

SLAVERY IN THE WEST INDIES

OR

A Description of One Semester Spent in Tripoli
College's Field Studies Program in Tropical Agriculture

CONTAINING

*a narrative of the author's trials in that program, and an
account of the events that led to her miraculous escape
from bondage, with observations upon the peculiar
manner in which the sugarcane is cultivated and processed on Big Anna plantations, and the oppression and
misery that results therefrom*

"MEGAN"

WRITTEN BY HERSELF

PART ONE

I was born in the small town of Haverstock, in the state of
New Hampshire, in the year 1990. As a child I experienced
no want of parental attention or care, nor did I ever suffer
from hunger or similar causes, so that my girlhood was most
pleasant, and withal almost free from fear. Later I was to
marvel that I could have been so wholly innocent of the evil
there was in the world, and yet I think I was. It was only on
rare afternoons, once or twice in a wondrous summer season,
when, the weather being delightsome and fair, I was surprised

to discover that my own spirits were low, and my sight was as it were clouded by an almost sensible depression of mind, so that I was moved to consider whether there was not some darker world beyond the world that I knew. But except for those days, so few as to fade from thought and memory in the long intervals that separated one from another, I enjoyed a happiness too fine for words, sporting about with my twin brother and eating Pop-Tarts, and I had naught but the most fleeting apprehension that man could be other than that noble and selfless creature which, to my innocent mind, he seemed to be.

When I had reached the age of eighteen years, not being the daughter of tradesmen or traveling performers, custom dictated that I should be sent from home in order to acquire that special knowledge which is called education. My brother elected to attend New York University, but I came to Tripoli College, desiring for myself a liberal arts education and having been so unaccountably derelict in my academic duties that Wesleyan, where I had very much wanted to go, would not admit me. Nevertheless, for two years I enjoyed myself well, delighting in the society of my fellows, the illuminating discourse of my professors, and the abundant food and drink. For me those years were the honeyed glaze on the bun of youth.

And yet it was under the following circumstances that I was made to suffer the outrages of Hell on a plantation in the West Indies:

In the autumn of my third year at Tripoli, I made the acquaintance of one Professor Kabaka, a teacher and scholar, who was to prove very important to me, for though our association lasted only about eight weeks, and though it never transgressed the bounds of propriety, yet he taught me what it meant to be a black girl in America, and he taught me the power of righteous anger, and, in short, I admired him very much.

But Tripoli College was at this time in a state of turmoil, and it was deemed necessary, by those who were empowered to make such decisions, that we form an attachment to the Big Anna corporation, without the assistance of which our financial fortunes must sink to nothing. This arrangement was intolerable to Professor Kabaka, who had his own reasons for despising that company, and thus he felt obliged to return to the Caribbean island of St. Renard, his birthplace, in order to take up arms against Big Anna, and fight for the liberty of those islanders who labored in servitude on Big Anna's plantations.

Though I cherished a deep sympathy for the banana and sugarcane workers of St. Renard, yet now I was preoccupied with my own sorrows, for not only had Professor Kabaka's departure left a void in my life, but I had also begun to feel a return of that gloom of which I had had the briefest intimations as a young girl. My mind felt closed to the beauty of nature, I could not take pleasure in the society of my friends, whose concerns had come to seem trivial to me, and I was filled with a loathing of my own body, to such a degree that I could hardly leave my room for the shame of being, as I thought, so coarse of feature, so dusky of complexion, and so ample of figure. At mealtimes I simply languished over a bowl of pudding or ice cream, cursing myself for that indulgence and yet powerless to subdue my monstrous appetite. I was at all times, or so it seemed, alone.

It was during this period that I began to think of coming to St. Renard myself, where, I hoped, a change of scenery might do me good, and for all I knew I might happen upon Professor Kabaka in the street. It was with these ideas in mind that I applied to be a student in Tripoli College's Field Studies Program in Tropical Agriculture, for not only would this bring me to St. Renard, but so too would it provide me with an opportunity to lose myself in charitable work, and it was my earnest hope that I might stir myself from that peculiar state of soul-sickness, and achieve a finer appreciation of all that was good in my life, if I labored to improve the lot of those less fortunate than I. The Field Studies Program, notwithstanding its association with Big Anna, an association of which I then had an imperfect understanding, seemed ideally suited to my needs, for the application materials available to me promised that it was a "broad-based initiative in resource management and community planning." I give the very words so that the reader may see how I was led astray. Participating students worked to "improve community organization, reduce the island's dependence on fossil fuels, and introduce sustainable methods of agriculture," and would themselves acquire "hands-on experience with tropical food crops."

O Reader, if I had but attended more carefully to that phrase, "hands-on experience," I might have saved myself so much grief! And yet what indication did I have that the Field Studies Program was not what it purported to be?

It was the eleventh day of January, in the year 2010, when I boarded a plane with six other students, to be joined on the island by nine more, and flew to the old colonial city of San Cristobal, on the island's Caribbean coast. Thus in a matter of five hours I was transported from the unutterable gloom of the northern winter, with its bitter cold and low skies, to the paradise of the West Indies, for so it seemed to be: The water shone an astonishing blue, the air was rich and exhilarating to breathe, and the sun, at its meridian, was almost directly over-head, and seemed but a distant relation to that fragile gray disk that hung in the skies over wintertime Tripoli for a few hours each day.

St. Renard lies twelve or fourteen degrees north of the line, in tropical waters, and has accordingly only two proper seasons, a wet season and a dry season, making it suitable for the cultivation of tropical crops like bananas, sugar-cane, coconuts, and cocoa, as well as coffee at higher elevations or in shaded groves. And yet, as I had learned from Professor Kabaka, the island's bounty is its curse, and these crops depart each day from its seaports, or are processed in facto-ries on the island, and provide no nutriment to the Renardennes. Indeed, with so much of the cultivable land, and so much of the farmer's own time, consumed in the production of these crops, the island is unable to produce food for its own tables, and later I often saw the local labor-ers eating tinned salmon or pale, canned vegetables, which were imported from the United States and Brazil. Our task, therefore, as it was represented to us in the only orientation meeting we were privileged to attend, was to help islanders make the transition from this manner of farming toward a model of subsistence agriculture. And yet such noble designs were quickly forgotten, and indeed were never mentioned again once we were in the island.

We had no time to explore San Cristobal, and promptly upon disembarking from the plane we were led to an ancient and rattling school bus and taken south to Tripoli's branch campus, which is called the Proxy College of the West Indies.

This beautiful house was to be our lodging for the first five days of the semester.

The Field Studies Program was at present the only educational program offered at the Proxy College, for the conditions of Tripoli's agreement with Big Anna had necessitated a reorganization of sorts. This was all to the good, for it meant that we had the place to ourselves. The Proxy College is situated on a former coconut estate along the island's Caribbean coast, from where it commands a majestic view of the water, which manifests, in its various depths, all the blues and purples of the spectrum. Our accommodations were spare but of the utmost cleanliness, with the excellent ventilation that is a necessary comfort in those latitudes. For the five days we were privileged to live there, I delighted in learning the names of the exotic plants that were in the grounds, and the wonderful variety of their colors and forms: the elegant disorder of the coconut palms, the haunting dream-purple blossoms of the jacaranda, the spreading banyan, the oleander, the pineapple plants, the salmon-pink ixora and the malodorous soursop, the silk-cotton tree with its buttressed roots.

I knew that Professor Kabaka was in the mountains, where he had raised a group of rebels, for he had written declarations and proclamations to this effect, and as my spirits rose I sometimes thought I might creep away and go in search of him. Yet each morning I delayed, thinking that I would lie yet a while longer under the great tamarind tree in the courtyard, for I was torn between my desire to see him and the blissful ease of this tropical Arcadia, where I might have been content to eat the bread of idleness all my days.

On the evening of the fifth day, we were enjoined to write to our families and explain that we would be leaving for the field the next morning, and that we would be gone some matter of weeks, and would therefore be beyond the reach of email or post. The Proxy College was to be made ready for some executives and shareholders of the Big Anna corporation, for that company was to be given the use of those facilities in exchange for providing us with accommodation on one of its plantations in the interior of the island. After all that Professor Kabaka had told me about the Big Anna plantations, it seems remarkable that I could have failed to grasp the evil portent of this announcement, and yet I think I did, for I supposed that the barbarities he described belonged to the twilit world of the poor, and though I might pass through that world as a tourist, yet I could never come to know it for myself.

We boarded the school bus once again and traveled east, over a range of low hills, into the flatlands which comprise the country's prime agricultural zone. During this trip I sat gazing out the window at the small West Indian houses, which were painted the most cheerful colors imaginable and which fronted sandy yards marked out with pink conch shells. At midday we came to a dusty crossroads distinguished by nothing more than a series of low wooden structures, whether houses or shops we could not tell, and there we stopped, supposing this to be one of those communities we had discussed in our orientation meeting. In fact, as we soon learned, the land and all that we saw about us belonged to the Big Anna corporation, and the structures along the road were, respectively, a tiny commissary, sick house, overseer's office, &c., &c. All about were the cane fields, and not far distant we could see the sugar mill and other structures essential for the processing of that evil plant. Farther still, as it was soon my misfortune to learn, were the banana groves and the packing sheds. We could see laborers passing to and fro, heavily laden with bundles of cane, and with expressions of the utmost severity and discomfort on their faces, which were much darker than mine, although at home I am considered very dark. Here and there a white man stood with his arms crossed. Indeed, it might have been a scene out of the dark past, and now I did experience a fleeting moment of apprehension.

During all this time, we were in the charge of Professor Beatrice Caponegro, our program director, and I cannot but express my feeling that she was one of those few who had some knowledge of the fate that awaited us on the Big Anna plantation, for it was she, and no one else, who led us into the rough stone longhouse in the back trace where we were to live for the remainder of our tenure on the island.

This structure, a ruin left behind by one of those empires which had preceded Big Anna, was only to become more hateful to me, and yet even on that first afternoon it was an abominable sight, with tuna cans, animals feces, and half-completed word-search puzzles scattered indiscriminately across the floor, lizards and other crawling vermin making free use of the space, and beds of the crudest design—no more than coconut-fiber mattresses moldering on irregular wooden frames. Above my own bed was a tattered image of Miami Heat star Dwyane Wade, upon which a number of small irregular hearts had been drawn, and it was among the saddest things I had ever seen. The lavatory was unspeakable and was, furthermore, like the dormitory, to serve all of us, men and women alike. To enhance the aspect of gloom, a tropical thundershower blew up quite suddenly, the rhythm of the wet and dry season being disrupted by global climate change, and we saw that the roof would not serve to keep out the rain.

Professor Caponegro delivered a few words of encouragement and enjoined us to do all that the Big Anna corporation asked of us, and more, for that company was fine and good and had our interests, as well as the interests of the Renardennes, at heart. It was a hollow and disingenuous statement, but it was her last word to us, for now she took her leave, never to be seen again by any of the students purportedly in her care.

The administration of our program was taken up by a Mr. Cavendish, who was to prove the most corrupted and licentious of all the men I knew in the island, and who presently made his appearance in the longhouse. Perhaps it had been his intention to welcome us, after his own fashion, and deliver the introductory monologue which would have been customary at that time, but in the event he was much exercised by the unseasonable rain, which is a great threat to the canes in crop time, and can rot them where they stand. Thus, in a mood of great anxiety, Mr. Cavendish led us through the fields of ripe cane to the sugar mill, which stood some three or four hundred yards from the longhouse.

The mill contained a variety of redundant apparatus, for it had at one time been fully mechanized, and dismantled machinery stood about in testimony to those happier days, when the demands upon the laborers were much less severe. Now that Big Anna was endeavoring to reduce its dependence on fossil fuels, and indeed to adopt sustainable environmental practices, it had reverted to a much older method of processing the cane. This was an effort, as Mr. Cavendish explained, undertaken not out of concern for the company's environmental impact, which he held to be negligible, but out of a need to impress customers with the illusion of that concern. The great problem, of course, as Professor Kabaka had taught me, was that sugar production is an arduous and labor-intensive process, and indeed nearly impossible without fossil fuel on the one hand, or, on the other, great suffering and loss of human life.

In the center of the facility were the great rollers between which the canes were crushed and their liquor extracted. These rollers were meant to be turned by oxen, and above our heads there were stout wooden projections to which those animals had once been yoked. But the oxen had all been slaughtered for want of food, the previous year having been one of privation and fear in the island, during which the plantations had been menaced, as Mr. Cavendish explained, by all manner of external and internal enemies, even including a gang of local children calling themselves the Number Ones, who had burned a toolshed and maimed an overseer.

The rollers were now geared to a treadmill, which had been salvaged from the ruins of an old jail or workhouse, and it was upon this terrible device that half of us were now set to walking. But the Big Anna treadmill bore little similarity to those machines upon which leisured people take their daily exercise, and upon which, indeed, I myself had so recently labored to slough off those sheets of flesh in which I had felt enrobed. It was a cylindrical construction, with thick boards fitted into it to form steps upon which we set our feet and walked, after a fashion, as if we were climbing a great revolving staircase. There was a rail overhead which we grasped in order to support ourselves and to which our wrists were tightly bound, so that we should not be crushed beneath the apparatus in the event that we lost our footing. The great difficulty consisted in keeping the feet moving from one step to the next at a pace consistent with the speed at which the treadmill was turning, for if one student was unable to keep pace with the others, then he would be left hanging from the rail, and then, though his life would be spared, with each incremental turn of the great cylinder he would be struck a blow upon the shins.

I walked the treadmill for what seemed to me an enormously long time, though I think it could not have been longer than twenty minutes, and then I was employed in gathering in the leaves and the crushed canes, which were together called cane trash or bagasse, and carrying them to the boiling houses, where they served as fuel. The islanders themselves were all this time engaged in cutting cane and preparing it for milling, or else in maintaining the fires beneath the great copper boilers, these being tasks that required more skill and knowledge than any of the students yet possessed. They did not speak to us, as indeed they had been instructed not to do, and yet we felt a kinship with them, and we felt at the time that we were a great help to them.

I must pause now to observe once again that although I had learned from Professor Kabaka about the insidious and coercive labor practices of the Big Anna corporation, and though I had been very much preoccupied with slavery throughout the previous semester, yet I did not even begin to suspect that I had myself been reduced to that hateful condition. In truth my mood was very much improved from what it had been at Tripoli, excited as I was to experience new things, form lasting friendships, and help others to achieve that high degree of material prosperity to which I myself was accustomed. It is remarkable what the eye will fail to see, and the mind fail to apprehend, when all the faculties are bent toward sustaining an illusion.

In the early afternoon, we were served a lunch of cornmeal porridge, and then we returned to the mill and were made to labor in growing discomfort until the early evening, for there was still a great fear that much of the cane would be lost if it were allowed to remain wet in the field.

Late in the day, an accident occurred which helped to establish the dark pattern of our semester abroad. There was a student, called "James," who was heavier and of a less robust physical condition than some of the others. He wore a T-shirt upon which were printed the words "Tripoli Mathletics," and on the back, in imitation of a sports jersey, were his name and the imaginary number $5i$. This unfortunate young man, growing more and more tired as he walked upon the treadmill, and calling out that he could not go on, soon lost his footing and hung suspended from the rail. Screaming in pain and calling out to Mr. Hertfordshire and Mr. Drax, who were two of the overseers, he received such a blow or series of blows upon the shin that his leg was quite broken, and he had to be taken back to San Cristobal that very night. Although it seemed in the event like nothing more than bad luck, still I might have observed how tardy were the overseers in stopping the mill and cutting him down from the rail. It did not occur to me, for indeed why should it have done?, that James had been fortunate in his accident, and had been spared much suffering, for he never returned to the plantation, and indeed was soon back at Tripoli.

In the evening, after James had been carried off and the urgency of the situation seemed to have diminished, Mr.

Cavendish returned, and was in every way a changed man, laughing and joking, offering reassurances, and saying how happy he was that we had arrived, for there was much here he was proud to show us. He led us back to the longhouse and there he made a kind of speech about the state of the Renardenne economy, the virtue of the Big Anna corporation, and his own commitment to what he called "low-carbon agriculture," by which was meant agricultural work in which the labor was done entirely by hand, without the use of mechanized transport, large cultivators, &c. &c. Thus he directly contradicted himself, or so it seemed, for not eight hours before he had minimized the importance of this initiative and characterized it as a burdensome requirement of public relations.

Mr. Cavendish was also a great believer in the virtue of sugar, as he explained: "He who attempts to argue against sweets in general takes upon him a very difficult task, for nature seems to have recommended this taste to all sorts of animals. To the influence of sugar may be, in great measure, ascribed the extinction of the scurvy, the plague, and many other diseases formerly epidemical."

He spoke in this manner for some time longer, describing with the greatest enthusiasm all of the uses to which the sugar was put, and we strove to listen with attention, though stupefied with exhaustion and fully sensible of the fact that he was not telling the whole truth, for we still believed that he might be a friend to us.

Later we were given a meal of plantains and salt fish, which I found myself too tired to eat, so I went to sleep in a state of hunger and great fatigue, only to be awakened in the dark of the morning by a great blast from a conch shell, at which we were turned out into the fields once again.

This time I was among a group sent to the banana grove some miles distant, and it was only now, laboring in a state of great weariness and uncertainty, that the peculiarity of my situation began finally to dawn on me. We were set to work carrying and packing the green bananas, while the islanders undertook the more specialized labor of digging ditches, managing the irrigation water, checking plants for signs of blight, &c. Though we worked side by side with them, still they did not speak to us, for, as I discovered later, Mr. Cavendish had forbidden it.

All day the sun burned most fiercely, and we were driven hard, with little to eat but a breakfast of cornmeal at ten in the morning, and salt fish with plantain later in the day. Twice during that long afternoon, an airplane passed overhead and sprayed the whole field, and those of us laboring in it, with the most noxious and horrible pesticides, bringing tears to our eyes, and causing more than one student to fall to his knees, struggling for breath. And now, reflecting that this operation did not accord with what I understood to be the principles of low-carbon agriculture, I worried again that much of what Mr. Cavendish had told us was untrue, and I wondered at the need for such misrepresentation.

We were so exhausted in the evening, bitten by flies and suffering from a kind of delirium of heat, that none among us could summon the strength to boil porridge for the evening meal, which we were now made to do for ourselves. We would have gone hungry had one of the overseers not taken pity on us and given us some bags of Big Anna plantain chips, adding that he would not be so obliging in the future.

The first sure sign that we were no longer free men and women came on the afternoon of the following day. There was a student among us, very strong and of the most pleasing proportions, who was called "Max." Having discovered a small stream on the banana lands, and passing by there quite often in the course of that day's labor, Max decided to refresh himself in the water. Thinking himself unobserved, he repeated the exercise several times before we were summoned from the groves by the conch shell. But upon arriving at the longhouse, we found Mr. Cavendish in a transport of rage, and immediately he began denouncing Max as a malingerer, and making the most absurd threats and insinuations, adding that we were not here to sport about in the water but to contribute to the prosperity of the island, and that Max had done the islanders great harm by taking time to bathe in the pond. In short order he became almost apoplectic, shaking his fist and crying out in an aggrieved voice that he supposed he was the only person on this plantation who cared about low-carbon agriculture. Then, to our great shock and horror, he compelled Max to take up a cowhide whip and actually strike one of the islanders, which, after much protest, with tears running down his face, that baffled young man consented to do, hardly knowing what he was doing and seeming to suffer almost as much as the islander under the lash, who suffered very much indeed. When this was done, Mr. Cavendish explained that each time we bathed in the pond, we did so much harm, and it would always be thus.

At this performance we were greatly shocked, and yet none of us raised a voice or made our objections felt, our exhaustion being so complete, and that special fear, which was the principal condition of our semester abroad, having already established itself in our hearts.

I will not say that we grew accustomed to our situation, but rather that we became so disheartened that life quickly lost its savor, and the spirit of rebellion was crushed within our breasts. We had little to eat, and our fare was of the very poorest, consisting of no more than salt fish, cornmeal, plantains, and, very seldom, the rejected or inferior products of the nearby Big Anna factory, such as *Bananaless Nut Muffins or Coffee Crisps*, which were hardly preferable. It was only the smallest consolation that I quickly became slim and lean on such a diet, for many was the afternoon when I saw Mr. Cavendish beating one of the local laborers himself, with a whip or scourge of tamarind rods, nor was it hard to imagine that he might do the same to us. Add to that fear the torments of insomnia, the agony of the prickly heat, the great danger of the sugar mill and the boiling house, and the degradations of our communal bathroom, and you will have some impression of the misery in which we lived.

Once I realized that I was a victim of the very evil from which Professor Kabaka had pledged to liberate the island, I felt certain that he would soon come to my rescue, and this hope sustained me for the first several weeks of the semester. As time passed, and still he did not come, I thought of sending him a message, but I could think of no method of doing so, for I did not know where he was, and we had no access to writing materials, nor could we trust those islanders privileged to travel on errands between the plantation and the city of San Cristobal. No doubt the reader will ask why I did not flee in the night, for indeed I soon realized that this was my only recourse, but the reason is that I did not know the road, nor was I certain that I could survive for long in the tropical jungle, and I had also a great fear that Mr. Cavendish would deal me some brutal punishment in the event I was recaptured. In short, it was terror that kept me rooted to the spot.

Our only solace was the knowledge that our term of indenture could not be greater than one semester, for afterward our loving parents would expect to hear from us, and one supposes that Big Anna could not hope to hold us over longer than that period of time. This, I think, is what preserved us from that despair which must be the true evil of such a life, for indeed our condition was but a temporary one, and not, as it was for the local labor force, eternal.

At first, we seldom found opportunities to speak to these islanders, for they were forbidden from addressing us, and we were mostly segregated from them. This precaution was no doubt intended to prevent an alliance between our two groups, and indeed to keep us in a state of mutual suspicion, for our captors lived in daily apprehension of a revolt, and no doubt they were afraid that we might incite the islanders to rise up and claim their rights as free people. This fear was increased by another circumstance, namely that there were at this time several groups of "maroons," or escaped laborers, encamped in the mountains. We heard wild stories of the maroons raiding other plantations and carrying off arms and provisions, and I often heard Mr. Cavendish and Mr. Drax speak the names of their leaders, among whom were Cudjoe, Mackandal, and Lubolo. And indeed, Professor Kabaka was among them, for once or twice I heard his name as well.

It was true that on those few occasions when I did speak to them, I found the islanders restive and discontented, but I believe that Mr. Cavendish need not have had much fear on our account, for most of the islanders suspected the students of colluding with Big Anna in exchange for the preferential treatment which they felt we received, and for that reason they would not have been inclined to listen to us.

As the semester wore on, however, and our captors grew more fearful of a general uprising, something seemed to give way in their hearts, and the subtle restraint they had exercised in their treatment of us was replaced with scorn and violence. Again it was Max, that most innocent and well-intentioned of students, who was the first to feel the bite of the tyrant's lash. One day he was working in the boiling house, a most infernal and abominable chore, and growing faint with exhaustion, he staggered out into the yard to catch his breath and steel himself for what remained of his eight-hour shift. Seeing him there, dizzy and gasping in the shade of a mango tree, Mr. Akins grew enraged and ordered several of the islanders to take hold of him, and there, without a word, he struck him several times with a tamarind scourge, and indeed laid his back open in several places, whereupon he ordered him bound to a molasses cask in the sun. There Max remained, blood running down his back, for another half or three quarters of an hour, before he quite fainted away and was carried off to the sick house.

I had myself largely escaped such treatment, being strong enough to do my work without calling undue attention to myself, and being careful to manifest an obliging disposition to begin with. And yet I will now relate those abuses which inspired me to fly, for fly I would have done, not content to wait for the end of the semester, even had circumstances not decided the issue for me.

But before I proceed to the events that led to my deliverance, I cannot forbear to pause a moment for reflection. How, one may ask, could the Big Anna corporation have hoped to make such a system profitable, and how could it have operated in this way without redress? I cannot answer the latter question, except by suggesting that it had not always been thus, and that I believe the slavery system, for that is what it was, had only just been reintroduced. On the one occasion when a Tripoli student, called "Mark," dared suggest to Mr. Cavendish that he intended to take legal action upon his return home, that evil man began screaming about the release forms we had signed prior to embarkation, at the same time begging Mark to reconsider, insisting that a student's testimony could not be admitted as evidence in a court on St. Renard, and finally pretending ignorance of the abuses that were the subject of his complaint. In short, it seems that Mr. Cavendish had a great fear of redress.

As for the profitability of the system, it is not easy to say what the truth was. Everything on the Big Anna plantation was done as rapidly as possible, and as cheaply. Because they did not have to pay for labor, the inefficiency of what the company called "Human Power Technology" was perhaps no disadvantage, as they were accordingly able to save themselves the cost of farm machinery and other equipment. I also know that Big Anna collected the substantial fees that our parents were made to pay as a condition of our admission to the Field Studies Program, and this no doubt was the principal reason we were suffered to remain on the plantation, for otherwise I am afraid we were a great burden, being so much less hardy and skilled than the islanders.

Moreover, I have heard the company praised for its "green" agricultural practices, the reason being that the operation of the plantation was said to require so little in the way of fossil fuels. On this basis, Big Anna claimed to be justified in charging high prices for its inferior snack products, which were supposed to be the result of sustainable agricultural practices. Never mind that the true cost of production was paid in human sweat and tears and blood, or that these products were so sweet as to be inimical to human life, for this claim, as I have already shown, was fraudulent even according to the most cynical and limited understanding of the word "sustainable": Not only did the company apply deadly pesticides, but its products had then to be shipped very great distances, an operation which required enormous quantities of fuel.

Mr. Cavendish, who used sometimes to stroll among us at night, often spoke of the desires of corporations as being more honest and pure than the desires of men, and used to impress upon us the very great good of profit, stating that if all men pursued their own self-interest, as corporations did, the world would be a superior place. But sometimes, in another mood, he used to become melancholy, and sought to justify himself as follows:

"Such a labor system as we have here on St. Renard is the only one which makes economic sense, for here indeed we have a situation exactly analogous to that faced by the planters of the eighteenth century, with the only difference being that we have eschewed mechanized cultivators by choice."

At such moments, it seemed possible that executives elsewhere in the company might have been unaware of the system in place on St. Renard, that system having been conceived by Mr. Cavendish himself as the only means of satisfying at least some of the requirements of low-carbon agriculture while at the same time making the plantation profitable, a challenge he would have been unable to meet without slave labor.

At still other times, he used to represent himself as an honest man engaged in a great struggle to exact a minimum of labor from an unwilling and exceedingly indolent labor force. Sometimes he seemed to forget the fear and suspicion that at other times nearly drove him mad, and I heard him speak thus:

"Why should they work, when indeed we are so indulgent, and the land so bountiful? The fact, I take it, is that there are too many good things in St. Renard for the number of laborers who have to enjoy them. If the competitors were more in number, more trouble would be necessary for their acquirement, and then we should see a labor force grateful for what work it can get."

In short, I cannot say what the truth of the situation was— whether Mr. Cavendish was acting on his own in running the plantation thus, or whether such practices were followed elsewhere in the company. I can only report the details of my confinement on that island as I myself recollect them, and if others can tell a different story, I invite them to do so.

From the local laborers, with whom, as our treatment worsened, we increasingly had opportunities to speak, we heard dreadful rumors about Mr. Cavendish, so that by the time he came to single me out, a misfortune of which I shall tell in time, I had already a good idea of his character. One story was that he used to gather a few of the younger men, make them drunk with cane liquor, and set them to fighting with one another for his amusement. Another story was that he would walk among the laborers' cabins in the dead of night, dripping and reeking with the noxious chemicals in which he soaked his clothing as a deterrent against biting insects, and in that state, drunken and tottering, he would attempt to force his affections upon the local women, who had but little recourse than to submit, fearing reprisals and harsh treatment. I had cause to believe this story, as the following will show.

As we grew more conditioned to the pace of the work, we were driven harder, working no less than fifteen or sixteen hours in a day, as well as three nights each week in the boiling house. One morning, when I was helping to truss a molasses cask, I was taken with a spell of dizziness and pitched forward onto my face. I had worked all the previous night in the boiling house, and all the previous day in the most infernal heat, and I had come to the end of my strength. But although I could not stand, and indeed was hardly aware of my surroundings, being half-dead with fatigue, the overseer, Mr. Drax, began jeering at me and making the most absurd insinuations, suggesting that I was a malingerer, and that I was intent on sabotaging the honest labor in which my fellows were engaged. When I did not rise to my feet after a period of three minutes, he was forced to relent, and instructed two of the other students to drag me off to the sick house.

I was confined for some days, being at first unable to stand, and there I regained some of my strength, but it was in the sick house that I was subjected to the first of those crowning indignities by which my semester abroad was made wholly and finally insupportable. For while I lay in bed, alone in that vile structure, Mr. Cavendish came to see me. He was much aroused, and paced rapidly about the room with his hands clasped behind his back. I should say that our clothes were at this time little better than rags, and sometimes not even that, so that we were compelled to labor in a state of shameful exposure, licentiousness prevailing among the overseers in consequence. Thus Mr. Cavendish, gazing upon me, and driven to lustful fantasies, began making pathetic entreaties, and asking me to pity him, as he was a lonely man. At any moment I expected him to become violent, nor was I fit enough to resist him, and I have no doubt that my honor would have been violated had there not come at just that time a cry from the field, in response to which he ran out again and left me.

I had no peace after this, fearing an outburst of that anger he so often vented on the backs of the Renardennes, and indeed those fears were soon requited, though in the event it was Mr. Akins who was the agent of evil. One day I had gone to beg a drink of water from some islanders when that man, surprising us together in the field, and perhaps taking me, dark as I was, for an islander myself, threw me down in the dust, saying that he would teach me to neglect my work, and dealt me two or three savage blows with a rawhide whip, as well as numerous kicks and punches. At this I felt something fall away within me, and I cannot easily describe my impressions, except to say that such treatment was the nightmare of which I realized that a part of me had always lived in fear, growing up, happy though I had been, a black girl in the shadow of American slavery. Thus the beating I received, in addition to being a surprise of the very worst kind, was also like a return to something I had known before.

The next day I was again at my work, cutting and processing cane, when Mr. Cavendish came upon me in the field, saying that he had heard about what had happened, and that he had been desirous of speaking with me. He asked that I come to see him in the field office that evening, and I had no choice but to consent, fearing the worst.

I found him seated behind his desk, his face horribly flushed, and his eyes the color of watermelon. He pretended to be much preoccupied with what he represented to me as "labor problems," and he delivered a most peculiar speech upon the nature and disposition of the island laborers, of which I will give a sample to show how little it touched upon the truth of things:

"When the Renardenne has eaten his banana," he said, "he goes to sleep, and though a hurricane destroys the hopes of the planter, though fire consumes the buildings erected at a vast expense, though subterraneous commotions engulf whole cities—what is all this to him! Enveloped in his blanket, and tranquilly seated on the ruins, he sees with the same eye the smoke which exhales from his pipe, and the torrents of flame which devour the prospects of a whole generation!"

He sighed and threw up his hands, very much as if he expected me to agree with him, and to establish with me some common understanding upon these grounds. I cannot say what he meant, nor what had occasioned these thoughts, and more-over, as I drew near, I saw that the papers upon which he had seemed to be writing were in fact X-Men comics, the margins of which he had filled with most obscene and childish draw-ings, and, further, that he was sitting with his trousers unfas-tened, in a state of firm and colorful arousal. I then made as if to excuse myself, pretending to think that I had surprised him in an intimate act, for the accomplishment of which he required privacy. With apologies, averting my eyes, I began to back out of the office, even as I heard him making entreaties and suppli-cations, begging me to stay with him and protesting that he did not deserve such treatment. If he made no move to restrain me, I soon learned the reason, for there were some men stationed outside the door, Mr. Akins and Mr. Drax among them, and as I passed through they grabbed hold of me.

Now Mr. Cavendish appeared in the doorway, laughing softly and joking with the other men. I have a good idea what he intended, for he came up to me and pressed himself close, and I could feel the metal buttons of his shirt on my face, to say nothing of the appalling manifestation of his desire. He began murmuring to me, though I could not understand him, and the abominable reek of his breath, sweet with cane liquor, was like an exhalation of Hell.

These men got me over a molasses cask and held me there, though they did not tie me. Then someone pushed my dress up around my waist, laughing all the while and making the most crude comments and suggestions.

At just this moment there recurred to my mind an incident I had witnessed earlier in the day. I had been walking past the field office when I saw Mr. Cavendish crossing the yard in the opposite direction. I quickly hid myself behind a small bush, and from there I heard an islander call out, and I saw my torturer stop and turn around. Crouching down and peering through the branches, I could see the islander quite clearly. He held in his hands a hammer and a nail. Murmuring to himself and tossing his head rhythmically, he knelt down and drove the nail into the soil of the yard. Mr. Cavendish seemed much affected by this event, and indeed grew very pale, and said not a word. Later, when both men had gone, I crept from my hideaway to discover for myself what the islander had done, and I saw that he had driven the nail into Mr. Cavendish's footprint.

Reflecting on this fact much later, I cannot but wonder what effect this ancient magic might have had, for now there came a sharp cry, and a confusion of voices, and Mr. Monthan, an overseer whom I did not know very well, came running in our direction, saying that the maroons were on the plantation, and they had set fire to the cane fields.

End of Part One

from

THE TRIPOLI COLLEGE TELEGRAPH
(APPROVED CONTENT)
March 10, 2010

Acting President Shows Clemency

Professor Richard Carlyle was released from custody late Tuesday night after Acting President Beckford announced that he was granting the troubled professor a full pardon.

"Artists are like children," said the acting president, "and must be treated indulgently."

Professor Carlyle was apprehended last Saturday while attempting to liberate the cowardly slave trader Bish Pinkman III, who is currently working off his debt to Tripoli in the service of the acting president.

Professor Carlyle explained that he had been feeling "desolate" about the role he had played in the Pinkman case but that he had not intended to lead Mr. Pinkman III to freedom.

"I was just thinking we could drink some NyQuil together and make amends," he said. "I wanted to apologize."

The acting president expressed disappointment in Professor Carlyle, although he insisted that he still considers the poet a friend.

UNDERCOVER DEAN: BLOG POST #7

A car came for me at about five o'clock on the evening I was scheduled to have dinner at Mr. Johnson Price's home. He lived no more than ten miles outside San Cristobal, but it was a different world out there in the country. His house, a huge Georgian mansion built from coral rock, was surrounded by five acres of terraced tropical gardens, and from the back porch he had an unbroken view of the coastal plain and the sea.

I was met at the door by an old black man who introduced himself as Affleck. I took him for a butler or a footman. He seemed very perturbed that I didn't have a coat to give him, but how could I wear a coat when it was almost eighty degrees in the dark?

I almost fell down as I stepped inside—the mahogany floors had been polished as smooth as a hockey rink—and I was gripping a hall table to steady myself when Mr. Price appeared. He was a boisterous and energetic person, running to fat but still light on his feet. He clapped me on the back and seemed very happy to see me, though at first he mistook me for a shareholder in the Royal African Company. It took him a moment to remember what Tripoli College was. I subsequently learned that it was his secretary who had sent me the invitation.

There were already about twenty or thirty people in the great hall, and everyone looked as if they'd been drinking for a few hours already. A very dark-skinned waiter named London brought me a glass of plantain wine, which was extremely strong, and I melted into the crowd and tried to fit in.

But it wasn't the kind of event at which you could fit in or not fit in. Everyone seemed to have come prepared for a different kind of evening. Some people wore T-shirts and shorts, others wore slim black dresses and suits in contemporary cuts, one man was wearing a bathing suit, and still others wore outlandish costumes—silk breeches with white silk coats and waistcoats, dressing gowns, ornate doublets, wide fur hats. Mr. Price was wearing a simple black suit when he met me at the door, but soon he slipped away and reappeared in a kind of tropical safari costume, complete with cork helmet. Some of the women were wearing bulky Victorian ball gowns, and at least two people were barefoot.

Almost as soon as I entered the hall, I found myself cornered by a disconsolate young woman who introduced herself as Lady Nugent. She had been on the island only a week or two. Like me, she was having trouble adjusting to the heat.

"This climate has a most extraordinary effect upon me," she complained. "I am not ill, but every object is, at times, not only uninteresting, but even disgusting."

"Where are you staying?" I said. "Don't you have air-conditioning?"

"I feel a sort of inward discontent and restlessness that are perfectly unnatural to me—at moments, when I exert myself, I go even beyond my usual spirits, but the instant I give way, a sort of despondency takes possession of my mind. I argue with myself against it, but all in vain."

"It helps to take a nap during the heat of the day. A kind of siesta, if you like."

She was wearing a large, lacy dress that hid her feet. No wonder she was hot! But there was no reasoning with her. I was dressed inappropriately myself, in a flannel suit, and I was sweating heavily even though the cold plantain wine was very refreshing.

"Add to these discomforts the great immorality of the European population," she continued, "debased by ignorance, licentiousness, and low, frivolous, and groveling pursuits."

To this I had no response. I stared at her over the lip of my wineglass.

I was saved from this conversation by the dinner gong, but my luck didn't improve. At the table, I was seated next to a man named James Cavendish, an even more committed mono-loguist than poor Lady Nugent. His only theme was "the color question," in particular as it applied to the treatment of labor-ers on the Big Anna® plantations he managed. This was just the kind of incriminating garbage I wanted to hear, but in the event I could barely stand to listen to him. Mr. Cavendish's contention was that locals were better off working in the cane fields than they would have been if they were left to fend for themselves. He seemed convinced that cane cutters lived idyllic lives.

"There are always those dissatisfied with their condition," he said, "whether because of the frustration of their personal ambitions or because of some innate defect in their character. But the great majority of the islanders are as happy as inno-cents in the garden."

He spoke in a wheedling and pedantic tone, as if trying to convince himself that what he said was true, and either he refused to make eye contact or else his eyes didn't point in the same direction. In other ways, too, he was a strange sight. He was bald in front, but he wore his hair very long in back and on the sides. This, combined with his small round spectacles, made him look disconcertingly like Ben Franklin, which irritated me. I have always been an admirer of Big Ben.

"Are the laborers of St. Renard capable of becoming happier in consequence of the gift of liberty?" he continued. "Are they capable of appreciating and enjoying its blessings, or would they even exchange their present condition for the turbulence, the dangers, the insecurity of a savage state of independence?"

I was finding it very difficult to dissemble my anger and disgust. Thankfully, the first course was served promptly. And what a first course! It consisted exclusively of beef: baked beef cheeks; boiled rump roast; an unidentifiable cut called "chine"; tongue and tripe baked into a pie with sweet minced herbs, suet, and currants; a Spanish dish called *olió podrido*, which was made from the head of the poor animal; and a dish of marrow bones.

To be polite, I ate little bites of everything, and even though I tried to pace myself, I was full by the time London came to clear my plates. I'd also had two glasses of plantain wine, a glass of claret, and a few sips of something called "mobbie." If I hadn't had so much practice drinking with Tripoli students that fall, I'd have been unconscious.

London and a few other waiters—a woman named Phinea and two men named Quaw and Bristol—now brought the second course, which consisted of two pork dishes, a dish of boiled chickens, a shoulder of mutton, a loin of veal, a shoat, three turkeys, two capons, two hens, four ducklings, eight turtledoves, and three rabbits. All this carnage! I found myself craving a bit of lettuce or a carrot. There were also several more elaborate dishes, including the shoulder of a young goat dressed in a sauce made from the animal's own blood; a whole kid roasted with a kind of stuffing or pudding in its stomach; and a suckling pig in a spicy sauce made from brains, sage, nutmeg, and claret.

Mr. Cavendish had emptied a huge tumbler of brandy and put away two ducklings and a dove, and now his face was brick red and his eyes had drifted even farther apart. He was gesturing at London and Quaw.

"I see them take up their baskets," he went on, "as if it were perfectly optional whether they took them up or left them there."

But now, maybe because I'd had so much to drink, I lost my temper:

"They haven't got any baskets! They're just doing a job, like anyone!"

A cockeyed smile crept over his face. It was the smile of a man who knows that the sun revolves around the earth.

"I can hardly persuade myself that it's really work that they're about," he said softly.

I tried to ignore him, and I made a special effort to thank London when he came to top off my glass of plantain wine. I was trying to thank all the servants by name whenever they did anything, but I kept getting their names confused.

"They saunter along with their hands dangling . . ." Mr. Cavendish continued.

"Stop it!" I shouted.

"They stop to chat with everyone they meet, and if they meet no one, they stand still and look round to examine whether there is nothing to be seen that can amuse them."

But London, who must have been listening, had a solution.

With a few deft movements, he pulled Mr. Cavendish's collar open and emptied a dish of chicken fat into his hair and down his back.

There was a moment of dreadful stillness as Mr. Cavendish struggled to process this astonishing development, and then he leapt to his feet and knocked his chair over. He was too slow: London had danced out of reach and was already on the other side of the table. Mr. Cavendish was left standing there, his long hair slick with chicken fat and his pink gumball eyes starting from their sockets. He literally wet himself with rage before charging out of the room.

I started laughing and looked around for someone to share this delightful moment with, but no one seemed to have noticed. Mr. Price was now explaining to London the many virtues of sea bathing, Lady Nugent was carrying on about the climate, and a man in a dressing gown was shouting about the maroons. Everyone was in his or her own world.

And there was more food to come. Phinea and Quaw and Bristol were carrying out dishes of ham, pickled oysters, caviar, anchovies, olives, some custards and sauces, and preserves made from plantains, bananas, and something called "gnaver." There was also a plate of dried neat's tongue, which was a little like beef jerky, and a bowl of dehydrated caviar that Mr. Price called botargo.

Everyone was talking at once, and everyone was blind drunk. The man in the bathing suit vomited into a trash can. Several people had fallen asleep.

Suddenly a wiry little fellow in a gray slouch hat and emerald vest grabbed my sleeve, jerked his head at Quaw, and hissed, "Do you think they've heard the revived name of Haiti, by which San Domingo is called at present?"

I felt like I was going crazy. I asked London for another glass of plantain wine.

"London!" I shouted. "London! I really admire your courage."

"Don't know what you mean, boss."

I winked at him, or at least I tried to. It would have made me a lot happier if I could be sure that he knew I wasn't a racist, but how do you say it?

Dessert was cheesecake, cream puffs, bananas, watermelon, prickly pears, anchovy pears, custard apples, and pineapples.

I called London over and whispered, "I don't really belong here, you know. I'm not one of them."

He poured my plantain wine without looking at me.

"I'm not a racist!"

"Me neither, boss."

So I let it go. What did he care anyway? The plantain wine was singing in my head, and outside the wind had come up. The dark crowns of the palm trees were dancing against a blue-black sky.

A sturdy middle-aged man sat down in Mr. Cavendish's place and introduced himself as Richard Ligon. He explained that he was doing some consulting work for Big Anna®, and somehow I got the idea that he was a botanist.

"So what's a gnaver?" I asked him.

"The seeds of the gnaver, or guava, have this property: that when they have passed through the body, wheresoever they are laid down, they grow. These fruits have different tastes, some rank, some sweet, according to the several constitutions they have passed through."

"That's crazy," I muttered. "A seed's a seed. What's the matter with everybody?"

I couldn't figure out how any of the other guests were connected with Big Anna®. There was no talk of company business.

"Does anybody know about the Field Studies Program?" I said. "Does anybody know how my students are getting on? I'd maybe like to head out there and check on them. Does anybody know Megan?"

Nobody heard me, or nobody cared. The man in the emerald vest grabbed my shirt once again and said, "The late Pope gave these islands and the content hereof to the Catholic sovereigns of Castile and Aragon, as is certified in writing, and you may see the documents if you should so desire!"

A few minutes later, I heard another man mention "that Indian-lover Morehead Tripoli," but John Morehead Tripoli had been dead for more than two hundred and fifty years.

Little did I know that the most mystifying and upsetting part of the evening was still to come. When we were through with dessert, Mr. Price rose and clapped his hands. It was now time, he said, for the ladies to adjourn to the withdrawing room.

And so they went, one after another, in silence and even with a kind of dread. When they were gone, a troop of female servants entered from the kitchen. They carried bottles of rum and brandy and Madeira. It was heartbreaking to see their forced smiles. The rest of the men shoved their chairs back and roared for more drink. One older fellow, sweating bullets in a black wool waistcoat and wool trousers, collapsed with a groan, and nobody moved to help him. Boxes of cigars were circulating, and bottles of "Kill-Devil" rum, and someone was playing a maniacal, seesawing waltz on the accordion. Later I was certain that I recognized former House majority leader

Tom DeLay, but by then I'd had so much plantain wine that I could hardly stand.

"Now to close up all that can be said of fruits," Mr. Ligon told me, "I must name the pine, or pineapple, for in that single name, all that is excellent in a superlative degree, for beauty and taste, is totally and summarily included . . ."

And so he continued, on and on, while the servant girls danced and the room filled with smoke and the world folded up around me.

I woke up in a big bed on the second floor. I never found out how I'd gotten there, but it seemed impossible that I'd made it on my own power. I was relieved to find myself alone and the house quiet.

I meant to sneak away—I thought I'd walk back to San Cristobal if I had to—but I ran into Mr. Price on my way out. He was wearing a nightgown and white silk breeches, and his big hard belly was mounded up in drifts and ridges on his abdomen. It looked like it had been sculpted that way and baked in a kiln.

He insisted that I join him for breakfast, and I didn't have the strength to refuse. I had to sit there as he drank two bottles of porter and wolfed down a leg of mutton. Pieces of glass and hunks of meat and bone lay all over the floor, and the man in the black wool waistcoat was still lying where he'd fallen. Was he dead? Bristol was poking at him with a mop.

Mr. Price himself was very cheerful. Evidently he thought his dinner had been a great success.

"And you, young man," he said to me. "Remember that shareholders in the Royal African Company are always welcome in my house."

I went outside and sat down on the steps. From there I could see the bright blue Caribbean Sea, ruffled slightly in the morning breeze, and the coral reef just offshore. I put my head in my hands and tried to gather myself. I was grateful for the violent sun, which seemed to quiet my nerves a little bit, and for the refreshing sea breeze.

After a while, London came up the hill from what I assumed were his own quarters. Seeing me in this wretched condition, and maybe remembering that I'd tried to be friendly to him the night before, he brought me a little tin bucket of water and sat down next to me.

"I am not happy with my life here, man. But it's a change coming."

"I hope so."

"It's a change coming," he said again. "It have a lot of angry people in the island and soon we go do something."

Excerpted from

A True & Exact Historie of These Ilands of the West Indies, with an Account of the Carwak Indians, and Observations upon the Newlie-Discover'd Iland of Saint Reynard, or Guanahani

BY

JOHN MOREHEAD TRIPOLI

CHAPTER 7TH

*Maroon'd on Saint Reynard ~ Frensy Feavor ~ Carwak Indians
Their Manner of Spending Time ~ The Bloody Flux ~ Monkie upon a
Chain ~ Vortex of Dissipation ~Yarico ~ Castrat'd by Land Crabs*

WE were put off that *floating Coffin* the ship *Tatterde-malion* about Noon, there being at that tyme 12 of us, including myself, who was the onlie Officer, and such a gang of stew'd and blackburnt scarcrows has ne'er been seen. Theyr was not a Man among us but was *stricken* with Agues, Feavors, Rotten Limbs, Contry Disease, &c., half or about 6 being so seek they would not rise from the sand, except if it were to scream & run about, tearing at theyr hare, and such is the Madness which is occazioned by these Frensy Feavors that a young Sailor this day with a short knife absolutely *castrated* himself & was dead as a haring by Sun set. Being very seek myself & nearly starv'd, I cant recall but one half of all that befell us that day, for I was in torments, pursue'd verily by *Ghosts* phantomes & spirits, and did repent of my actions aboard the shippe, on account of which I was landed heare. In all that day we did not shift more than 10 ft. from the *Ocean See*.

But tho I have said that on this day I was Seek, and hardlie expect'd to see the Sun rise, but the next day I was well and now survey'd all that I saw about me, being well-pleased by Saint Reynard that greene isle, esp. by the *Coco Tree* which grew there in abundance. But hardlie had I collect'd my Wits and roused my companions /, tho two had died in the night, and were sweld like Drown'd Carion by the heat of the Climate / but we had Guests, viz. about 10 of the *Carwak Indians*, who live upon this the iland of *Saint Reynard* tho they be all but extinct on many of the other West India illands. They were quite naked with not even that strip of linnen to conceal what decency forbids us to expose. We held our posishun, as indeede we must, for wee were cutt off in our retreat by the See, and the waves, & by seekness, but wee gave evidence of our extreame weakness by the circumstance that a *Young Sailor* /, being the verry same Hapless Youth who on board shippe was punish'd for his part in the Mutiny by having all his teeth brok'n out / chanc'd to *dye* at that instant tumbling into the sand so that our whole number was now melted down to about 8, and most of us in a verry weakly condition indeed.

In as little time as a Girl might lose her Maidenhead we were surrounded & all things being hopeless I suddenly took hart & thanked Heaven in the expectation of now being dispatch'd to Eternity, my sufferings end'd at last, for which end I now in eagerness heartily composed my soul. Yet now I had a great Surprize, namely that the Carwak chief address'd me in my own tongue, and bid me well-come to *Guanahani*, which is how the Carwak call Saint Reynard. He had learnt English I know not how, and also spoak French which he had learnt off the *boucaniers* who infest the iland at a sertain season. Also as I must not omit to mension that one of our number /, a Sailor nam'd Brigg /, being Extremely Fat, & Corpulent, & no more able to support the fatigues and Excessive heat than snow the sunshine, dyed as we spoke with this Carwak chief, his Desolution hasten'd by that dreadfull Distemper the bloody flux, which was now come among us, and our hole number now reduc'd to I think about 7.

The Carwak are now grown verry few, because of the Inhuman Cruelties inflict'd upon them by the Spaniard, and in the worst of tymes are reduc'd to these theyr onlie amusements, namely, *Lamentation* and *Toaping*. Firstly, they drink *Perino*, which is a spirituous liquor made from the *Cassavie* / the *Cassavie* as I have discribed is a Poysonus Shrub or Bush, but from the rut can be obtained a farinaceous substance which is also theyr chief food, and supplys the want of bread /, and secondly they have a grate love for *Kildevil*, this being a strong liquor which is made from the dregs and feculence of the sugar boylers and which they have from the *Boucaniers*, who bringe it from the other ilands to trade with them for the Ghost Apple, of which I will say much in time. Also they drink *Mobbie* and *Oui-cou*.

Despite the grate bounty of the iland, where, as it seem'd to me, Nothing is wanting that Nature can afford, many of the Carwak do truly die of affamation, if not of Ilnness, for they say that the iland is all over run by Annimals of all kinds, viz the Goat, Wild Hogge, and others, which trampel theyr gardens wherein they produse the *Cassavie*, and dye from eating of it, and further, these Annimals not having existed in the island before the European came, the Carwak do not believe them eatable, tho I believe *all* Quadrepedes are eatable, tho they be frivivorous or Man-eaters. Another thing I will say upon this subject, is that, tho the Carwak profess'd themselves hungrie, yet I did find myself well-nourish'd during my days with them, for often there was spred out before me such Frutes, namely the *prickled apple*, queene pine, & *Zapote*, that made one composition of Charm and Ambrosia.

In the Carwak village I now again relapsed, and was verry Seek, as before, but the Chief gave me to drink the ground dried pisle of the *Green Turtle*, and by this I was cured, at least for the day. The girls treat'd me kindly also and I was much taken with theyr charms. They nursed me & bathed me & never in all my time in the West India ilands was I so happy, for who would not undergo a little Pain to see the Pretty Girls sigh for their sufferings? I will also say, that, though they are call'd in Englande the *Troublesome Sex*, on the iland they are the most gracious & smiling Angeles, and trulie the *most* beautiful I had seen since leaving *Englande*, having been none too favourbly impress'd by the Pumpkin-colour'd whores I had seen upon other ilands in that tropick Sea. Let prudes and Coquets say what they will, but I b'lieve there are grate practical arguments to plead in favour of going Quite Naked, as they do, for to a Natural State is annex'd a superior *mobility*.

One thing I ought not to omit which is very remarkable viz that one morning I saw a Carwak man who keep'd as a pet to a Silver Chain one monkie, which was a most noble and dignified Creatur, like to a *Judge* in manners, except that he was as great a Toaper as the Carwak Indian himself, who is the greatest toaper of all the species of *Man*, drinking of the Kildevil as he dos from morning til night. I have never seen a monkie so drunken as this one upon Saint Reynard.

Sleeping in the *Carrbet*, which is the Carwak Hutt, & lieying about all Day, & finding my needs all provided for by the

Grayshus Indian, I now descended in a *Vortex of Dissipation*, being nearlie as full of *Despaire* as the Carwak, for I knew not how to get off the iland, and lament'd my verry distress'd Situation. Yet all in all I was us'd well, and found each day many several ways I mite beguile the tyme, so that I was happie indeede, in spite of my despayr.

One evening tho the *Muskitos* be inconceivable numerous we went down to the See, which in the darkness flickers with a thousand lites, and there I fell to talking with a young sailor / Copplestone was his name, / and recalling with him Merrie Englande. Soon we were joyned by a marine Bamfield was his name and all together with the Carwak we empty'd a dozen Calabashes of the Kildevil & weep'd such teares as evidently weaken'd poor Copplestone beyond hope of recoverie, for he now had a verry stiff way of walking, as I notic'd /, like a Gouty Puritan /, & this I took to be an Evil Omen, for so it was, and the next moment he was lying upon his face in the sand, dead. Yet here I tolde myself, & determin'd, that I would Forcibly keep my spirits from sinking, by Laughing, and Singing, while all my companions were dying around me.

So I now joyned Bamfield, and some of the Carwak girlles, who stood upon the shoare looking out to See. Bamfield offer'd them the Calabash, thinking they must refuse, for onlie the Carwak men, by custome, are permitted to drink of spirituous liquors, & yet they took it from him and eatch drank, for the Carwak live in dailie expectation of the *World's End*, and none of them now carres for what in older dayes was the custom among them. I will not omit another observashun I made upon Carwak girls viz. that many of them are marvelously possessed of that anterior extuberance which is so wanting in the Lacker-fac'd Creolans I had known elsewhere in the ilands.

Thus we disported ourselves all that night with these 3 girlles and I in particklar with one lovely Girl *Yarico* /, for such was her name, and this indeede was my first meeting with Yarico my true hart's love / and verily it was as debauched a tyme as we had yet had in the iland, tho I must draw a Sable curtain over it.

Next morning Barnfield was gone without any conjecture could be formed what was come of him. Yet soon I found him in a grove of *Coco-trees* where he lay upon his face in the sand, & when I levered him to his backe I saw a *Horrible Thing*, namely, that his skin was stretched tight as a jacket to a Dutchman, & he had been *absolutely castrated* by the Land Crabs, but of course this Misfortune would not trouble him now, for he was *dead*. There being nothing more I could do for him, I now went for my Breakfast of Maize or Indian Wheat, which Yarico cook'd for me over the smoak of a swinging fire, the grain being of a shining yellow or orange, as large as Marrow Peas, and also theyr was fishe of a lubricative texture. This ended our gratest Revel, and heare I put an end to the Chapter.

CHAPTER 8TH

Life Among the Carwak ~ The Ghost Appel ~ Their Method of Extract'ng Sap ~ Desire to Make an Ende ~ Pennington or Codrington ~ Diseases Peculiar to the Climate ~ These Wonderfull People the Carwak

Now I lived as the Carwak did, for eatch morning I bayth'd in the See, after which I sat to drie upon a log, & breakfast'd upon *Cassavie*, Indian Wheat, or it may be crabbes, and some tymes I shared this fud with the *Macaws*, which are a kind of Tropickal Crow. Then a girl often Yarico my love paynted me all over with a dark paynt, after the fashun of the Carwak /, and I hope the reader will forgive me that I did not speake of this custome before now, for it is a verry conspicuous circumstance, and not onlie protects against Insects, but preserves the skinne against the Sunne / and when this was compleated my next care was to walk about the Iland.

Now I must tell of a *Singular Item* which I knew upon the Iland, & that was the subtile liquor or as they say *Medisin* which is made from the *Ghost Apple* Tree, call'd also the Carwak Apple Tree. This tree is very like to the *Mantionell*, yet is not half so poyson, tho if the sap fly into the eyes as it is said it makes a man to be stone blinde for a month. Its frutes are round and greene, in bignesse very much like the Crab Appel of the old Continent, and yet in theyr vertues not so, for the Carwak make a drinke from it which is most Miraclous. How it is made, is this, viz. that the fruit, leaves, & it may be some small twigs or flours, are pounded till soft, then pressd in a wooden vessel below which is a kind of bucket, into which it dreeps, and heare the *Sap* is collect'd. Then it is boyld for some tyme, this being essenshal to destroye the poison which is in the Sap, for I have eaten of the frute which I pluck'd fresh from the tree, and, first, it is by nature so Restringent that it drew my mouth up like a Hen's fundament, and, two, that it verily swept my Guts clean, from which circumstances I conclude that boyling is essenshial.

The Carwak have a grate *Reverence* for this drink of the Ghost Appel Tree, which they make in tyme of *Seekness*, or else when some one among them has died, but at other tymes they touch it not, for it is a *Slow Pernicious Poyson* & may not be consum'd but once in a fortnight. However, the circumstances being that the Carwak, not long after we came to the iland, grew seek them selves with the dreadfull *Bloody Flux*, this was when I observ'd them preparing the Sap. I must not omit to menshun that the Ghost Appel is also used for many other purposes, viz to whit'n the teethe, and extirminate the *Okoba*, whitch is an insecte which infests the *Cassavie*.

The Chief, who alone of the Carwak spoake Englishe, tho others made them Selves understood wel enough, gave us the juice in a calabash dipper, and we dranke. Tho I had been sick-lie all that day, yet this drinke frighted away the ague & now I was as if strucke by a *Thunder Bolt*, the drink being so verry powerfull. Trulie my hed swam with lite, from which I conclude that with-in the sap is that verry substance which, in the darkness, causes the See to glowe with lite, many of these trees being plant'd on the beech, and the sap falling in the water.

This drinke had produs'd such an effect in me, that, I thought it would be meet to drowne my Self in the See, yet at this tyme I had grate difficultie in moving forward, as I want'd to do. Yet the sap or juice, tho it gave me feet of clay, and so too a *Desire* to make an ende, had here a quite diffrent effect on others of our number, who were now dwindl'd, I think, to 5 men. There was one Sailor, Pennington I think was his name, or Codrington, that was in a Hectick Feavor, and drinkeing of the juice he would not leave off talking:

Now *Rain* / , said he / and other phenomena of which the
Atmosphere is theatre, does owe its geniture, as the
Ringworm does, Sir, which being an afflictshun consisting
in scarlet patches upon the Under Parts, & at the same
tyme gloweing with a Scrufulous Halo, dryves a man

nearlly mad with the iytching, yet as I said Rain, my
Friend, and Ringworm, tho I sense it will be difficult to
obtane belief of this, both phenomena, &c. &c.

Poor Pennington, or Codrington. Perhaps even then he felt
the approach of *Death*, by the lowness of his Spirits, or the
want of Bodily Vigour, for I, tho nearlie blinde, could see it
writt'n in his face. Perhaps also he thot to frustrate God's
intension by draweing out his speach thus, and ne'er coming
to the poynt.

I was muche distract'd now by two things, namely vomiting, for I was sicke, and, second, I had a grate desire to open a
Coco-nut, of which the eatable part is secured within so strong
a Magazeen that I could not, for all that I tryd each day, make
a passage to the kernel. Yet now I thought I mite have recourse
to a stratagem, viz. that I would go to a hill I knew, and from
there jump into the See, clutching the *Coco-nut*, & would
lande among the rocks belowe with my full weight an emasiated 9 stone upon the *Coco-nut*, and there burst it open. This
wood have the double effect of ending my Life, which was all
to the gud, and much desir'd, for this Frute the Ghost Appel
does produce such a powerfull inclination to take one's Self off
to *Heaven*, or to *Hell*.

Pennington, or Codrington, now having left off talking, he
propos'd we drink to the healths of those our friends in the old
Continent, and so we did, each of us emptying a calabash, so
that I quite forgott my desire to open the *Coco-nut*, and instead
I was driv'n nearlie Madd, and wish'd very much to see my
lovely *Yarico*. And as Pennington, or Codrington, was now
suddenlie quite dead at my feete, there for I went off in search
of her, intending to make her my *Wife*.

It was quite darke, & all alone in the nite I went downe to the *See,* where I could here voices, and singing, for indeede it was a lovely Musick. The Carwak some of them were sitting upon the sand, tho the sand flees which are there did not molest them on the account of the painte with whiche they cover'd themselves, as I have said. I watch'd threw the Coco trees, and wen I came among them they did not remark me, but only gave me to drink some Perino, so that it struck me, that, in all truthe I loved these people the Carwak, for there too was *Yarico,* and she *smyled* at me.

Findings: *Mosquito Masterminds* Professor Jana Brewster has just published a paper that may prove shocking to anyone who cherishes a sense of human exceptionalism. It details unequivocal evidence for intelligent community organization and sophisticated group decision-making in mosquitoes, focusing primarily on their use of malaria as a way of controlling the size and geographical distribution of human populations.

Malaria is a disease of the Old World tropics, and its importance in the New World—particularly its influence on the development of New World plantation slavery—has only recently been acknowledged by historians of the colonial period. Once it was established in the Americas, it wreaked havoc on both indigenous and white European populations, and the labor vacuum thus created in malaria zones was what motivated some colonists to begin importing enslaved Africans. Not only were slaves easier to replace, according to the cynical logic of early slaveholders, but people from West and Central Africa were much more likely to have some resistance to certain forms of the disease. Although early colonists did not understand the biological mechanism, the results were obvious: Planters with African slaves ended up with a larger and more vigorous workforce than planters who employed European laborers.

Physicians have known for more than a hundred years that malaria is a vector-borne disease spread by infected mosquitoes. Until now, however, those mosquitoes have been dismissed as little more than passive transport for the malarial plasmodium—in effect, a feature of the climate. But this summer, while doing research for an unrelated project, Professor Brewster made a shocking discovery. She learned that *Anopheles quadrimaculatus*, the species of mosquito that serves as North

America's main malaria vector, can't be found in most northern states. The effective limit of its range is, incredibly, the Mason-Dixon Line.

"South of the line," Professor Brewster says, "we used to see malaria and thus we saw plantation slavery as well. North of the line, there were essentially no infected mosquitoes, no malaria, and therefore no plantation slavery. What this means is that anopheline mosquitoes must have understood and respected this artificial human boundary."

Mosquitoes, she argues, must have decided *as a group* to confine themselves to the Southern states, which means that they were complicit in the creation of a Southern plantation society.

But the reality may be even more extraordinary. If mosquitoes were capable of recognizing human political boundaries, might they also have been capable of helping to establish such boundaries and thus to engineer that plantation society? They had much to gain by doing so: Unprotected, closely quartered slave populations provide a reliable source of blood meals for female mosquitoes. Since females require mammalian blood for egg production, they would have had an interest in maintaining and reinforcing the slavery system. Professor Brewster has postulated that they "managed their human herds as we might manage our cows and sheep," probably in order to keep slave plantations close to favored breeding sites.

This also means that the insect was instrumental in creating a situation that led to civil war. It is therefore reasonable to ask whether mosquitoes consciously brought about that conflict as well, just as they may have helped to create plantation society in the first place. Mosquitoes thrive in wartime for the same reasons they thrive on slave plantations. Large groups of people with inadequate clothing and little or no shelter provide a veritable buffet. Additionally, the deformation of the landscape tends to produce depressions that collect rainwater and provide breeding sites free of the fish and other predators that typically threaten mosquito larvae.

"I've always had a horror of bugs," Professor Brewster says. "This just makes it worse."

In the last hundred years, humans have developed many effective methods of mosquito control, but this doesn't mean that these insects no longer pose a threat. Malaria is still hyper-endemic in equatorial sub-Saharan Africa, and there is no reason to imagine that we here in North America will be safe forever.

"They're cooking up something dreadful," Professor Brewster says. "They're just waiting for their moment."

An Open Letter from
THE ANTILLIA LIBERATION ARMY
MARCH 16, 2010
to
THE PEOPLE OF ST. RENARD

———

Brothers and Sisters:

The philosopher Hegel, who was himself no friend to the enslaved Africans of his day, nevertheless provides us with these words:

"Even if I am born a slave, and nourished and raised by a master, and if my parents and forefathers were all slaves, still I am free in the moment that I will it, when I become conscious of my freedom."

We have willed it. We are free. But our protests have fallen on deaf ears. We know now that Big Anna and the United States will fight to keep us marginalized, dispossessed, disenfranchised.

The great Toussaint-Louverture wrote these words during the Haitian revolution, and we make them our own:

We have no other resource than destruction and flames. The soil bathed with our sweat shall not provide our enemies with the smallest aliment. We will tear up the roads with shot, we will throw corpses into all the fountains, we will burn and annihilate everything in order that those who have come to reduce us to slavery may have before their eyes the image of that hell which they deserve.

Commandant Kabaka, the Antillia Liberation Army

From
SLAVERY IN THE WEST INDIES

OR

A Description of One Semester Spent in Tripoli's Field Studies Program in Tropical Agriculture, etc.

PART TWO

Though I had all but given up hope of rescue, yet as soon as Mr. Monthan had delivered his news, namely that the maroons were on the plantation, and that they were burning the cane fields, I was certain that Professor Kabaka had come to set me at liberty.

But I was not yet a free woman. Indeed, I had a terrible fear that I was now in greater danger than I had ever been, for I did not know what fresh evil my tormentors might conceive, or how carelessly they might discard my life, now that their own lives were in jeopardy.

After Mr. Monthan had gone, someone picked me up by the hair and stood me next to Mr. Cavendish, who, though he looked as if he had just been startled from a lewd dream, grabbed hold of my arm and said nothing. It was the consummation of a fear that had pursued him, for all I knew, as long as he had been in the island, but now that his fear had become a reality, he was the very picture of self-control. Mr. Drax and the others went into the field office in order to arm themselves, and Mr. Cavendish began to walk in the direction of the long-house, dragging me along beside him. At every moment I expected him to strike me or sink a knife into my back, or else throw me down and do what he had long been threatening to do.

Soon we came to the yard of packed earth where the other students had been cooking their evening meal, and we found them very much agitated by the shouting and the smoke, for they had not yet learned the reason for these alarms. Here, still holding my arm in his moist but irresistible grip, Mr. Cavendish seemed to become quite cheerful, and he commenced a species of oration on the subject of globalization, which he held to be a great good, though inevitably, as he said, there were disagreements such as that which was now being adjudicated in the fields. As he spoke, I felt one of his red eyes upon me, goggling, as it did, apparently free of regard for its fellow, in his large and misshapen head. Later I came to believe that he had gone quite mad, for he seemed perfectly insensible to the disaster that was unfolding around him, and of which the other students were just now becoming aware. He insisted once again, as he had so many times, that he could not trust the local labor force, for though they were "tinctured with the language and outward bearing of piety," yet they remained capable of anything. Indeed, he said, if they purported to love the Bible, they loved it only "as a Roman Catholic girl loves the doll of a Madonna, which she dresses with muslin and ribbons.

"And yet what shall I do? Shall I set them at liberty? As two-thirds of them have been born upon the plantation, and many of them are lame, dropsical, and of a great age, to do so would, of all misfortunes that could happen to them, be the most cruel."

We listened with a kind of awe to these absurdities. The infernal glow of the burning cane was now visible in the sky, and this in addition to the great quantity of sweet smoke, which had a very distinct smell, like burnt caramel, gave the night the appearance of a region of Hell.

But now, at last, Mr. Cavendish seemed to come to himself, for he turned suddenly and squinted into the smoke. Huge shadows rose up and flickered and died away again, so that it was impossible to say if there were men in the fields, or if these were only the fantastic shapes thrown up in the firelight by the dancing cane.

Now several things happened. First, Mr. Cavendish released me, and I retreated immediately to the edge of the yard. Next, Mr. Drax and Mr. Hertfordshire came around the corner of the longhouse, both of them now armed with rifles, and commenced firing into the smoke. Then Mr. Cavendish started toward the longhouse, no doubt to take cover, but he had not gone more than a few steps when he was lifted off the ground in a most peculiar way, as if tugged off his feet by a receding wave, and before my eyes, so slowly that I could watch every change of expression on his face, he was pulled gently apart, an arm now detaching itself from his trunk, and then an ear spinning slowly into the night. A moment later I realized that the noise of gunfire had alarmed my hearing, for now sound returned in a murmuring rush, even as Mr. Cavendish fell to the ground. His head was broken like one of the clay pots we used for cooling sugar, and blood covered all.

Mr. Drax and Mr. Hertfordshire had fled without my seeing them go, and suddenly there were men all about. I knew at once that these were the maroons, and indeed they were a dreadful lot, for they had wild hair, and were tattooed all over, and had no shirts upon their backs, nor shoes, and their speech was so rough that I could make out only one word in three.

So often, lying upon my worm-eaten pallet during my first weeks in the island, I had dreamed that Professor Kabaka might descend from the mountains and carry me off to freedom. Yet now, when I had every reason to believe that he was upon the plantation, and indeed when I might have expected to see him at any moment, I experienced a feeling closely allied with heartbreak. Indeed, I think I can say that I was quite heartbroken, for I had before my eyes the tangible proof that he was not the man I thought he was, nor indeed a man with whom I would have willingly spent even a moment of my time. My crucial realization was this, specifically that not until that moment had I allowed myself to believe that he might make so bold as to translate his thought, and his fiery speech, into bloody action. Now that he had done so, I saw that whatever love or admiration I had felt for him was based upon the fiction of his good nature, and now that my cherished image of him was extinguished, I was left, in a manner of speaking, bereft.

But I could not pause to savor this exquisite disappointment, for I had a decision to make, namely whether to stay where I was and trust that I should be used well by the maroons, or else to flee and take my chances upon the wild paths of the jungle. And indeed it was not an easy choice, for although I could not be sure who these men were, nor whether they served under Professor Kabaka or under another maroon leader, I nevertheless had good reason to believe that they wished me well, and that they had come to free me from the tyranny of the Big Anna corporation. Yet at the same time, their probable intentions notwithstanding, I did not like the idea of remaining dependent upon the desires and calculations of others, nor did I relish the prospect of meeting Professor Kabaka here, in this dismal place, after what I had just seen.

Before I knew what I was doing, and almost without having decided to do so, I was running through the rows of smoky cane. The ground was hardly visible beneath my feet, and I was cut all over by the leaves of that terrible plant, but I pushed on, heedless of these discomforts, and made as near as I could guess for the eastern boundary of the plantation. I could not have fled west in any case, for the fields in that direction were all aflame.

I ran for some twenty or thirty minutes, until I had put at least a few miles between myself and the plantation. When I had recovered my wits, having come by now to the wasted and poisoned fields beside the Big Anna factory, and supposing myself secure in that desolate place, though of course I had a great fear of snakes and other ravenous beasts, I sat down and hugged my knees, and there I wept for some considerable time, while the sky to the west was all alight, and the factory continued its nightmarish work some distance away. In truth I felt that Mr. Cavendish had deserved what he had gotten, nor was it difficult to recall innumerable examples of that man's cruelty, even excluding the events of that very night, but at the same time it had been an awful thing to see him picked apart by gunfire, as it would have been awful to see any human being thus mutilated, for it reminded me how provisional and how fragile is our life in this world.

After a period of ten minutes, or perhaps much longer, I succeeded in banishing that dreadful image from my mind, and at the same time I realized that I could not stay where I was, for I was quite without shelter in that field, and there was every reason to believe that Big Anna employees in the factory would soon learn of what had happened nearby, and would shortly be abroad, so I picked myself up and continued on.

I traveled all that night and into the morning. I was horribly confused in my mind, but I understood that it was better now to avoid giving the slightest advertisement of my condition, and not to make myself conspicuous in an attempt to remain inconspicuous, for I did not know who I could trust in the island, or who might be an agent for Big Anna. Therefore I tied a rag around my head as a sort of head scarf, after the fashion of the local women, whom I resembled enough at a glance, and I continued east, first across newly harvested cane fields and then, in the first light of dawn, along a dirt road. I was at least an hour upon this road before I encountered another soul, it being still very early. This was a young man, an islander, and when he asked me where I was going, I explained that I was going to visit my sister, who lived not far away. As my accent was unfamiliar to him, he became suspicious, but I persuaded him that I was not from the United States, as he had guessed, but from another island to the north, and that my sister had come here with her husband some years before. It was a preposterous story, and I had little hope of its being believed, deciding that if he expressed further suspicion, or if he attempted to lay his hands upon me, I would pick up a rock and therewith attempt to crush his skull, but he let me pass, saying only that if I wanted to have some experience of a real man, I had only to ask for him in San Pedro. He seemed to have no knowledge of the events of last night, and though he must have smelled or seen the smoke, which was impossible to ignore, he did not ask me about it.

I walked for another hour or more, until I was in a more densely wooded place. Here I had less fear of being seen, but I was afraid that my presence would occasion more suspicion, there being nowhere I could plausibly be going to, so I kept off the road and made but slow progress through the jungle, which grew thicker as the land rose toward the mountains. There were enormous silk-cotton trees hung all about with great vines and creepers, and there were tree ferns, palmettos, and all manner of unfamiliar flowers, nor was the place at all silent, for birds and other creatures made a great racket as I passed. Later that day, a gray parrot addressed a greeting to me, saying, "Hello," in the distinct voice of a woman in her mature years, and I was much impressed by the oddity of that event.

By evening, I came to an abandoned estate, which I knew to be a cocoa estate, having read of such places in the program materials I had received before coming to the island. The cocoa grew in the shade of tall trees, and the pods were of many colors, reds and purples as well as greens, and there was a scent in the air which I took to be vanilla or some similar pod or bean. But it was plain that no one had lived here in some time, for the paths were all overgrown, and the plants had not been tended, and there were shaggy coffee bushes growing abundantly among the cocoa, their red berries very striking in the green dusk. It was cooler among the trees, though still very warm, and the scent was delicious. I pressed on and soon came to the old estate house, which was a sprawling edifice of a single story, with elaborate woodwork and a verandah on three sides. It was mostly overgrown now, and even collapsed in places, the white ants of the tropics having done their work.

Beside the house were fruit trees, which were derelict and unsightly after long neglect, but upon which there was some fruit nonetheless. Only now did I realize how hungry I was, for it had been at least twenty-four hours since I had last eaten, and perhaps longer. I ate some grapefruit, which is here called "the forbidden fruit," and also a small soursop, as well as some of the coffee fruit, which gave me the same thrill that a cup of coffee might have done. It amused me to spit out the coffee seeds, which elsewhere are considered the only useful part. At some distance from the house I also found a jackfruit tree, the bulbous and irregular produce of which recalled to my mind the shape of Mr. Cavendish's head. I had already begun to hammer at the fruit with a rock, splitting it into two irregular hemispheres, when suddenly my sight was oppressed by an image of that man, and the terrible grimace I had seen on his face as the bullets tore his life away, and though I was still ravenously hungry, yet I could eat no more. I picked my way up onto the verandah, where I went to sleep on a bench, for it was too hot to sleep inside the house, and the mosquitoes would have had no more difficulty getting at me inside than out.

I woke early the next morning, oppressed by cramps and wind as a result of having eaten so much fruit on an empty stomach, and yet I could not remain to luxuriate in that discomfort, nor would I receive any sympathy from the beasts of the jungle, so I left that place and continued on my way. By afternoon I had reached an altitude from which it was possible, by the fleeting glimpses I had through the trees, to see the flat-lands stretched out below me, and to gauge their extent, and mark out a path toward San Cristobal in the north.

I saw a few Ghost Apple trees, which were heavy with fruit, but thankfully I knew enough to disdain them, for they are said to be poisonous. Then I came upon a sapodilla tree. Though I had seen this fruit before and I knew it was much prized, I had never tasted it, and I did not know how important it was to eat it only when it was perfectly soft and ripe. I placed one of the small, firm fruits into my mouth and began to chew, and the milky white sap was so powerfully adhesive that I thought I would choke, my throat having been glued shut. I was forced to scrape the sticky pulp out of my mouth with my fingers, and only after some ten minutes of coughing and spitting did I succeed in overcoming this discomfort.

After this I was wary, though I soon found another stunted grapefruit tree and refreshed myself well enough. Thus I kept from starving, although the reader who, perusing this chronicle of woe in the safety of his armchair, supposes that a diet of tropical fruit may be counted a luxury, is advised that the body continually cries out for something to accompany it, even if it be only a glass of milk or a crust of bread, for the sweetness of the fruit seems to suck the strength from the blood. I was all this time in a state of the most unendurable discomfort, moreover, having been bitten all over by insects, and suffering greatly in the heat, for St. Renard is so hot that one may pick a mango green and find it ripe when one has raised it to the mouth, and spoiled after a few bites. It might have been a consolation that the night was cooler upon the hills than it was in the lowlands, but I could not sleep for thinking of Mr. Cavendish, his image now linked grotesquely to that of the battered jackfruit. In my exhausted state I saw the fruit splitting open again and again, and felt it yield under the rock, and imagined that I had been the one to break apart Mr. Cavendish's head, and that his head was filled with fibrous pith and fruity seed pods.

With the dawn I felt somewhat cheered, if not refreshed, for I soon chanced upon a kind of pass in the hills, and came through and down the other side, from which slope I could see the ocean, which was a glittering sunlit blue. From the position of the sun that morning I knew this to be the north coast. As I have said, my idea at this time was to make for San Cristobal, which was not far distant, for I knew there would be hotels and resorts, and tourists in whose company I should feel safe, and in that place I could contact my parents. I also held out a hope of meeting with my friend William Brees, who was the dean of students at Tripoli, for he had told me he might be coming to the island, and though I did not believe him at the time, knowing how slowly he moved, and how indecisive he was, yet now I was ready to believe anything.

I had only a few hours' journey left to me, for I could see the city well enough, and there were signs of habitation now: men and women among the trees, at work on their provision grounds, and crude shacks with palm roofs, and all manner of garbage scattered in the undergrowth. But I had not seen any fruits that morning, nor had I collected any to carry with me the day before, and hunger soon lay heavy upon me, for I was not used to going very long without nutriment. I tried eating some sea almonds, but I could not separate the hard rind from the nut. Later I came across a stand of very small banana plants and, thinking myself saved, I picked their diminutive fruit, which was quite red, and ventured to taste it, but it was like chalk and ash in my mouth, these plants being, as I later discovered, an ornamental variety gone wild. So I had nothing to eat that morning, nor did I want to appeal to those islanders I saw now and then, for I did not feel that I could place my trust in the Renardennes if I did not know to whom their allegiance was compelled.

At last I came to the shantytown which is known as "Buzzard Point." This neighborhood extends east from the margins of San Cristobal and swarms up the slopes of the hills. I kept to the less trafficked parts of that neighborhood, where dogs and children scrounged among the garbage or slept beneath rusted sheets of corrugated iron. At first the houses in this place were little better than the derelict huts in which the islanders on the plantation had lived, and there were many that were as bad, but the aspect of the place improved as I walked west, and soon I came to a paved road, and I began to see shops and stalls offering items which were plainly intended for tourists, such as T-shirts, carved pieces of mahogany, alarm clocks fashioned from conch shells, and pieces of coral rock.

I intended to throw myself upon the mercy of the first tourists I met, eager to bring my ordeal to a close by whatever means I could. And now, to my great joy, I saw Americans again, being able to identify them at a glance by their complexions and their glossy hair, as well as by their general exuberance. I went up to the first of these people that I saw, a couple in their middle years, and with tears in my eyes I began to describe my condition, and to beg them for assistance. But no sooner had I opened my mouth than the eyes of the man went dark, and he began shaking his head, at the same time taking his wife by the upper arm and conducting her across the narrow street. In torment, I followed after them, almost shouting now, and indeed hardly able to control myself for the exhaustion, hunger, and anger that I felt. And yet I was too filthy, and my general appearance too incredible after days in the jungle, to convince them that I was an American like themselves, and only temporarily disadvantaged. Nor did it help that I was nearly as dark as the peddlers and beggars who oppressed tourists in these places, shouting entreaties and demands as they passed. I still had my head scarf, moreover, having found it useful not only as protection against the sun, but also for the pressure it exerted on my forehead, that pressure helping to alleviate the discomfort of my headaches, from which I had been suffering in the last day.

I made a second attempt to engage the attention of some tourists, and this time, although they might have been deaf for all the attention they paid my cries of lament, a woman snapped a photograph of me as I stood beseeching her with my arms outstretched.

Thereafter, downhearted and very much exhausted, I sat down on a broken crate in the shade of a sea almond tree, its rusty leaves scattered all around me. Upon the crate I saw the hateful emblem of the Big Anna corporation. At this time, it seemed as if there were no place in the world I might turn to for help, my clothes having turned to rags and my shoes having fallen apart, leaving me with no outward sign of my identity, and indeed, save for my accent, which had gone unremarked by the Americans I had confronted, no manner of proving who I was, and where I had come from.

Though I was very much distracted by hunger, and indeed wretched in every respect, it did occur to me to wonder why there were no more visible signs of the chaos that reigned in the interior of the island. Indeed, it might have been a day like any other, with tourists snapping photographs, and locals accosting them, and policemen with saturnine expressions lounging on the street corners. I had only the smoke, and a brief glimpse of a Big Anna military convoy, to convince me that the events of the last days had been no dream.

Upon the corner opposite was a coconut seller of East Indian appearance, as indeed there are many East Indians in the island, descendants themselves of coerced laborers. I fancied that this man was now looking at me with an expression of particular attention, though all this time he was speaking most demonstratively with an

American woman who stood sipping the coconut water from a colored straw. When she had gone, he stood watching me for some time longer and then took up his machete and began cutting the rind from a coconut, and making an opening at the top, and then he came over to where I was and presented the coconut to me, saying that I looked as if I could use it.

I drank the coconut water, which was not sweet, but rather of a cooling, astringent mineral flavor, and directly I felt stronger, and told the man thank you. He said once again that I looked as if I could use the coconut, and he asked if I knew that coconut water was the most healthful substance to be found in the natural world, being almost identical in the balance of its minerals to the humors of the body. I replied that I believed it. He then divided the empty coconut into several sections and cut the meat from the rind, handing it to me piece by piece, and I ate it, though it hurt my stomach, for never had anything tasted so wonderful.

The coconut seller did not press me to give an account of myself, but my eyes filled with tears at the kindness he had shown me, and feeling that I could trust him, there being nothing but goodness in his eyes, I revealed myself to him, and told him my story, omitting only that part which concerned the killing of Mr. Cavendish, for I could not bear to think of that now. He was amazed at my relation, and could scarcely believe his ears, frequently asking me to repeat myself, and to elaborate a point, and to return to a previous one, talking all the while in an excited voice. When I had finished, both of us had tears in our eyes, and he insisted that he would do all he could to help me, and more.

Though I had intended to call my parents as soon as I was able, yet now, much to my surprise, I found that I did not relish the idea of such a phone call, for indeed how could I explain to them what had happened? I will go so far as to say that I felt a kind of embarrassment, as if my predicament had been some fault of my own.

For this reason I resolved to determine whether William Brees was still in the island, if indeed he had come in the first place, and to do that I had only to find a computer, for I knew that he updated his Facebook profile religiously, thus preserving a record of all that he did and thought, and of everywhere he went. Therefore I asked the coconut seller if he could lend me a few pennies so that I could buy myself a few minutes in a nearby internet café, and this he was most eager to do.

I can hardly describe the delight I felt when I set my fingers upon the computer keyboard, and watched the glowing windows flicker and dance before my eyes, for it was as if I were home already. In a matter of moments I had the information I sought, for I discovered, to my great relief, that William Brees was indeed still in the island, and that he was staying nearby, in a bed-and-breakfast called A Piece of the Indies. I was greatly comforted, for I had no doubt that he would be eager to help me, and now I could delay that conversation with my parents, the thought of which was the source of such complex feelings, and painful emotions.

I asked the coconut seller to direct me to A Piece of the Indies, which he promptly did, and I arrived there after a walk of no more than ten minutes. It was a pretty house, embosomed in sweet-smelling shrubberies, and in the brilliant sunshine it seemed so far removed from the plantation upon which I had lately toiled that for the briefest moment I felt as if I had come to a different island altogether, and I remembered those dreams of tropical sunsets and soft air that had so enchanted me as I sat beside my radiator at Tripoli three or four months before. This impression was confirmed by the sense I had that no one in the city had any information about the violence in the interior. Indeed, were it not for the smell of the burning cane, I might have thought it had all been a dream.

I found Dean Brees in a state of prostration, so sick was he with an unnamed fever, and indeed I will venture to say that he was made sicker still by the abhorrent prescriptions of his physician, who had forced him to swallow all manner of foul tinctures and suspensions, and indeed to violate his nether-parts with a most curious instrument, for the doctor had diagnosed a venereal complaint, when in fact Dean Brees was probably suffering from nothing more than the flu.

Here, at last, after all my trials, I wept, and I wept not because my ordeal was at an end, though of course I felt the greatest relief on that account, but because I was now in the company of a man who had never been anything but kind to me, and who respected the choices I had made, and in front of whom I knew it was safe to weep. Nor did he fail to comfort me as best he could, though he was very weak, and feverish. Thus it was that sitting there with him, and looking down upon him where he lay sweating and shivering, I realized that although we could hardly have had less in common, he, and not Professor Kabaka, was the person after whom I ought to model myself, for he had taught me that simplest and most valuable of human lessons, the importance of kindness.

I placed a cold washcloth on his brow and then I took some money from his wallet and purchased him some Tylenol at the corner store. Then I undertook the preparations for our departure, purchasing two plane tickets with his credit card, packing his suitcase, and obtaining for myself some new clothes. He was soon feeling much better, and though he was not yet well we took ourselves off to the airport, whence we departed that very night. But of this I will say no more, for my deliverance was at hand, and my own sufferings at an end. Thus I bring my narration to a close, leaving the island of St. Renard stretched out below in the warmth of the Caribbean night, suspended as it were between the bloody past and the uncertain future.

UNDERCOVER DEAN: BLOG POST #8

Even though I hadn't seen any of the plantations or factories, my dinner at Mr. Price's house seemed to confirm all the worst things I'd ever heard about the business ethos of Big Anna®. It made me embarrassed to be an American. So I can't say I was surprised when I began to hear rumors of strikes and other conflicts on the island.

Commandant Kabaka had made it clear that he wouldn't shrink from violence, but he didn't post news about actual events, and I was having trouble getting concrete information about the situation in the interior of the island. One day the air was full of sweet smoke, and another day I saw three fierce-looking black men tramping down the street with rifles on their shoulders, but the *Saint Renard Times* was always full of the same tourist stuff: "Peggy Nutmeg to Perform at High Times Casino!" "Pompey's Makes the Best Conch Fritters in the Caribbean!" Every day I was more concerned about Megan and the other Tripoli students, but it was impossible to arrange transportation to the interior.

One morning, two or three weeks after the dinner at Mr. Price's house, I woke up feeling a little strange. There was a kind of echoing or reverberating noise in my head, and I almost fell over as I got out of bed. I chalked it up to a bad night's sleep and went down to the courtyard for some coffee.

Downstairs, I saw a group of young men and women I didn't recognize. They were dressed formally—the men in carefully pressed suits, the women in lacy gowns of the sort that Lady Nugent had been wearing—so I assumed they were here on business and I decided to ask if they knew anything about the political situation. I called one of the young men over and put the question to him directly:

"Can you tell me anything about the strikes and conflicts in the interior? I'm concerned about a friend of mine."

But my voice sounded strange to me, and suddenly I began to sweat. It was like a light going on. One minute I was dry and comfortable, the next my clothes were soaked. I was also keenly aware of my pulse, which was strong and fast, like the ticking of a watch.

"We represent the Free Produce Society of Pennsylvania," the young man said. "We're organizing a boycott of all slave-grown produce, and that includes everything marketed under the Big Anna® trademark."

He passed me a flyer, which I'll reproduce here because it made a powerful impression on me at the time. In my feverish state, I felt certain that I'd found a way in which I could contribute to the struggle against Big Anna®. The flyer read as follows:

WHEREAS there are many persons, who while they deplore the existence of Slavery, indirectly contribute to its support and continuance by using articles derived from the labor of Slaves:— And whereas we are satisfied, that by a proper union of reasonable efforts, articles similar to those which are thus produced, may be obtained by *free* labor:—And believing that the general use of such articles among us as are raised by Freemen, will gradually establish a conviction in the minds of those who hold their fellow-creatures in bondage, that their own interests would be promoted by the increased quantity, and more ready sale, of their produce, resulting from the change of the condition of their Slaves into that of hired Freemen:—

Therefore,—We whose names are hereunto subscribed do agree to form an Association under the title of

THE FREE PRODUCE SOCIETY OF PENNSYLVANIA

The anachronistic language seemed just right, and I had a wild idea that by making this analogy with the bloody past, which we were all supposed to have transcended, they'd have no trouble shaming people into joining the boycott. How could any good person argue against it, after all?

But then, almost as quickly, my spirits fell once again. One of the young men was outlining his plans for the boycott, but although I strained to listen, it was like I had couch cushions tied to my head. I was still sweating buckets, and now I worried that my tongue had started to taste funny. I could hardly tell if it was today or yesterday or two hundred years ago.

"We think the practice of slavery is morally, religiously, and economically indefensible . . ."

There was a mango tree next to the pool, and for the first time I realized that it was hung with miniature fruit. It came to me suddenly that it would soon be dropping big sticky mangoes all over the pool deck.

"Who'll clean it up?" I said.

I thought I should tell someone to snip the little mangoes off right away, before they could cause any trouble.

"Just bring me a ladder and I'll do it."

But suddenly the mangoes started to swell and burst, and hunks of sweet fruit fell into the pool with an offensive *plop plop* sound, and I thought I was dreaming, and do you know what? I *was* dreaming!

When I came to, one of the young men was holding me by the shoulders and another was standing very close, looking into my eyes. The sharp shadows of the royal palms seemed to bite into my skin.

A doctor had been summoned. Mr. Codrington, the proprietor, brought me a cup of sage tea.

I spent the rest of the morning in bed, alternately sweating and freezing, clicking the air conditioner on and off, and drinking cup after cup of this mysterious sage tea, which was delicious. When I slept, I had ferocious nightmares. In one of them, two slave girls cut Bish Pinkman III into small pieces and fed him to me. I kept trying to refuse, but they wouldn't hear of it, and eventually I decided that it would be impolite to disdain this food they'd taken so much trouble to prepare, so I ate the bloody hunks with a smile of gratitude.

I woke up later to find the doctor standing beside the bed with Mr. Codrington.

"I sometimes think this island is incompatible with virtue," Codrington was saying. "A young man arrives, and no sooner has he stepped off the boat than he feels he can now drink, wench, and blaspheme without a sigh or a blush."

There was no doubt that he was talking about me, even though I was older than he was.

"He simply continues until a premature death puts a period on his sufferings and excesses."

Seeing that I was awake, the doctor gave me a very stern look and offered me a slip of paper. It was entirely filled with dark, cramped handwriting—a prescription—and even now, back home at Tripoli and restored to health, I can only make out the first two lines:

R. Vin. antimon. Zip.   *sign.* puke.
R. Sal. catt. amor. Zip.   *sign.* purge.

"The prescription," the doctor said, "is one vomit, two boluses, one phial of injection, an electuary, and a purge, all marked thus, and you are to be rigidly strict in taking them as follows: The first night you are to take the vomit by swallowing a tablespoonful every ten minutes by a watch until it operates, then to work it off with large and repeated drafts of lukewarm water, until you puke seven or eight times . . ."

I tried to interrupt him, but he raised his hand and continued. He went on and on. Codrington was writing it down. I simply closed my eyes and concentrated on my breathing.

"At night repeat the bolus," the doctor was saying, "and the third day repeat the purge. If in six days you do not find the discomfort much abated, repeat the boluses and electuary. You must not omit every day to bathe and wash the parts two or three times . . ."

"What parts?" I said.

". . . and every night when going to bed to rub a small bit of the ointment to the butt and under-part of the penis."

"I think there's been a misunderstanding," I said. "It's just the heat, the mosquitoes. I caught a bug or something."

The doctor rolled his eyes. "Intemperance destroys many more constitutions than anything inimical in the climate."

He gave me some dietary advice. I was to avoid greasy foods, windy and flatulent foods, spicy and salty foods. Bread, *panada*, barley gruel, and linseed tea were to be my only nourishment for a few days.

When he'd gone, Codrington went out to have the prescription filled, and I fell asleep and dreamed that Megan and I were married, and Bish Pinkman was our child.

Codrington came back to deliver the mysterious medications, but now that my fever had spiked again, I was so disoriented that my only concern was to follow the doctor's instructions to the letter. I didn't want him to be disappointed in me.

Codrington prepared the so-called "vomit" himself, and reminded me to take it by the tablespoon until it operated. I'll spare the reader a description of this part of my ordeal.

The next morning I was well enough to come downstairs and drink a cup of weak tea. The Free Produce people were there again, now dressed in shorts and T-shirts. They were very polite and kind, asking after my health and trying to include me in their conversation, but I still felt weak. After about fifteen minutes, I went back to bed.

The fever returned in the early afternoon, and in my delirium I wandered into the bathroom and ate at least half a tube of toothpaste. I vomited for what seemed like forever, and when Codrington found me I was curled up on the floor of the bathroom, encrusted in dried toothpaste. I was dreaming that I was a naked slave girl! I remember worrying that Codrington could see the inside of my dreams, and I was very ashamed.

The next morning the fever was gone once again, but I was feeling wiped out. I tried eating some oatmeal, which tasted wonderful and wholesome, and then I got into the pool and tried to relax for a little while.

But the fever returned, and Codrington kept forcing me to take the bolus and the electuary—a kind of sweet paste—and it seemed like I'd never get better as long as I was taking all that medicine. I had bizarre, vivid dreams once again, so that when I woke up late the next morning and saw Megan standing at the foot of my bed, dressed in rags and thin as a rail, I was certain I was still asleep.

"Pinch me," I said.

But she started crying. She hugged me. I didn't know what to do or think or feel and I just hugged her back and told her that everything would be okay. And in that moment, after everything that had happened, I believed it. Everything would be okay. I missed my wife so much that I could hardly stand it, but I *could* stand it.

From: "Maggie Bell" <mbell1990@tripoli.edu>
To: "Chris Bell" <cfb456@mercurylink.net>
Date: March 24, 2010, at 1:00 PM
Subject: (no subject)

Mr. C,

It's only because I worry about how Mom and Dad will react.
Dad would say all the wrong things, call people up, yell at them,
cause trouble. All I want now is quiet, so don't worry. I know maybe
I didn't make sense on the phone. I'm just exhausted. But yes, that
is what I need you to do. Don't say anything. Just think good
thoughts about me and I'll be home in a few days. I'm staying with
the dean this weekend.

I don't know. A person could go crazy trying to think through to
the truth of it. Plenty of good people eat Big Anna junk food and
wear underwear made by kids in Southeast Asia, and the same
people spend their time writing petitions to raise the minimum wage
and ban plastic grocery bags. It doesn't make them hypocrites. It
makes them people living in an imperfect world. The only lesson is
the basic one, which you don't have to work on a sugar plantation
to learn: Just try every day to be better, and never stop trying.

Capitalism. I don't know. Capitalism means pain and fear but also
a walk on the moon and a hybrid car and this email and all the
comforts that make life less bad. Capitalism is just people and when
we say it's evil, we're really just expressing our disappointment with
people. In the fact that people are not better than they are. That
they're just people.

I've spent the last day or two sitting out on the porch in the cold,
drinking tea and staring at the melting snow and the spring rain. I

feel fine. I've decided that I'm allowed, after everything that happened, to feel fine. The thing I learned is that I'm tough. I always thought so and now I know for sure.

Jeez, man. We'll be okay. I love you,

M

Christina Montana
Prof. Collier, English 401b
Creative Nonfiction Assignment
April 3, 2010

AT HOME WITH PRESIDENT BECKFORD

Inside the museum it was unendurably hot, the walls were running with moisture, the hygrothermographs had been destroyed and the pieces were scattered through the ravaged galleries, a scroll here and a needle there, and someone said that he'd said that humidity was good for the paintings, but maybe he despised the paintings, it didn't matter, the truth was that in the unbearable lethargy and mortifying reek of that museum there was no room for motive or decision or even impulse, there was only the roaring silence of a haunted orchidarium and the overwhelming musk of a perfumery in flames. We didn't know where to turn in that disorder of violated sarcophagi, it seemed as if time had stopped, nothing moved, nothing mattered to us any longer, certainly not the minor procedural concern that had brought us here, a matter of getting our schedules signed, of getting him to sign off on our course selections for the fall, because after everything he was still acting chancellor of the English Department, such things were his responsibility, paperwork was paperwork and paperwork must be done, we couldn't expect Tripoli's antique computer systems to adjust to the capricious whims of mankind.

A filthy derelict of a man, dressed in the uniform of a porter or footman from another time, met us in the prehistoric gloom of the Brewster Gallery and introduced himself as Mr. Bish Pinkman III, associate director of the Vocational Writing Program. He asked if he could bring us something to drink, coffee or tea or wine, and he offered us handfuls of sinister white tablets, which he had arranged on a dull salver from the college's collection of antique silverware. To satisfy the demands of our anxiety, we ordered wine, we ordered chilled white wine, we hoped it would cool us down, but even more we hoped it would calm our hammering hearts and enable us to keep our heads long enough to navigate out of that evil paradise of smoldering Dumpsters and indistinguishable trash-heap exhibits and early American paintings covered with the most obscene graffiti. Only when he turned to go did we see that Mr. Pinkman III was hobbled, there were small dumbbells bound to his ankles with chain and baler twine, it was ghoulish, and we listened with horror as the ghastly thump of his homemade shoes died away. In the quiet that followed we could hear impossible sounds, we could hear children talking softly, dogs whimpering, tormented birds singing show tunes, the martial rhythm of construction. We could not swear to the reality of any of this and we had already begun to accept that what we heard and saw in that place was only as real as we made it, no more, so that when Mr. Pinkman III returned and handed us trophy cups filled with cane liquor, we drank and drank, we felt an animal thirst, we didn't care why he'd asked what we wanted if he was only going to bring cane liquor, it turned out that cane liquor was just what we wanted. We helped ourselves to some of his white tablets, why not, to hell with it, we'd follow the slope all the way to the bottom.

In the entry hall we saw maintenance trucks parked among the garbage and the medical waste and the ruined antiques, we saw stuffed flamingoes from the natural history collection twisted into impossible contortions, we saw a blind man striking his twisted knee with a gavel. Mr. Pinkman III walked ahead of us without asking where we needed to go and what we needed to do, he walked ahead without guiding us, talking to himself, weeping softly, arguing a point, but he could only be taking us to him, where else was there to go, so that when we reached the furnace heat and jungle damp of the upper floors, when we saw the huge continents of mold on the walls, when we thought we could not go any further because of the swelling in our feet and the fluttering of our hearts, we knew these could only be his own private rooms and offices, and they were not guarded by a three-headed jaguar, as we had heard, or by a statue with eyes that could burn a student to cinders within her clothes, as some of us had read, but only by a clacking bead curtain drawn across the doorway. We went in, withdrawing our folded schedules from our pockets, we remembered now why we had come, it was absurd but it was a requirement, the fine for a late schedule was twenty-five dollars.

And there he was, it was him, he had a fine mist of white hair and delirious blue eyes and teeth like we had never seen, they were like piano keys, and he was sitting on a throne in that riot of broken Mayan stelae, of dead orchids, a potted banana tree, a dismantled vehicle, so many other things, treasures of pre-Columbian art, junk and trash, a portable toilet stuffed with prints from the looted gift shop. He asked us if we wanted some coconut wine, he was just about to enjoy a thimbleful, the stuff was packed with electrolytes, and we said sure, why not, to hell with it, and how about a few more white tablets? Mr. Pinkman III came hurrying across the gallery in his madman's shoes, those shoes that were made from rawhide and loneliness and duct tape, and he distributed the coconut wine, a trophy cup for each of us and a thimble for him, he didn't require more, he was pickled in the brine of his unconquerable scholastic ambition, he was mummified by time passing, always passing, he was only a man after all, and he was petrified by his stony asceticism. Everything had been said of him in his very long life and we wondered what could be true. He had been a pirate in the Cayman Islands, a smuggler in the Florida straits, a wrecker on Key West, he had witnessed the advent of steam, he had been a founding partner of Standard Oil, he had conceived of the Tropical Fruit and Rail Company during a night of lunatic sweats and visions, he had taught Benito Mussolini to play the clarinet, he and Teddy Roosevelt had sealed a blood pact by shooting each other in the thigh, it went on and on, what did it matter, the coconut wine was like the chill vapor of death, we knew that we would never leave that place, the past was more real to us than the world outside, that springtime world of radiant rain, so close and so remote in the tinted window.

He motioned for us to sit and we did, cross-legged in the garbage, pouring sweat and not looking at him now for fear that he had the faculty of bewitching students with his eyes, and then we handed our schedules to him and we heard his astonishing pronouncements, and they were astonishing because they seemed so clear, because they had a hallucinatory lucidity. Don't take this class, have you satisfied your pre-1800 requirement, avoid Carlyle, have you taken English 125a. His voice had a hypnotic quality, we could hardly keep our eyes open, it was impossible to say what time it was, or what day, or what season of the long academic year. He spoke without pause, telling us to extend ourselves, Latin is of great utility, you'll want to take three credit hours of English 565, you'll need a senior seminar, have you taken Math 215, do you have experience in weapons manufacture, you may want to check out Hertfordshire on postcolonial theory.

He was still talking when Mr. Pinkman III arrived and motioned for us to follow. The birds were singing their show tunes, the orchids filled the air with their whore's perfume, and he was still talking, he was unfazed, he had a great passion for requirements, he knew all the abbreviations, he knew the course catalog by heart, but he hadn't signed our schedules, we'd have to pay the fine after all.

MINUTES / APRIL 2010
FACULTY MEETING

The dispassionate secretary, who had missed the last two faculty meetings and had been looking forward to this one, at least insofar as he was capable of looking forward to anything, took too much Malpraxalin® beforehand, fell asleep on the toilet in the hallway bathroom, and arrived twenty minutes late. There were only six or seven faculty members in attendance, of whom several presented an even more dissipated appearance than the secretary himself, who had not bothered, or who had perhaps been unable, to fasten more than two of the six buttons on his shirt, and who wore a pair of filthy slippers instead of shoes.

There had been some trouble on St. Renard. The acting president was explaining that at least two sugar plantations had been forced to suspend operations following terrorist attacks by Professor Kabaka's Antillia Liberation Army (ALA), although he assured us that everything was now under control. His loyalties, of course, lay with Big Anna®, which he characterized as a "bulwark against the evil of colonial nationalism." In the same spirit, he moved that we condemn the actions of Professor Kabaka and the ALA.

At this time, or perhaps later, the secretary noticed a wet area on the front of his—that is, the secretary's own—trousers. Struggling to focus his eyes, and making full use of his still-reliable sense of smell, he determined that it was not urine, as he had expected, but only coffee. It was also interesting to see that steam was rising from his lap, which was an indication that the coffee was boiling hot. He felt no pain.

Ginnie Hampton, professor and chair of philosophy, was inclined to wonder if the situation on St. Renard was not more serious than the acting president would have had us believe. She apologized if her concerns seemed "hysterical," but she had read an article suggesting that conditions on Big Anna® plantations were actually quite frightful.

The acting president nodded gravely and responded as follows: "It would be improper to assert that all the narratives of whippings and mutilations that have been told here at Tripoli are absolutely false, but allowance must be made for the exaggeration so seldom disjoined from a description, and in general terms we may be sure that the treatment of laborers on St. Renard is mild and indulgent."

He added that we ought to pay no attention to "the perverted and exaggerated statements of the islanders themselves, who are particularly artful and dexterous at misrepresentations of this nature."

Francis Amundsen, sycophant and professor of English, tipped over in his chair and fell heavily to the floor. The acting president paused momentarily, and Professor Hampton took advantage of this pause to ask whether we had any information about our students in the Field Studies Program. She assumed they were "perfectly safe," but it was just as well to make sure.

The acting president responded by saying that the students displayed "few indications of being deeply affected with their fate." The truth was that "from being divided into watches, and plentifully fed with syrup and ripe canes, they preserved their health remarkably well."

This was probably not the response that Professor Hampton had expected—indeed, for anyone not overcome with dispassion, it was cause for alarm—and she was perhaps justified in asking what he meant by "their fate." But the acting president declined to elaborate. He said that he would answer that question with another question, as follows:

"How much is a single human life worth?"

No doubt this question was supposed to be rhetorical, but Lincoln Harcourt, professor of economics, who was no more troubled than the secretary by the grim implications of this reply, immediately undertook to answer it.

The simplest solution, he explained, would be to quantify a particular attribute like earning potential or the capacity to do physical labor. Provided that some scale of value were determined beforehand, one could then rank people according to their economic importance. But the virtue of such an approach was only relative or comparative, and it would not enable one to compare people from different environments. Alternatively, one might attempt to compute the integral value of all the expenses— e.g., food, education, clothing, housing—associated with the production of a given human person. But no—and here Professor Harcourt tittered and slapped his forehead—this was, again, only good for comparative purposes. Perhaps one could calculate some "absolute value" like the energy content of the body—a value which could be expressed in joules or calories, according to preference, just as one would express the energy content of a snack product. According to this model, however, the largest people would prove the most valuable—a potentially objectionable outcome.

He concluded by saying, "It's probably best to go back to the basics. A person is worth whatever another person is willing to pay to get him."

The secretary, who had been following the discussion closely for several minutes, must have allowed his attention to wander, or perhaps the foregoing had been a dream or hallucination. When he came to himself, the acting president was speaking once again, and speaking loudly. His theme was Big Anna® and the island of St. Renard. Several times he referred to himself as "president of the Ocean Sea."

Peering myopically around the room and looking, as it were, for clues, the secretary spotted a tarnished salver of white tablets on a table by the door. They seemed to glow and pulsate, a source of brilliant light in that atmosphere of gloom. He knew intuitively that these were Malpraxalin® tablets, for which he had lately developed a substantial need. How he had failed to notice them when he'd entered the room, he will never know. He now rose and began to stagger forward, realizing as he did so that he had gotten up too fast: Darkness, thicker or of a different quality than the darkness that now enveloped him at all times, descended quickly.

When the secretary regained consciousness, he was prostrate on the gray carpet, with what he hoped was only blood—and not, for instance, a liquefied portion of brain matter—leaking from his nose. Surely his collapse was a misfortune, but it was not a misfortune that it would have been profitable to dwell upon. Therefore he began to crawl forward on his hands and knees. From that position, he spied the unconscious form of Professor Amundsen stretched out beneath the table.

The secretary will never know how long this journey took— perhaps moments, perhaps days—but when he had finally managed to knock the dish of Malpraxalin® to the ground and force a few tablets into his mouth, he felt much better. That is to say, he felt much different.

The acting president was now making excuses for those Big Anna® executives who were stationed on St. Renard and who, "in some small way," had overstepped their authority and contributed to the atmosphere of confusion and disorder. But it was important not to get bogged down in individual cases. The critical thing was the long-term viability of the system. What could be done to strengthen the plantation complex on St. Renard?

In the first place, new legislation was called for. One suggestion that had gotten a lot of support in Big Anna® boardrooms was some form of "pass law" requiring laborers to obtain written permission from their employers whenever they left their plantations. Anyone, even a tourist, would be able to challenge a laborer and demand to see his or her pass, and if that laborer could not produce it, he or she would have to spend a night in jail. Laborers would thus be accountable to their employers at all times.

Professor Harcourt suddenly appeared before the secretary, who was now sitting beneath the table and whose first instinct was to bleat in a threatening manner and strike out with his fists. Professor Harcourt took no notice of this. He was not wearing shoes—a telltale sign—and his skin was bright yellow, like a lemon. He scooped some Malpraxalin® tablets into his mouth, began to chew with gusto, and walked unsteadily from the room.

And now, at long last and after who knew what extraordinary trials, William Brees, former or perhaps—who could say?—still current dean of students, made his return to Tripoli College. He materialized in the doorway like a man risen from the dead, a tall and crooked figure with watery eyes.

Was he surprised by the gruesome spectacle he saw before him? If he was, he gave no sign.

The acting president—or should one say the president of the Ocean Sea?—folded his hands and gave the dean an indulgent smile. No doubt encouraged by this sign of tolerance from one whom he may have regarded as an antagonist, the dean said he had some discouraging news for us. Were we ready to hear it? He said: "Big Anna® has enslaved our students on St. Renard!"

To this there was no reaction. Indeed, it was hardly a shock. One felt it to be true just as one feels, at the end of an intricately plotted murder mystery, not astonishment at the identification of the killer but satisfaction at the final exclusion of alternatives.

"There's no time to lose," he said.

He was dressed for the tropics in soiled linen and wicker sandals. He was not an impressive figure, nor indeed one who could hope to inspire much outrage, whatever the news he'd come to report.

The acting president bared his improbable teeth and said nothing.

Dean Brees wanted to propose a boycott of all Big Anna® products, as well as a boycott of all other products known to have been produced by slave labor—shoes made in East Asian sweatshops, for instance. He moved that we establish the "Free Produce Association of Tripoli College," which would set up an informational website through which one could purchase "free labor" alternatives to slave-produced goods. Could anyone, in good conscience and with an untroubled heart, continue buying Big Anna® products when they knew the real human cost? Could we make people understand that taking responsibility was not the same as accepting blame?

With this, the dean sat down and waited expectantly. There was something almost admirable about him, resolute and clearheaded as he was in this moment.

The acting president rose and thanked Dean Brees for his suggestions. In what seemed like a magnanimous gesture, he said that we could all applaud our colleague "for his tireless efforts on behalf of the downtrodden, etc." Needless to say, there could be no question of boycotting Big Anna® products—we were ourselves a Big Anna® product—but that didn't mean we couldn't heed the spirit of Dean Brees's remarks.

And that was all. The acting president simply pressed the meeting forward.

As for Professor Kabaka and the ALA, he said, Big Anna® Shock Troops™ had been dispatched and order had already been restored. The ALA was not a sophisticated fighting force, nor was it well supplied or well provisioned, and it had been a short campaign.

The bigger question was this: Was St. Renard, in the end, worth fighting for? Some Big Anna® executives had suggested that it was not, that it would be more sensible, in the long run, to move the bulk of the operation elsewhere. Given that we were better able to manage the disease environment than we'd been in the fifteenth and sixteenth centuries, there was talk of reestablishing the plantation complex on São Tomé or the "fever coast" of West Africa.

The secretary waited to see how Dean Brees would respond to this, but the old man had subsided into a placid slumber. There were to be no more objections from that quarter.

The acting president reminded everyone that Big Anna® also owned the Pacific island of Moahu, although the soil there was poor and the island itself very remote.

He said many other things besides, but the secretary could not be bothered to listen. Although the evening was well advanced, there was still an hour of daylight remaining. Spring had come and summer was not far behind. Indeed, it suddenly occurred to him that another academic year was coming to an end. Fatigue had set in, as it always did at this time, and exhaustion told on all the faces, both real and imaginary, that he saw ranged about him.

It was true also that he found himself prey to melancholy reflections. Everyone was a year older, after all, and death closer than ever. But there was a certain satisfaction in all of this. It had been a year of great changes and upheavals, to be sure, but it would end as all years must end, and in that sense it would have the same unvarying rhythm. No doubt time would smooth the wrinkles, homogenize the texture, and render it indistinguishable in memory from the years that had preceded it and the years that would follow. The secretary was a geologist, after all, and he knew better than anyone that the wild dreams of men were no more than a brief tingling on the skin of the earth. All of it, in the end, would come to nothing.

So he lay back, staring up at the underside of the table, and idly pressed Malpraxalin® tablets between his teeth. The light upon the wall was golden, or so he imagined. He heard the acting president faintly, as if through a long cardboard tube:

"The grand argument," he was saying, "against the continuation of the plantation system in general, is undoubtedly the terrible waste of life which it occasions, yet if we consider the alternatives . . ."

But the secretary had drifted off to sleep. And thus, no less surely than any other—though some questions were left unanswered, and some problems unsolved—the semester came to an end.

From: "Maggie Bell" <mbell1990@tripoli.edu>
To: "William Brees" <wbrees@tripoli.edu>
Date: April 8, 2010, at 4:15 PM
Subject: RE: Checking In

Hi, Bill,

I wouldn't get too discouraged. You're not going to draw any water at that well. I think your idea of a website is very smart, and these days it's easy enough to publicize these things.

I told Chris, but I didn't tell my parents anything. And then do you know what happened? Chris told Mom and Dad he was gay. Dad said, "Shit!" Practically the only time I've ever heard him swear. Then he hugged him and said he loved him, simple as that. I was amazed. I guess Mom already knew. She said, "Thank God that's over with!"

I'm actually doing very well. You know how when you get back from camping, you can't get enough of the hot shower and the clean towels and the food all right there in the fridge, no sand in it, no bugs? That's how I feel. Because it was bad, yes, but it wasn't the end of the world. It wasn't as bad as it could have been. And now I'm here, just sitting here, and aren't I allowed to be mostly okay? Of course I am.

Nothing in my life has ever tasted as good as the piece of carrot cake I ate in your house the day we got back.

What am I supposed to make of it all? As soon as you get past the immediate context, the things people do and the reasons they have for doing them begin to seem outrageous. Human life becomes a sinister cartoon. But maybe the truth is that we just invent or impute these complex motives, and really the only motives that matter are fear and love. And how do you know that love isn't just a kind of fear? This doesn't seem like a very satisfactory lesson, does it?

But how do you know, on the other hand, that fear isn't just a kind of love?

Do you know what I find strangest of all? The strangest thing is that one day, maybe not next year but maybe in five years or ten years, these last months will be nothing but a wan memory. Vague images, the impress of horror, nothing more. I won't remember that it was this particular bug bite on my ankle that itched more than any of the others. And that's nice.

For your help, your kindness, I can never say the right kind of thank-you.

Love,
M

Excerpted from

A True & Exact Historie of These Ilands of the
West Indies, with an account of the Carwak Indians,
and Observations upon the Newlie-Discover'd
Iland of Saint Reynard, or Guanahani

BY

JOHN MOREHEAD TRIPOLI

CHAPTER THE LAST

I am Rescued ~ Brotherhood of Man ~ Seekness and Climate
My Method How to Disarme the Planter ~ Sorrow to Depart ~ Farewell
to Guanahani ~ The Future of the Carwak

Now I was brought on board shippe, and indeed these men thought they were doing me a great service, viz rescewing me from the Carwak. My cloathes had long since rott'd from my body, and now I wore, in all truthe, nothing more than that in whitch I had come into the world, tho I was painted all over to keep off the muskitos / which torment'd the sailors e'en to Madness /. But this is above all the most Sensible garmet in such a Climate, for tho my Rescuers gave me some things to ware, yet I could not, it being too hott. And being long accustomed, too, after One Year among the Carwak of Guanahani, to walk barefoot, my feete could not bear the confinement of shoos.

Many tymes in these years that have pass'd away have I asked my Self why I *did* go with them, for shurely I was happyer upon Guanahani than e'er I was in Merrie Englande, and shurely they would not have compelled me aboard? And to this great question I know not the answer, except to say that I had liv'd all this year in the hope, or so I thought, of rescew, so that suche a hope was but a habit of mind, and ne'er examin'd, with the effect that onlie in the fullnesse of tyme did I discover that I want'd it not, & then it was to layte.

I will now offer some thots on the *Englishman*, for having been among the Carwak for so long a time, I coud now see the Englishman as it were with *Fresh Eyes*, viz. that he is exceading filthy, esp. after long confinement a board shippe, and stank like the verry Devil. His eyes seem like those of the *Abouri* or *Swamp Weasel*, and his complexion in the tropicks is of pink, and white, for he dos not know how to painte his bodie as the Carwak do. And finally there is a worse circumstance, namely, that he is cover'd over with Vermin.

But now I thought, that, I had bin *my Self* an Englishman, and after one year, as it seem'd to me, was one no longer, and how could that be, for in that argument what was I? And so, tho dreading Prolixity of which, perhaps, I have already been to often guilty, I cannot forebare to offer some thoughts on the Indian, or rather on Man. For the Indian, as I judge, is like to the Russian, who is like to a combinashun of the Chinaman & the *Pole*, who are like to others in theyr turne, and others, &c &c, which leades me to believe that there is but 1 Set of Men on the globe, such diffrences of height & breadth, &c., as there are from one to another, and most particlerlie of the darkness, liteness, or redness of the skinne, are produced according to the Soil and Climate in which he livves, from which I conclude, not onlie that the Indian is brother to the Russian, and perhaps is latelie come from the Russias by Canoo, yet so am I brother to the Indian, & the Russian, and also that shoud I remaine in this iland I shall be as brown and red as these the Carwaks, by the action of the Soil, and also of the Sunne. For that is the reason the *Ethiope* is become soo darken'd, and the Swede, who is no more expos'd to the Sunne than a *Cave Louse*, is white.

I will saye, if the reader will be pashent, another thing, viz. that tho I had been sicklie when I was first come to this iland of Saint Reynard, or Guanahani, yet I regained my health wonderfully, and when I had been one week a board shippe again, I grew sickly, from which I conclude, first, that it is not this *region* of West India that is so deadlie, but onlie our shippes, or, as it may be, our cloathes, or, even, tho I know there are many will protest, it may be that the verry *Sugar Cane* imits some subtile malarious poyson, for on those ilands, such as *Iamaica*, where it is cultivat'd, there is great mortality, and on this iland there is *none* either of the cane or of the seekness but what we bringe with us. For me this yet remains to be controverted, for the truth is that when all my companions had dyed, & I alone was left to shift for my Self among the Carwak, & the seekness had all burn'd its Self out, *then* no person among us whether it be Man, Woman or Childe grew seek. From which I conclude that Guanahani is a bless'd Isle.

It may well be hop'd that the Sugar Cane is never brought to Guanahani, and, that the iland is preserv'd in its Virgin State, to be a *Paradize* for the Carwak, and for the European /, not I shud say the dregs and dross of all Europe, but those more gentle Souls, or perhaps the infirm, who may yet regane theyr health heare marvelouslie well /. Yet I know not how to exclude the Cane from this iland my true hart's Home, for as long as **A** profit is Religion, & **B** money is pope, & **C** sugar be the most dear of all the produce of these ilands, then **D** the sugar planters will controlle that gratest share of power, being the *Priests* of theyr Religion of Profit, and the commanders of Money, and all this region will be annex'd to theyr interest. Yet it may be, that, in this matter of Money lyes the answere, for wee can turne the Planter's Religion to *Our Profit*, viz that **A** suche Monies as they do have must be had in exchange for theyr produce, so that **B** we need onlie restrane our Selves from the purchase of Sugar to pinch off the flowe of Money, and to robb the Planter of his power. So, I saye to you, Reader, if like me you have enjoy'd this time among the Carwak, then take your Tee with *Honey*, which is neare as sweete, and it may be you will preserve poor Yarico and these others, her contry Men the Carwak, from the ravages of the *Sugar Cane*, and keep Guanahani as beautiful as ever it was, so that others our posteritie may enjoy it for ever, along with the Carwak.

Yet it now comes tyme to say my farewell to Guanahani, or, as it is so call'd by the Englishman among whom I was now come once more, *Saint Reynard*. A board shippe I was given food, for it was suppos'd I was hungrie, being *marooned among the Savage*, but the soop was smoaky, & the beef was old, & my face was bedued with tears. Long and tearfully had I plead'd with my *Yarico* to come back with me to Englande, yet tho I wept, and cry'd, and beat my breast, she would not, saying that her place was among her people the Carwak. O Yarico!—kind Reader forgive me this Ejaculation—would God that you are happie, my Great Friend!

Yet one consolashun was mine, as the shippe wayed anchor, and the sails grew big-belly'd, and my belov'd *Yarico*, and indeede my true home of Guanahani, slid away over the See, and, it was this—namely, that tho it be a tyme of great

Despaire among the Carwak, & great Mortality, when seekness is on board with every English shippe, yet mayhap the reason is onlie that this be but a tyme of change, when all the world seeks for a new balance and harmonie, & shurely in the course of tyme suche a balance will be found, or as t'were restor'd, and then they are shure to become, in the space of years, as wonderfull numerous as in dayes gone by, for they knowe well how to live on the lande, which is theyr ancient home. And that is the best I can wish for them, and my true and greatest hope as long as I live, for it should make my hart gladd to know that such peopll as the Carwak are there, just so, across the wyde blue See.

But now I must say Good Bye to Guanahani, Good Bye to the yellow'd *Coco-nuts*, Good bye to the colours of the Tropick sunne Set, & to the Perino, & the wite sands, & the watter of Guanahani which is inconceivable Blue & clear & bright, and Good Bye, Good Bye, my Yarico! For I will saye, that, Yarico, tho it tooke me some tyme to know it, yet now I *do* know that if I had it all to do again, I would have staid with you, and many was the tyme that I lament'd that curs'd hour when I allowd my Self to be taken, and put a board the shippe, for tho I vowed to return, yet Life swallow'd me up, and gave me a new wyfe, and I ne'er saw you more.

SOURCES AND ACKNOWLEDGMENTS

There were many historical William Beckfords, several of whom were writers, one of whom wrote *A Descriptive Account of the Island of Jamaica*. My Beckford is a fictional creation. He does not quote directly from this book, but its spirit, its casual cruelty, is a part of him. He does, however, speak lines written by Teddy Roosevelt and Benito Mussolini. His e-mail to the college is a messy collage of Mussolini's speeches and articles, in particular "The Doctrine of Fascism," a 1935 translation of an article Mussolini co-wrote with Giovanni Gentile. Later, Beckford and James Cavendish both pick up bits of language from eighteenth- and nineteenth-century writing about the West Indies. Both of them speak lines from *The West Indies and the Spanish Main*, an infuriating book by Anthony Trollope. One or the other also speaks lines from *The History, Civil and Commercial, of the British Colonies in the West Indies*, by Bryan Edwards; *The History of Jamaica*, by Edward Long; *An Account of Jamaica*, by John Stewart; *Journal of a West-India Proprietor* and *Journal of a Residence Among the Negroes in the West Indies*, by Matthew Gregory Lewis; and *Memoirs of a West-India Planter*, by John Riland.

Richard Ligon was a real person who traveled to Barbados in the seventeenth century and wrote a remarkable account of his journey, *A True and Exact History of the Island of Barbados*. He speaks some lines from this book when he appears in the novel and the menu of the Big Anna® banquet is taken from him as well. Lady Nugent quotes her own journal, Professor Carlyle quotes "The Futurist Manifesto," and the *Constitution of the Free Produce Society of Pennsylvania* is a real document. Commandant Kabaka's dispatches are modeled after the writings of Subcomandante Marcos, which are collected in *Our Word Is Our Weapon: Selected Writings*. Kabaka acknowledges his sources but it's worth emphasizing that John Gabriel Stedman's *Narrative of a Five Years' Expedition Against the Revolted Negroes of Surinam* is a wonderful and humane book, still very much worth reading. I borrowed phrases from Stedman and Ligon, as well as from Ned Ward's astonishing *Trip to Jamaica*, for John Morehead Tripoli's own travel narrative. The letters of Israel Framingham Tripoli contain a few phrases from letters written by Thomas Jefferson and Ephraim Williams.

With very few exceptions, the treatments described in the *Field Studies Handbook* are, or rather were, real medical practices. I quote without attribution from the following: *West African Hygiene*, by Charles Scovell Grant; *On Duty Under a Tropical Sun*, by S. L. Hunt and A. S. Kenny; *Tropical Trials* by A. S. Kenny; *The Stranger in the Tropics*, by C. D. Tyng; *A Few Words of Advice to Cadets*, by Henry Kerr; and *The Soldier's Pocket Book for Field Service*, by Viscount Garnet Wolseley. The treatment to which the dean is subjected on St. Renard comes from *West India Customs and Manners*, by J. B. Moreton, who offers this prescription as a cure for venereal disease.

Most important for the spirit of this book are the slave narratives, which I think have more to teach us about the nature of the United States of America than do any of our founding documents. I will list the names in no particular order: Henry Bibb, Charles Ball, Olaudah Equiano, Frederick

Douglass, William Wells Brown, Moses Roper, Mary Prince, Harriet Jacobs, Sojourner Truth, Solomon Northup, John Brown, William and Ellen Craft, Henry "Box" Brown, James Albert Ukawsaw Gronniosaw, James Williams, Ottobah Cugoano, Briton Hammon, John Marrant, and Venture Smith.

I relied on a large number of secondary sources as well, among them *Plagues and Peoples* by William H. McNeill; *Ecological Imperialism* and *The Columbian Exchange*, by Alfred Crosby; *1491* and *1493*, by Charles Mann; *Sweetness and Power*, by Sidney W. Mintz; *The Sugar Barons*, by Matthew Parker; *Sugar and Slaves: The Rise of the Planter Class in the English West Indies, 1624–1713*, by Richard S. Dunn; *Hegel, Haiti, and Universal History*, by Susan Buck-Morss; *The Middle Passage* and *The Loss of El Dorado*, by V. S. Naipaul; *From Columbus to Castro*, by Eric Williams; and *The Traveller's Tree*, by Patrick Leigh Fermor.

I am very grateful to everyone who read early drafts of this book or provided assistance of some other kind. Many thanks to David Leavitt, Michael Hofmann, Ed White, Audrey Thier, Peter Murphy, Rob White, and David Weimer. Thanks also to my agent, Cynthia Cannell, and my editor, Rachel Mannheimer, and thanks to everyone at MFA@FLA.

I'd be living in a cardboard box with a squeeze bottle of malt liquor if it were not for my wife, Sarah Trudgeon, who also read many many drafts and provided invaluable editorial advice. Thanks are not enough, never enough. I can offer only my love.

A NOTE ON THE AUTHOR

AARON THIER was born in Baltimore and raised in Williamstown, Massachusetts. He and his wife have just returned from Florida, where they lived in Gainesville and Miami, and they are now hiding in western Massachusetts once again. His essays have appeared in the *Nation*, the *New Republic*, and the *Buenos Aires Review*. He is currently at work on his second novel.